System of Secrets

by
M.B. Smith

Justice M. Hill Publishing
Ashburn, VA

Second Edition

ISBN: 978-1-105-53675-5

Other books by M.B. Smith:

Chancy, Queen of Ashes
Love or a Safe, Sterile Life
System of Secrets
ZON
Purity
The Secret of Hawk's Talon House

Prologue

High Prince Aden Cade sprinted across the clearing with a taal less than seventy meters behind him and closing fast. With the ten-ton, seven meter high feline-like creature bearing down on him, he forced himself to remain calm and keep his mind blank. If he let down his guard for even a second, it would know his plan and fade back into the impenetrable jungles of Seti. Aden pushed his body harder than he thought possible. Only twenty more meters and he would succeed in luring the taal beyond the protection of the xanide crystals.

A root grabbed at his foot and he stumbled briefly before regaining his stride. He imagined he could feel the creature's breath on his shoulder, but it was still 20 meters away when he crossed the xanide boundary. Having reached his objective, he allowed it to get even closer. Just as it leaned down its massive head with its jaws open intending to snatch him off the ground, he ducked behind a large tree at the edge of the clearing and watched the behemoth sprint past.

It was impossibly agile for something so large, but even it had to obey the laws of physics. It had to stop before it could turn around, and when it did, Aden had already taken the bow off his shoulder and was drawing back his arrow. The taal didn't fear the puny weapon and charged straight at him. He calmly released his arrow and watched it disappear.

It took the young prince three days to reach his camp. It was empty except for the taal, now imprisoned within a force field. He had tipped his arrow with an extraction beacon, and used it to beam the beast to its confinement. As a precaution, he had ordered his men—who knew nothing of his true purpose for coming to Seti—to wait for him on board the *Kila*, in orbit above the planet.

He approached the force field to get a closer look at the creature no human in memory had ever seen. He didn't know how he knew it, but she was female. As he got a good look at her, he realized she only vaguely resembled a cat. Her head was blocky, with stubby ears, and a short muzzle framed in massive fangs. She had slanted, pale yellow eyes, and a broad, black nose. Her brindle fur was thick and even across her body, and formed a mane around her head. Aden thought she looked far more suited to a cold environment than a jungle.

As his eyes worked their way down her body he saw she had no tail to speak of, and her four, thick limbs terminated in massive, five-toed paws. He had the distinct impression that if she wished, she could have stood upright.

From his research of the old stories, he believed she was telepathic and capable of manipulating thought. Therefore, he thought it best his men be out of range, so they could beam him out quickly if necessary. He realized what a wise precaution that was, as the taal bombarded his mind with thoughts that ranged from freeing her to committing suicide. He was sure she had attempted to reach out to others of her kind, but the force field most likely limited her telepathic range.

When the taal reconciled herself to the fact that Aden knew she was telepathic and was able to ignore her efforts to control him, she lay quietly in her cage. He attempted to feed her, but she refused to eat. He stayed with her for two days hoping she would come around. Instead, she lay sullenly in her confinement, growing weaker by the hour.

Knowing nothing about taal physiology or psychology, he became concerned she might prefer death to captivity. He realized she was quite capable of feeding him sympathetic thoughts, but in the end he decided to free her anyway. He went over to the console controlling the force field and paused with his finger on the button. He knew that if he was wrong he was about to remove the only thing keeping her from his throat. He smiled grimly, then pushed the button and held his breath as the force field flickered off. If the creature could indeed read his mind, she would know that he had meant her no harm.

At first she stayed where she was, as though she didn't believe he was setting her free. When she saw that the field remained down, she stood up. She was wobbly at first, not having had food or water for days. When she regained her equilibrium, she strode over to Aden and looked down at him, as if to intimidate him. When he remained where he was, unflinching, the creature leaned down until her massive head was less than a centimeter from his. Then she struck him across the face with her paw, turned, and ambled slowly toward the jungle.

The force of the blow knocked Aden off his feet. He stood up and watched as the taal retreated toward the jungle, no longer concerned about the human who had captured her. When he saw blood dripping on the ground, he held his hand to his face and found a gaping wound. He yelled after her, "I'm sorry I tricked you! I will keep your secret safe! This is your planet. It is for you to decide when we are ready to know you again!"

The creature paused, then turned and deliberately retraced her steps. When she was once again face to face with him, she opened her jaws wide and roared. When Aden continued to stand his ground, she dragged a front paw across the dirt and snorted as if in disgust. Then she turned and left for good. After she disappeared from sight, he found a medkit and closed his wound. He had always believed that reward followed a good deed. For the first time he realized punishment could as well.

When he later contacted his ship, he learned that his father, King Edris, had found out about his adventure and ordered the ship to stay where it was until he arrived. When he got there the next day he was furious, not only at Aden, but also at his men for helping him. Feeling responsible for their trouble, he pleaded with his father to go easy on them.

Fortunately Edris was a kind man and he quickly relented, after chastising Aden for hunting in a forbidden area. When he asked him about the gash on his face, Aden told him he'd received it grappling with a huge life form he'd never seen before. While this was true, he declined to describe it or admit he knew what it was.

Pleased his son hadn't suffered a more grievous injury, and secretly admiring his crew's loyalty, Edris granted them all leniency on the condition that Aden promise he would never try such a thing again. He readily agreed; after all, he had accomplished his goal of proving that taals existed, even if it was only to himself.

Father and son remained on Seti for the next week engaging in a traditional hunt in a safer part of the jungle. When it came time to leave, they took one last look around at the royal hunting lodge. Neither realized how many years it would be before they saw it again.

While Kealt surgeons could have repaired the scar on his face Aden let it be; it would serve as a reminder that doing the right thing might not always be easy.

Chapter I

An almost universal sigh of relief issued from Ardalan and Kealt delegates when a member of the Kealt Royal Guard burst into room shouting, "Esteemed personages, you must evacuate immediately! The royal palace is under attack!" For over eight hours the delegates had been negotiating the mind-numbing details of the arranged marriage between High Princess Sia Selarney of Ardala and High Prince Aden Cade of Kealt. Even a xanide bomb would have been a welcomed distraction. Had the guard realized how badly the negotiations were going, he would not have been surprised when the participants ignored his directions and ran toward the source of the commotion.

It was Princess Celesta Mar, the adopted daughter of Aden's sister, Princess Glyn Habaret. At one time Celesta had been one of Kealt's most promising young scientists. She was as beautiful as she was smart, and considered by many to be the most desirable woman in the solar system. That was before her life fell apart when she and a group of fellow scientists found themselves caught in the event horizon of a black hole during a deep space expedition. A nearby Ardalan space fleet attempted a rescue, but could only save Celesta before the ship was destroyed. The strain of having lost so many friends and colleagues under such terrifying circumstances was too much for her; her mind snapped and she became violently insane. To protect herself and others, the Kealt Government kept her confined in Kealt's most secure mental health facility. Despite the security and the use of strong sedatives to keep her under control, she had escaped twice before. Each time security forces quickly recaptured her, but not without casualties.

Sia doubted the official version of Celesta's misfortune, which never sounded right to her. She believed the Kealts were covering something up, and her own government was participating. Whatever it was it had to be significant if even her own father, King Ivege, wouldn't budge from it.

When Sia reached the plaza, the Celesta she saw before her bore little resemblance to the beautiful, intelligent woman she'd once been. She was completely naked and her thick, curly orange hair was matted and filthy, as was her pale, mildly freckled skin. Sia had never seen her in person before. She was surprised at how small she was, especially compared to the typical Kealt woman.

Despite her diminutive stature, the guards had failed to subdue her, as evidenced by the pile of unconscious officers at her feet. As she fended them off, she screamed Aden's name.

While Sia watched, one of the guards hit her with a blast from an energy weapon intended to stun. Although it would have knocked a man twice Celesta's size on his back, it only succeeded in enraging her—she waded into the remaining guards and forced them back with a series of lightening quick blows.

She might be crazy, thought Sia, but she could fight like a Halsation fire demon! She was grudgingly impressed; however, as more guards poured in, their sheer weight began to force her back toward the waist-high railing that ringed the plaza. On the other side, 100s of meters below, was Rilan, the capital of Kealt.

The crowd gasped when Celesta jumped up on the thin railing. It seemed impossible that a human being could stand on it at all, but she not only stood on it, she kicked at any guard brave enough to get close to her. A second attempt to stun her nearly knocked her off her perilous perch.

The guards ignored Glyn's increasingly desperate pleas to leave her daughter alone. Angered by the damage she had inflicted on so many of them, they edged their way closer and closer to the now weakening princess.

Sia despised most Kealts. Even though she'd never met her, she especially hated Celesta, who was rumored to be one of Aden's favorite lovers. As she watched her standing naked on the railing, she uttered under her breath, "Well, at least she's a natural redhead!" When the second stun blast hit her, it occurred to Sia that the furious guards didn't care if they killed her.

She looked over at Glyn, who was sobbing helplessly as other guards held her back. She liked the older woman, who was the only real friend she'd made during her nearly six months on Kealt. She pitied her as well; no matter what Sia and others thought of Celesta, Glyn loved her and stood by her while she struggled to regain her sanity. Despite everything, Glyn was proud of her and would be devastated to lose her only child.

Almost against her will, Sia stepped forward and forced herself between Celesta and the guards. She held up her arms and exclaimed, "I am High Princess Sia Selarney of Ardala! As the future queen of Kealt, I demand that you put away your weapons and leave this area immediately!"

When the guards froze, but held their ground, she added, "I will consider any further acts of aggression against this woman as an act of war against Ardala!"

The guards looked at one another uncertainly, and at Sia. After what seemed an eternity their captain said, "Come along then, there's nothing to see here!" Rubbing their assorted bruises, they helped their fallen comrades to their feet and began shuffling away.

When the guards released Glyn, she ran to Celesta, held up her arms and said, "Come down sweetie! Mother is here, no one is going to hurt you!"

The effects of the stunning and the energy spent fending off dozens of guards had taken their toll. As Celesta woozily stepped off the railing, she slipped and fell onto Glyn.

"I'm sorry mother!" she exclaimed as they tumbled to the ground.

"It's OK sweetheart!" replied Glyn, helping her to her feet and embracing her. "I love you dear; everything's going to be all right!" Then she let go of her, took off her ceremonial robe and wrapped it around the now shivering woman. It was fall in Rilan and growing colder each day.

"I must see Aden!" implored Celesta.

"He's a long way from here," replied Glyn, "but he'll be home soon."

"He promised me he would keep them from giving me drugs! I'm almost better. I can't hear the voices anymore. They tried to force me to take the drugs. I won't be controlled anymore, not by the doctors or the…"

"No one is going to control you anymore," interrupted Glyn. "You're coming home." She put her arm around her and began to lead her away. When she saw that Sia was still there, she paused.

"Sia, my family owes you a great debt. I wish there were some way we could repay you."

"Cancel this wedding!" she replied tersely.

Glyn shook her head sadly. "Only you or Aden could do that; but if you took the time to know my brother you'd understand what a good man he is. You might not be so eager to discard him. Nonetheless, I trust that when the time comes he'll do the right thing." Then, with the now oblivious and drooling Celesta in tow, she turned and walked away.

Sia did not understand Kealts, largely because she refused to make the effort. Still, it was obvious Glyn was trying to tell her something. While she was still trying to sort things through, Minister Ledo Alt, a minor Ardalan bureaucrat, approached her nervously.

"Your Highness," he said uncertainly, "these Kealts are unmanageable. They insist that we go back inside and finish the negotiations."

"Today I have had my fill of petty politics," snapped Sia. "Since it is unlikely that Princess Glyn wishes to return either, it would be unfair for me to attend and disadvantage the high prince, who would be without his primary representative. Therefore, I trust you will represent my interests admirably."

If the minister recognized her obvious sarcasm, he was wise enough to ignore it. "As you wish, Your Highness," he responded doubtfully.

Then he bowed slightly, turned, and walked back toward the palace.

Although it was only early evening, Sia suddenly felt very tired and returned to her quarters. She had never imagined that arranged marriages were not just distasteful, but exceedingly hard work. She cursed Aden, not for the first time. From her brief experience with him, she considered him nothing more than a huge, ugly baboon. While custom forced her to participate in arranging the terms of their marriage, he was serving a comfortable, symbolic tour in the Ardalan military under the command of her brother, High Prince Polis Selarney. She imagined that even now they were drinking the day away and enjoying the company of beautiful women.

She also thought of her best friend, Gabo Sin. Did he miss her, or had he forgotten her? She comforted herself with the thought that soon she'd be going back to Ardala, where she would enjoy her last three months as a free woman. At the end of that period, she would return to Kealt and be married.

She supposed her parents would understand if she decided to break the centuries-old tradition that had kept Ardala and Kealt from all out war. Seemingly for the hundredth time she balanced her needs against the wellbeing of Ardala. She thought of her brother Polis. He was a proud and capable warrior, but in a confrontation with Kealt there would be many casualties and he could be one of them.

She also thought of Aden. While she despised him, she knew inside that Glyn was right: He also possessed good qualities. She didn't want him to die either, and surely he would die before allowing Kealt to fall to Ardala. As she prepared for bed, she said a prayer for Polis…and for Aden.

Chapter II

As the console exploded, throwing Aden to the deck, Admiral Polis Selarney bellowed, "Get those shields back up!" Aden staggered to his feet and found a working console, then rerouted power and exclaimed, "They're back up, but I don't know for how long!"

"Why are my fighters still in the hanger!"

Aden grimaced at the screen. "The hanger doors are damaged, they can't launch!"

"If we can't get them out of there soon, this won't be much of a battle!"

Aden hustled off the bridge in reply. The *Kreg* was the Ardalan flagship. It was tough and its main weapons were devastating the zon, but without fighter support to distract the zons' own weapons, she was being pounded. Her shields were on the verge of collapse and she was suffering structural damage. Polis was right, if

Aden didn't get her fighters into space quickly, the fight would be over soon.

When he reached the hanger deck it was in chaos. Fire control teams were attempting to put out blazes and secure ordnance, repair crews were trying unsuccessfully to force open hanger doors, and pilots sat by helplessly in their fighters. Aden ran up to the nearest fighter and ordered its pilot to leave. Then he climbed into it, secured the canopy, and ordered all personnel not in a fighter to leave the hanger deck immediately.

Once the hanger was empty except for pilots secured in their fighters, he initiated his weapons systems, directed a fusion cannon at the hanger doors, and fired. When the blast destroyed the doors and opened the hanger to space, Aden engaged his engines and flew out through the gap. Realizing what he'd done, the other pilots followed him, and the additional firepower quickly turned the battle in the humans' favor. With defeat now inevitable, the zon mothership summoned what was left of its fleet and retreated into hyperspace.

With the zon vanquished, Aden returned to the *Kreg*, whose hanger doors had been temporarily replaced with a force field. Once he secured his fighter, he disembarked and headed back to the bridge, where Polis was waiting for him.

"Are you crazy?" he exclaimed. "You're supposed to defend this ship, not attack it!"

"I'm sorry Polis, uh, admiral. There was no other way to open the hanger doors in time!"

Polis laughed and slapped him on the back. "I guess not," he replied. "Good going."

The two men spent the next several hours assessing battle damage and reporting to their respective home worlds. At evening mess, Polis looked across the table at Aden. "So, Kealt intelligence was right again. We were headed into an ambush. Are you ever going to tell us your source?"

Aden put down his fork and smiled grimly. "We have several," he replied. "Most are among the aliens the zon have impressed to do their bidding."

The zon were man-sized, insect-like creatures that had appeared three years earlier from an unknown portion of the Poseidon Galaxy. They were intelligent, but due to their physiology, were largely unable to actually operate, manage, or maintain the machinery that made them so dangerous. For that, they often depended on members of other species, whom they controlled by fear and other means only vaguely understood.

At first the zon were satisfied with the handful of planets they had captured from some of the galaxy's less numerous and powerful alien races. Apparently these planets were merely way stations for them, places they used for resupplying as they made the journey from wherever they came from to wherever they were going.

However, recently they had begun taking a greater interest in the region of space occupied by Kealt and Ardala. Instead of passing through it, they were expanding their holdings, and now their ships were returning from wherever they had gone. Many appeared to be damaged. Both Kealt and Ardalan intelligence believed that somewhere out in space the zon had run into an even more formidable enemy and were being forced to retreat. This was not good news for humans, whom the zon enjoyed as food.

While zon technology was in many respects superior to other species, they were a manageable threat when the humans had an advantage in numbers. Now that the zon appeared to be in the process of making their home closer to Kealt and Ardala, that advantage was diminishing rapidly. Colony after colony fell to their forces. While neither side would admit it, it was only a matter of time before the zon turned their attention directly to Ardala and Kealt.

"Most?" queried Polis evenly, in response to Aden's answer.

"Come now Polis, you don't expect me to give up all our secrets any more than we would expect you to give up yours! However, I can assure you that Kealt does not actively spy against Ardala. On the other hand, our intelligence minister is quite convinced there are Ardalan spies in our own midst, perhaps planted among our refugee population."

Polis raised his ale and replied, "Turnabout is fair play on both our worlds, I suppose! Very well then! You are a politician *and* a soldier—a most dangerous combination."

Aden lifted his own glass and touched Polis's. "Yes," he laughed, "but surely such a combination of qualities exists in the Selarney family as well!"

"You're a good man Aden. I will be proud to have you as my brother in law."

"Ah, if only Sia shared your enthusiasm."

"Maybe not yet," replied Polis, "but I'm sure in time she'll come around."

"Perhaps," said Aden. "Arranged marriage is such a primitive custom. A prize such as your sister should be free to choose her own mate."

"I agree," responded Polis, "and you yours, and I mine; but as barbaric as it is, it has kept us from each other's throats for a long time."

"I suppose," replied Aden, "but isn't it time we treated each other like brothers, not enemies?"

Polis finished his ale and put down his glass. "Past time," he agreed, "but there are many on both sides who would enjoy nothing more than to bath in the other's blood."

Aden refilled his glass. Then he lifted it and said, "Here's to peace, if only to save me from a knife across my neck as I sleep!"

"It would undoubtedly help my fair sister's humor if she knew the truth about Celesta."

"The truth? To what are you referring?" replied Aden, who suddenly seemed uncomfortable.

"Celesta herself entrusted her secret to me when we rescued her." When Polis saw Aden continue to fidget, he quickly added, "You know, she was in a delirious state at the time, and I doubt one could put stock in anything she said. Besides, she swore me to secrecy! Still, if such a thing *were* true, it would be wrong to keep it from Sia."

Aden smiled crookedly. "I see," he answered. "I'm sure we all have secrets. One day she will know all of mine, but not today. I too swore an oath—to my father. I must honor it. For now she will have to go on considering me to be nothing more than an ugly, oversized, oversexed baboon!"

"Well then!" replied Polis, raising another toast, "here's to my future brother in law the baboon!"

Aden tapped Polis's glass. "Here's to my remaining time aboard the *Kreg*!" Changing the subject he said, "Your fusion cannons are most impressive. I've never seen an energy weapon cut through the shields of a zon heavy cruiser so easily. It is true we too have powerful weapons, but in battle I would much prefer yours. What say when this is over you give me the plans to bring back to Kealt?"

Polis choked on his ale trying not to laugh. Fusion cannon technology was among Ardala's most jealously guarded technologies. When he recovered sufficiently to speak he quipped, "Well, I suppose as soon as Kealt hands over its precious cloaking technology! Anyway, you do have free run of the ship. If you want the technology so bad, you could always steal it."

Now it was Aden's turn to laugh. "You know I would never do that!"

"Of course, that's *why* you have free run of the ship!" Polis held up his glass once more and said, "Here's to honest Aden! The best enemy first office I've ever had! I'm sorry we'll be taking you home shortly."

Aden raised his own glass. "I can assure you the pleasure has been mine. You run a fine ship. Let's hope this is just the beginning of a lasting collaboration between our peoples!"

Unfortunately, Aden's last days aboard the *Kreg* were mind-numbingly dull. The zon appeared to have taken a break from raiding human colonies, and he spent most of his time catching up on his reports and overseeing mundane tasks around the ship. In his free time he often thought about his first encounter with Sia.

It was at the cultural exchange ceremony on Ardala. He had expected she would look like Polis—short, with a stocky build, swarthy complexion, and round features. He was shocked by how beautiful she actually was.

She was tall for an Ardalan, lean, and wearing a thin, yellow, ceremonial dress made of silk that did little to conceal her perfect figure. She had long, wavy, white-blond hair, and pale blue eyes that sparkled. Her face was alabaster, and perfectly complimented by her full lips, fine nose, and dazzling smile. While most Ardalan women smoldered, she glowed. She captivated him as no woman ever had.

To his chagrin, she treated him like a filthy weep hog. She refused to talk to him except when she had to, and most of the time refused even to look at him, as though she was trying to pretend that he didn't exist. He guessed that she might already be in love with someone else. However, if she were, no one, even Polis, would admit it.

When the ceremony concluded, he thought for a moment that she wouldn't even stand with him under the centuries old acardia tree, which was part of an old Ardalan tradition. Beneath its sweeping boughs, betrothed royals were expected to kiss each other on the cheek and say goodbye prior to embarking on their respective cultural indoctrinations. When, to his relief, she appeared, she gave him the coldest kiss he'd ever received and walked off disdainfully when it was over.

Aden himself had enjoyed numerous paramours over the years, but had never met anyone who could keep his interest. While Sia was certainly beautiful, she would never love him. He now regretted he had missed his chance to know, at least, what real love was.

Sia aside, he had enjoyed his time with the Ardalans, so much so he had almost forgotten the purpose of his visit. Now that the clock was running out and he would soon return home, a sense of dread filled him. Sia was beautiful, bright, and extremely desirable. Given the choice, she might have fallen in love with him on her own. As it was, she was a caged bird whose only thought was to escape. It made him sick to think that he was forced to be the one holding the key.

Chapter III

Kealts loved parties and used any excuse to throw one. Although Sia was looking forward to going home, even if only for a short time, she had mixed feelings about the celebration that marked the formal end of her six-month cultural familiarization period.

On the one hand she dreaded the event, because it meant that she would have to socialize with Aden. The thought of it made her want to take a sharp utensil and ram it through her heart. On the other hand, she would celebrate her reunion with Gabo, who would have recently arrived on Kealt as part of the Ardalan delegation. She hadn't seen him since she'd left Ardala, and was looking forward to dancing with him all night, no matter what Aden and the Kealts might think. She doubted Aden would care anyway—an apparently rejuvenated Celesta was on the guest list.

As Sia gathered with the other Ardalans before entering the great hall, she found herself amused by the sheer opulence and pomposity of the event. The Kealts had arranged that the royal families of both planets would enter the hall separately, while their respective national anthems played. Since they were on Kealt protocol required the Ardalans to enter first, followed by the Kealts. As they waited, Sia embraced her parents, King Ivege Selarney and Queen Sarin Hebrid, and said, "You don't know how much I've missed you both!

"Oh, I imagine about as much as we've missed you!" replied Sarin, beaming at her.

Before Ivege could reply, one of his aides pulled him aside. Sia said, "I'll be so happy to go back with you, mother. I hate this place!"

Sarin released her. "Have you forgotten that I am the daughter of King Hebrid of Kealt?" she asked. "Believe it or not, some of these people are your relatives, although distant ones. Granted Kealt is different from Ardala in many ways, but if you gave them half a chance you'd find that they are big hearted and generous." She smiled and added, "Besides, if you look around, I think you'll find you look more like a Kealt than an Ardalan. Where do you think you get your height from? Ardalans tend to be smaller than Kealts."

Sia had always thought Sarin was a little too tall, too awkward, and a little too self-conscious. Now that she was back among her own people, she realized what a fish out of water she was on Ardala. She had never actually looked at her as a woman before; for the first time it occurred to her that she was indeed beautiful, an older version of Sia herself. Her mother was right: She herself also looked more Kealt than Ardalan. Unwilling to admit it, Sia said, "I don't care if that's true or not; I don't like Aden, and when I see Kealt I see Aden!"

Sarin held Sia's hands. "I once felt exactly like you do about your father. We had a very difficult start, to say the least. I'm sorry you and Polis had to suffer through it as well. However, over time your father's real character asserted itself. He turned out to be a wonderful man! I can't imagine what my life would be without him. Still, arranged marriage is a barbaric business and one day it must end. Sia, you must know that if you don't want to go through with this your father and I will support you. You mean more to us than all of Ardala and Kealt combined."

Sia wiped away the tears that were beginning to seep from her eyes. "I know; but this arrangement has helped prevent the massive, destructive wars we've fought over and over again. In my dreams…my nightmares…I see Polis going into battle and being killed by Aden and others I've met here. I would do anything to prevent that, even marry a brute like him!" When she calmed down, she realized Gabo was nowhere to be seen. "Where is he?" she asked.

"Where is who?"

"Gabo, of course; he's supposed to be here!"

Sarin replied, "He asked me to pass on his regrets. He has pressing duties he must attend to on Ardala."

"Mother that's not fair!" exclaimed Sia, unable to hide her disappointment.

Another aide came and whispered something in Sarin's ear. When he left, she admonished Sia and said, "Look, the celebration is about to begin. Let's not keep everyone waiting! We'll go to our seats so they can come in and we'll discuss this later."

Reluctantly she stood next to her parents and the formal procession began. When the table was settled, Aden, who had just completed his service aboard the *Kreg*, and his family entered to raucous applause. When he reached their table, he took her hands and greeted her warmly. "High Princess Sia Selarney!" he exclaimed. "You are indeed the Jewel of Ardala!" Sia almost blushed in spite of herself. When they took their seats, she was still upset that Gabo was absent. In an effort to get her attention Aden gently touched her arm and said, "Hello Sia!"

She replied distractedly, "Yes, uh, hello."

"I'm sorry, is something bothering you?"

Feeling guilty for ignoring him she said, "I'm so sorry high prince. I was expecting to see a dear friend of mine. I just learned he won't be here."

"If you're referring to Gabo Sin, I was looking forward to seeing him as well. I've become quite fond of him."

"He's a friend of yours?" replied a surprised Sia.

"Yes, while I was on Ardala I worked with him quite often. He mentioned you and he were friends. He's a good man; I heard he was called away at the last moment."

Sia tried her best to mask her disappointment. She smiled and said, "Yes he's been a close friend of my family's for years. I haven't seen him for a while and I was hoping we could catch up."

"Ah," replied Aden. "Well, the good news is you'll be heading back to Ardala shortly and will have plenty of time to 'catch up.'"

Sia blushed. Maybe Aden wasn't as stupid or unfeeling as she thought, or as crude. Once they all were seated Danil Reinis, the Kealt First Minister, took the podium that stood on the edge of the large, raised dance floor located in the middle of the hall, and introduced King Edris.

"Welcome treasured guests," he bellowed. "I would like to extend an especially warm welcome to the king and queen of Ardala, and their handsome family." When the applause died down he said, "Today we celebrate the return of High Prince Aden, and bid High Princess Sia goodbye. We all know King Edris finds long speeches boring…" He paused when the crowd erupted in laughter. "…so, Your Highness, I happily turn the podium over to you."

King Edris stood up and walked slowly to the podium amidst more applause. When he reached it, he faced the audience, placed his hands on the sides of the podium, and smiled. He waited until the ballroom grew quiet, then said, "Today is indeed a momentous occasion. Not only am I welcoming my son home, I'm saying goodbye, for now, to my future daughter in law. She is a fine young woman whom I will be proud to welcome into my family." This time the applause came primarily from the Ardalans. "I am also pleased to welcome King Ivege Selarney, and his beautiful queen, Sarin Hebrid, both old and dear friends."

As the Ardalans cheered, Sia winced involuntarily. It sickened her to think that her parents had any affection for the barbarian king; surely he exaggerated their relationship.

When the Ardalans quieted down King Edris continued: "I'm sure many of you noticed the *Kreg*, the proud flagship of the Ardalan fleet, which just this morning landed in the royal spaceport. For the first time in Kealt history, an Ardalan warship has landed on our home world, only not for war, but for peace. It took a lot of trust and good faith on both sides for this to happen. It is my sincere hope that this event marks a turning point in our relationship."

This time both the Kealts and Ardalans applauded.

"While we have more or less been at peace for 200 years," he continued, "there is no denying that we have had our differences; I will not attempt to downplay them. Still, I say that it is past time we put aside the blame, anger, and mistrust and address these differences honestly and candidly.

"Although some of us may feel comfort in these emotions, the fact is, if we don't overcome them we may both be doomed. Three years ago, a ravenous, evil species called the zon began to invade our section of space. For the most part, we have been content to protect our own parochial interests. This must end. The Kealts and Ardalans are brothers. We have a common ancestry, religion, and language. For two hundred years, our planets have been ruled by leaders born on both worlds. And now we are both committed to democratic reforms that one day soon will hand over full governmental authority to officials elected by the people. With so much in common, there must be a way for us to find our way past that which keeps us apart, so we can focus on our common enemy, the zon."

The ballroom erupted with the loudest applause of the evening. King Edris held up his hands. When the crowd again quieted he said, "I think we can all agree these are fine sentiments, but they will never come to fruition if each side waits for the other to make the first show of good faith. Therefore, with the backing of the Council of Commons, I have a proposal to make."

Silence enveloped the hall as representatives from both planets awaited King Edris's next words. After a brief pause he said, "There is one issue that for millennia has served as an insurmountable barrier between our peoples—it is Seti, the land of our origin. We have fought over it, shed blood over it, and never fully accepted each other's right to it. That must change."

Sia noticed that many Kealts looked uncomfortable as King Edris went on.

"When Kealt last retook Seti during one of our many wars, we vowed to share it equitably. I am ashamed to say that despite a treaty negotiated in good faith, we never did. Therefore, to rectify this great injustice, and as the leader of Kealt, I formally and respectfully request that Ardala send a delegation to Seti for the purpose of negotiating a new treaty that will truly guarantee fair and equitable access to this planet, which means so much to both of us!"

Pandemonium broke out among delegates from both sides at the audaciousness of King Edris's offer. He held up his arms to silence the crowd and said, "King Ivege, will you please join me."

Ivege made his way to King Edris and embraced him. Then he turned and stepped up to the podium. "King Edris," he began, "I know that Seti also is a sensitive subject amongst your own people and that by offering to honor the promise Kealt made centuries ago you are taking a great risk. However, it is a crucial step toward the reunification of our great cultures." He turned back toward the audience and said, "The enmity between Ardala and Kealt must end, for once and for all, or neither of us may survive. As King Edris noted, the zon threat is growing.

"When they first appeared they were content to maintain a handful of bases, which, we believe, were used primarily for rest and resupply before they moved on to their ultimate destination.

"Last year we began to notice that more zon ships were returning to Poseidon than leaving. No longer content to prey on just the weaker native species, like the qrell and the traque, they began attacking Ardalan and Kealt colonies. At first they failed, but only because we outnumbered them.

"However, as their numbers increase our forces are becoming stretched thinner and thinner. Many of our smaller colonies have fallen or been abandoned. Most recently they attacked Trolaxia, one of our most heavily fortified military installations. They were repelled, but only at great cost. Before that, only intervention from our Kealt friends saved a major scientific colony on Bort. Kealt too has lost several colonies and others are under siege.

"Our sources tell us that somewhere out there, in the depths of space, the zon have encountered a species even more violent and powerful than they, one which is intent on annihilating them. We believe they call themselves the tayron. We also believe that the zon home world was somehow destroyed. Therefore, with no place to go to or return to, they are attempting to make our piece of space their new home. We all know how the zon sustain themselves—this cannot be tolerated. Ardala will not become food for any species, no matter how great and powerful, nor will Kealt."

King Ivege turned to face King Edris. "Your Highness," he said, "we appreciate the personal and political risk you are taking. In return, may I propose an exchange of military technologies? My son tells me you are quite intrigued by our fusion cannons."

King Edris stood next to King Ivege, smiled, and replied, "Very well. It shall be done. Let us pray that our good will is not eaten alive by the details of what promises to be a most challenging and lengthy undertaking. Therefore, we have no time to waste; at the conclusion of this grand celebration, let us begin planning for the negotiations without delay.

"Speaking of eating, I believe we've bored these people enough. Your Highness, with your permission, may the feast begin?"

"Of course my good friend," replied King Ivege.

The tremendous applause quickly ceased as the music resumed and hungry guests rushed to the buffet table, a massive affair that lined one wall of the hall and was divided in the middle by a substantial bar. Sia remained in her seat, horrified at the thought of any cooperation between Kealt and Ardala, let alone the transfer of Ardala's most sensitive technology. She leaned over to her mother and whispered, "He can't be serious! We can't work with these savages!"

"Sia," Sarin replied, "these are dangerous times. The Kealt aren't savages. They've proven on multiple occasions that they're willing to risk their lives to protect even Ardalans from the zon. Your father is a great man. So is King Edris. We need to trust them."

"If they're so great and we're such good friends, why must I subject myself to this sham of a marriage?" sniffed Sia.

"It is an old tradition and old traditions die hard. I'll tell you this—I've known Aden since he was a child; you could do a lot worse." She pointed to an angry looking young man who had not applauded during Edris's address. "Had Aden not been born you might be marrying that man. As it is, Aden pushed off the wedding as long as he could, hoping Edris would finally implement the last of his reforms, making it unnecessary. But, with Edris aging, the Kealt Council of Elders was concerned that if he waited much longer, Edris might not last until Aden produced an heir." She gestured toward the sullen man and added, "They were ready to elevate him if Aden didn't stop delaying."

"He's better looking than him, what would have been so bad about that?" she huffed.

"His name is Kux Mar, high prince of the Mar clan. They are an odious, mean-spirited, conspiratorial, dishonest, and cruel lot. If he were to one-day take the throne there would be no peace anywhere in the galaxy, nor would his queen ever know love. The Mars are the opposite of Aden and his family, who are wonderful, decent people."

"You *like* Aden?" exclaimed Sia.

"Yes," replied Sarin. "I also trust him, and that's more important."

Sia felt a tap on her shoulder. It was Aden himself. "Excuse me, Your Highness, but are you going to eat? I can assure you the food is excellent. Perhaps I can bring you something?"

"No thank you high prince," she replied curtly, "maybe in a while. Please, don't wait for me! "

Aden left, doing his best to hide his irritation, and Sia resumed her conversation with her mother. When the Kealt musicians began to play popular dance music, she felt another tap on her shoulder. Now irritated herself that Aden would continue to bother her, she said without turning, "Please! I told you I wasn't hungry!"

"I'm not either," replied an older and coarser voice.

Sia turned and was startled to find Gris Habaret, Glyn's husband and Aden's brother in law, smiling at her. She did not recognize him at first; she had never seen him in formal dress before, clean-shaven and fresh, with his short, salt and pepper hair plastered back. He was far more presentable than she'd ever thought possible.

"Gris, I'm so sorry! I thought you were…someone else."

"Yes, I'm sure you did," he replied, wearing an amused expression. "If my good for nothing brother in law won't ask you to dance, might I have the pleasure?"

Once such a disrespectful address would have horrified her, but having spent six months on Kealt she realized that often the more gratuitously insulting someone was, the greater the affection they felt toward the person being insulted. In spite of herself, Sia's face reluctantly cracked into a grin. "I will grant you that pleasure," she replied, then stood up and took Gris's arm.

As the evening went on Sia found that she was enjoying herself, much to her disappointment. She was especially pleased that for the most part Aden kept his distance. Maybe she had indeed underestimated his intelligence, she thought wryly. After a particularly strenuous dance, she excused herself and headed for the bar. She ordered a glass of Ardalan wine, and then she turned and promptly spilled it onto King Edris himself.

"I'm so sorry!" she exclaimed, ineffectually trying to dry his tunic with her handkerchief. "I'm so clumsy!"

"Think nothing of it my dear!" replied the smiling king. "It's not often I have a woman as beautiful as you laying hands on me."

Sia drew back in embarrassment. Since she'd been on Kealt she'd rarely seen Edris, and never this close. He was huge, even bigger than Aden. He was closer to 80 than 70, but still fit, broad-shouldered, and athletic. He wore his long, thick gray hair in wild, uneven braids. His face was craggy with age, and covered with an unkempt beard. Despite his age, he was undeniably handsome. She noticed that he had the same steel-gray eyes as his son. She was sure that in a foul mood those eyes could crush an army; but that would be another day. Today they danced. To her surprise she felt her knees wobble.

When she continued to gawk at him speechlessly, Edris smiled kindly and said, "I'm sorry, that was rude. I love to dance. Would you mind?"

"Ya ya yes, ah no, ah, of course I would…love to dance with you!" stammered Sia, who felt like a giddy schoolgirl in the presence of such overwhelming virility.

"Very well," he replied, tactfully ignoring her nervousness. He took her glass and placed it on the nearest table. Then he extended his arm. "Shall we?" he asked.

To her surprise Edris was a graceful and skilled dancer. She almost forgot that he was literally twice her size. When it was over, she was almost sorry to let him go. He put his hand gently on her shoulder and asked her to join him by the fireplace at the back of the hall. Like everything else on Kealt it was outsized, and filled with enough burning wood to generate an inferno. It was so hot no one could stand within five meters of it. Edris grabbed a glass of ale off the tray of a serving girl. "Anything for you my dear?" queried the king.

"I'll have some wine," she replied.

"Excellent!" exclaimed Edris. He caught the attention of another server and chose a glass for her. As he offered it to her he said, "I hope you like this. It's a rare type of wine made by one of our religious orders. We call it Kag. It's somewhat of an acquired taste, but I admit I have a weakness for it!"

Sia took the glass and held it briefly to her nose before taking a small sip. "This is wonderful!" she said, before taking a second sip.

"Your father is a great man, Sia," answered Edris. He raised his glass and added, "I will be most honored to welcome his daughter into my family."

"I wish I could share your enthusiasm, Your Highness," she replied, without raising her glass, "but this custom of arranged marriage is awful. I will find no joy in it."

Edris lowered his drink. Sia expected him to rebuke her, but to her surprise he said, "I can see that in addition to your great beauty you're honest.

You are correct: It's past time for this archaic practice to end. Sadly, this is a difficult time between our peoples. There are forces on both planets that would enjoy nothing more than another war, and would gladly use any excuse to start one.

"These arranged marriages have kept the peace, such as it is, for a long time. To stop them now might be the match that would ignite the hatred that still smolders. Aden is as opposed to this union as you are, but despite the supposed peace between our peoples, he's lost two brothers to this hatred and I've lost two sons. We've been equally brutal to your people. I've met your brother Polis. He is a fine young man. I lose sleep at night thinking he could one day kill Aden in battle, or the other way around. Your parents and I have failed to stop the bloodletting between us completely. Perhaps together you and Aden can finally unite our worlds."

"We killed your children and you would still have peace with us? I'm not sure I could ever be so…magnanimous."

Edris smiled wanly. "More death will not bring them back. I wish to be remembered as a king of life, not death, by both worlds."

Sia had always prided herself on being a good judge of character. Certainly she had been wrong in the case of King Edris, who was far from the gluttonous, lecherous brute she had imagined him to be. She raised her own glass and said, "There is wisdom in your words. Here's to Aden and I, that we may inherit the wisdom and strength of our parents."

Edris met her toast and replied somberly, "May you have them in greater abundance, for that is what it will take for us to live in peace!"

Sia eventually excused herself and made her way back toward her table. Sarin intercepted her and said, "There you are! Why so serious looking?"

"I'm sorry!" she replied. "I just had a long conversation with King Edris."

"Quite an impressive man, isn't he?"

"He certainly isn't what I expected."

"Oh, did you think he was going to try and eat you?"

Sia smiled in spite of herself. "No, of course not," she said, "but he's actually a gentleman."

"And that disappoints you?"

"It certainly does," she said, wearing a mock frown. "I so wanted to despise him!"

When Sarin laughed at her expression, she laughed back. Then Sarin said, "You know, I had quite a crush on him when I was young. He was so handsome and charming! Still is, for that matter."

"Mother you didn't…!"

"No dear, of course I 'didn't!' I'm much younger than he is and he was married to a woman he adored; but our families were quite close and I did see him frequently." Sarin caressed

Sia's shoulder and added, "If you give Aden a chance, you'll find that he isn't an altogether an unpleasant fellow. In fact, he's a lot like his father."

"Perhaps," she replied, "but he's in love with someone else."

"To whom are you referring?"

"It's no secret he and Celesta Mar are lovers!" Sia replied caustically.

"I know they're fond of each other," agreed Sarin. "After all, they grew up together; but I doubt they're really lovers." She gestured toward the dance floor. "Right now I'd say your own dear brother is vying for that role."

Sia followed her glance. Sure enough, in the middle of the dance floor were Celesta and Polis, locked in a close embrace, oblivious to those around them.

"That is disgusting!" she exclaimed. "I'm going to put an end to it right now!"

She took a step toward them when Sarin grabbed her arm. "Leave him alone. He's an adult. His own marriage has not yet been arranged. He can associate with whomever he wants."

"But she...she is so horrible! Do you know what kind of reputation she has here on Kealt? She's mentally unstable, has no morals, is a drug addict, and shiftless!"

"Oh, I think you're exaggerating just a bit," replied Sarin gently. "She's really quite pleasant."

"You sound like you know her too," observed Sia.

"As I said, the House of Hebrid was quite close to the House of Cade. Glyn and I were good friends. I've known Celesta since she was a child. In fact, I'm her Godmother. She was such a precocious child! Glyn adopted her not long before I left Kealt, so I didn't have much contact with her as she was growing up, but not long ago she spent considerable time on Ardala as part of a joint Ardalan/Kealt science team. I found her to be bright, friendly, serious, and ultimately, courageous."

"Don't tell me you like her too?" asked Sia incredulously.

"She's a very likeable woman."

"How come you never told me about her?"

"I would have, except every time I've ever tried to speak to you about my life on Kealt you quickly grew bored and stopped listening!"

"I'm sorry mother I didn't mean to be so gruff. It's just that I have such a visceral dislike for her. Since today I feel like talking about her, there is something that's always bothered me."

"Oh, and what would that be?"

"Whatever happened to her had nothing to do with a black hole, did it? For one thing, it's too convenient to believe that a fleet of Ardala's most advanced warships just happened to be in such an isolated region. Also, I've seen her take on an entire squad of Kealt's royal guard, literally without even the shirt on her back. She would have let them kill her if I hadn't intervened. I can't believe that being stuck on a ship trapped by a black hole would be nearly enough to drive *her* mad."

Sarin smiled crookedly. "I'm sorry Sia. I have to admit I share your skepticism, but I don't know any more than you. I suspect your father and brother promised King Edris they would protect her secret, whatever it is."

"Secrets, secrets everywhere!" replied Sia, with a touch of humor. "It seems this solar system is full of secrets. Very well then, enough about her. I want to dance!"

Two hours later Sia was exhausted and more than a little intoxicated. The Kealts did indeed know how to throw a party. She was sure she had danced with every man in the ballroom--everyone except for Aden. She almost felt sorry that she had gone to such great lengths to ignore him, especially since Celesta was commanding Polis's attention. The feeling quickly passed; there were plenty of beautiful women trying to make up for her lack of attention. He seemed particularly attracted to a young, voluptuous, raven-haired girl who took every opportunity to dance with him.

When she finally left the dance floor, she needed a drink. She went to the bar when she couldn't find a server. While she was standing in line, a tall, doughy, greasy-looking old man tapped her on the shoulder. When she turned, he said, "A future queen should never have to wait for anything. What's your pleasure?"

Sia provided her request and he waved to a bartender, who immediately filled his order. He handed her glass to her and said, "Your Highness, I am Abeg Mar, once an exalted high prince and potential heir to the throne, and now just a faded old man and your humble future servant." He bowed slightly, then held up his glass and said, "Cheers."

Sia nodded politely, took a sip, and was about to walk away when he said, "Times have certainly changed when a woman of your station must wait in line along with those who aren't even of royal blood. Do you know Edris even invited some of the rabble from that farm colony, Epsilon II? And provided them appropriate clothes on top of it! On behalf of all well-meaning Kealts, I apologize for the rudeness of the Cade clan. They have become a weak, cowardly, and, dare I say it, corrupt family who have made every effort to reduce the monarchy to just another creaky, old, toothless bureaucracy. Soon I fear it won't exist at all. I trust that on Ardala the monarchy remains a robust institution and is not as serious about democratization as Edris. I hope that when you become queen of Kealt you will bring that wisdom back to us and restore the proper order of things."

Not long ago Sia would have agreed wholeheartedly with Abeg's assessment. However, after meeting the regal and proud King Edris, she knew the Cades were anything but weak and cowardly. The fact that Abeg was willing to defy him in front of his future daughter in law told her that he must have significant support from within the Kealt political structure. Edris had his hands full, that much was certain. Perhaps that was why she'd seen so little of him.

Before she could answer Abeg's challenge, Celesta and Polis brushed her on their way to the bar, nearly spilling her drink. As they went by Abeg added, "Surely you've heard the rumors about the high prince and his so-called cousin?" When Sia just stared at him mutely, he wrinkled his brow, shook his bald head disapprovingly, and said, "A most unpleasant business."

She'd had enough of Abeg's impudence. Regardless of their merits, his comments were most inappropriate. For better or worse, she was going to be the queen of Kealt one day, and needed to set the tone for the kind of queen she was going to be. However, before she could rebuke him, Celesta inserted herself between them.

"Hello Your Highness," she said cheerily. "I'm sorry I bumped into you a minute ago, I can be so clumsy at times." She looked scornfully at Abeg. "Beware of this one, you're talking to the traitorous weep hog who killed Aden's brothers."

"You should be careful whom you call names, Celesta," replied Abeg condescendingly. "'Crazy bastard' comes to mind when I think of you, and I mean that quite literally."

From her stunned expression, Sia could see that Abeg's cruel words had stung her deeply. She almost felt sorry for her. When she threw her drink on him in response, Sia decided she'd had her fill of political intrigue, Kealt style. "I find you *both* revolting," she exclaimed angrily. "Kealt has to be the ugliest planet in the universe!" With that, she turned and stomped off.

It was after midnight and she decided that whatever fun she'd been having had been spoiled by Abeg and Celesta. She told her parents goodnight, and declined their offer to walk her back to her quarters; she needed some fresh air and time to think.

As she crossed the plaza where she had saved Celesta, she savored the crisp air and the moonless, clear, starlit sky. She was lost in thought when she caught sight of a large man leaning over the railing gazing at the lights of the city below. Even in the starlight and at a fair distance, there was no doubt it was Aden.

Still feeling tipsy and a little guilty that she had barely even said hello to him, she decided to tell him goodnight. Before she reached him, out of the corner of her eye she caught a glimpse of a female figure gliding toward him from another direction. Gliding was the best way to describe how Celesta moved—confident, graceful, and almost feline in nature. She was as easy to pick out in the dark as Aden.

Sia was herself beautiful and knew it, but for a moment she felt diminished as she watched Celesta sidle up seductively next to the high prince. Neither had seen her, and she decided to keep it that way. She turned to leave, but felt compelled to stop at the sound of Celesta's voice.

"What is such a handsome young man doing out here all alone?" she asked Aden with mock concern.

He turned and hugged her gently, leaned down and kissed her on the forehead, then released her. He caressed her arm and said, "We've been through so much together, good and bad. You've always been there for me. I don't know what I'm going to do without you."

"You're not dying, you're getting married!" she replied.

Aden snorted in amusement. "In this case I'm afraid they're one in the same. She hates every cell in my body. I'd almost rather go to war than have to live with her; I'd probably have a better chance of surviving!" He absently touched the scar on his face. "She is a taal. She can neither be tamed nor trusted."

Now it was Celesta's turn to laugh. "You and your taals! You still believe they actually exist, don't you? Anyway, she can't be that bad! I'm sure she feels the same way you do. After a while she'll find herself falling madly in love with you; what woman wouldn't?"

Sia put her hand on her mouth to stop herself from retching. Fall in love with Aden? She would rather have a zon suck her dry.

Aden embraced Celesta and said, "No matter what, don't ever forget that I love you. Nothing can ever change that."

Sia thought she heard a catch in Celesta's voice when she replied, "No, nothing can!" She pulled his face down to hers and kissed him on the cheek; then she said goodnight and walked away, as did Aden.

Sia had never thought of Aden and Celesta as human beings, people with feelings, hopes, and dreams. She was beginning to see them both in a different light. For the first time she found herself questioning her own feelings. She turned to head back to her quarters and found herself face to face with Celesta. Sia was stunned. She didn't know how it was possible for a human being to cover so much ground so quickly and quietly, but there she was. And she was angry.

"How dare you spy on us!" she demanded.

"I'm...I'm sorry," sputtered Sia, at a loss for words. "I was on my way back to my quarters…"

"…and you decided to spy on us!" interrupted Celesta.

Quickly overcoming her initial shock, Sia forcefully replied, "I'm sorry, I shouldn't have done that. It wasn't my intention. I saw Aden standing there and thought I'd go over and talk to him. He's going to be my husband, as repulsive as that is to all of us. Before I got there, you slithered in. I know you two are lovers, and I doubt even our marriage will stop that. Just know that I am no fool. I will marry him only to prevent war. You two deserve each other. I'll never be a proper wife to him. If you want to continue being his lover we'll all be happier."

When Celesta's anger gave way to unbridled laughter, Sia thought she was becoming unhinged. Then she caught her breath and exclaimed, "Lovers? If you knew how ridiculous that was, you'd be laughing too. I didn't think I'd like you Your Highness, but I must admit you're growing on me. You say what's on your mind."

"Are you mocking me?" replied Sia testily.

Celesta snickered. "Certainly not; it's nice to know that Aden's charm doesn't work on *every* woman." She turned as if to leave, but paused and said, "I never thanked you for saving my life. I know you don't like me, but you did it anyway. Aden could do worse than marry you! I may be the last person on this planet you'd take advice from, but here it is anyway: Trust Aden. He always puts others first and *always* does the right thing, no matter the cost."

Before Sia could answer, she walked off into the darkness.

Two days later, Sia leapt out of bed—in four hours she would be boarding a ship back to

Ardala and she didn't want to be late! Except for a small bag she'd carry with her on her trip, most of her things were already stowed away. When she finished her shower, she took extra care to ensure she looked perfect. She would be meeting Gabo soon, and she wanted to get back in practice. She cursed intra-solar system travel—for technical and safety reasons nonmilitary vessels traveled so much slower than military vessels within solar systems; it would be over a week before she got home. She took one last look in the mirror, then picked up her bag and left her quarters. She had arranged for a hover car to take herself and her aides to the spaceport, which was 30 minutes from the palace.

As Sia rode to the spaceport, she leaned back in her seat, soothed by the low, steady hum that emanated from the xanide powered antigravity plates. Hover technology was ubiquitous on planet bound vehicles on both Ardala and Kealt. It was an exceedingly clean and efficient technology. Based on the driver's input, a computer manipulated the amount of power fed to various sections of the antigrav plating, which increased or decreased the antigrav effect on the plates. The net effect was that when a hover car was in motion, it slid along the gravity variation, following the path of least resistance. It was essentially going downhill, like a sled on snow. Depending on how the driver applied the power, an antigrav vehicle could attain astonishing speeds and maneuver sharply at whatever speed it was going.

When Sia and her entourage arrived, they quickly made their way through customs, then queued up for boarding with other VIP passengers. She was just about to step onboard when two serious looking Ardalan security officers approached her. "Your Highness," spoke the senior officer, "I am Captain Sulok of the Ardalan Royal Guard. Your father has instructed us to bring you to his quarters immediately."

"But I'm about to leave!" she protested.

"We're sorry, but we have our orders," he insisted.

When it was clear they wouldn't take "no" for an answer, she stomped off after them. She kept looking anxiously at her timepiece—if she got this over with quickly, she could still make it back to the ship in time. When she got to her parents' quarters, Sia burst through the doors and exclaimed, "Father this is really too much! My ship will be leaving shortly. What is so important you had to drag me back here?" When she realized Sarin wasn't with him she said, "Where's mother, has something happened to her?"

Ivege smiled wanly. "No dear, she's fine. She simply didn't have the stomach to tell you."

"Tell me what?" asked Sia apprehensively.

"The zon have attacked another of our colonies and are moving on two more. They are too distant and we don't have the forces to protect them. We are in the process of evacuating them."

"Why don't we ask our 'good friends' the Kealt for assistance?" she replied sarcastically.

"As a matter of fact we did," said Ivege. "They are already helping us transport personnel to Dacat V, which is in a more heavily fortified sector, and have promised to send more ships immediately."

"I'm very sorry father, I really am," answered Sia impatiently, "but what has this to do with me?"

Ivege pointed to a chair and said, "Please, sit down."

Sia remained standing. "I don't have time for this! My ship will be leaving!"

"Sia," replied Ivege sadly, "I'm afraid you're not going to be on it. The zon threat is unsettling our kingdom. We need to show our subjects that we're doing everything in our power to meet this encroaching menace. Therefore, I would like you to go to Dacat V and take personal charge of refugee resettlement."

"You can't be serious!" she huffed.

"I am quite serious," he assured her. "You will leave within the hour."

"These are the last three months of my freedom!" she huffed. "I will not spend them attending to the affairs of distant colonies I've never even heard of!"

"I'm sorry Sia, but we were born to certain duties. We must not appear callous or disinterested in the face of such devastation."

She began crying and exclaimed, "This is so unfair!"

"It is indeed," he replied.

Before the day ended, she was en route to Dacat V.

Chapter IV

Aden sat at his desk, awash in paperwork he had been avoiding for months. There were performance reviews, requisition requests, personnel transfer notifications, requests from charities, and countless other administrative minutia. He didn't know where to start. Just when he seriously thought a small office fire might be the answer, he was jolted by a knock on the doorframe.

"Yes Tock!" he enthusiastically greeted the desiccated, nervous-looking old man who stood hunched in the doorway wringing his hands. For reasons Aden never understood, Edris employed the bird-like Tock Horat as his senior aide. "What can I do for you?"

"I'm so sa sa sorry to bother you, Your Highness," he stuttered, "but you wanted to know when the remainder of the Ardalan royal family departed Kealt. Their ship sa sa safely departed an hour ago."

"Very well; is there anything else, and I mean *anything*, you have to report that could mercifully delay me from diving into this mess before me?"

"Ya ya yes, there is one other thing…"

"Oh?"

"A young woman is sitting in the atrium. She came by yesterday as well. She said her name is Drusa Prine, that you ma ma met her at the dance, and wished to see her again."

"Ah, the well-rounded raven-haired girl!" he replied enthusiastically. "Excellent Tock! Please tell her I'll be right out!" He had forgotten her name, but remembered her well. She wasn't especially well brained, but she'd been fun to dance with and had gone a long way toward helping him forget Sia's inattention.

While he couldn't remember having asked her to visit him, he didn't care—any excuse would have served to get him out from behind his desk. He picked up a fist full of papers hoping to accomplish something before he left for the day. He quickly grew fed up, tossed them onto the desk, and went to look for Drusa.

When he stepped into the atrium she stood up, smiled broadly, and said, "There you are! I thought you were avoiding me!"

She was small, almost petite, but full-figured, wearing a short, black skirt, and a white, very low cut, almost sheer blouse that did next to nothing to conceal her well-constructed bosom. She was holding a black and white checkered purse, which matched her outfit perfectly. She had her thick, straight black hair pulled back in a ponytail, and her dark, almost black, almond-shaped eyes were framed in just the right amount of makeup. With her dusky, clear skin, full lips, perfect teeth, and strong cheekbones, he noted that she was quite attractive and even exotic looking. He had never seen anyone quite like her before.

"Nothing of the sort," he answered cheerfully, "I have been fully occupied trying to sort through the mountains of paperwork I have been unable to delegate to others, many of whom actually resigned rather than take it on."

"You are so funny!" she said giggling. "You must have an important job. This is a really nice building."

Aden was incredulous. Was it possible she really didn't know who he was? "Ah, yes," he replied. "Are you hungry?"

"I could eat a sogalot!"

"A what?"

"Don't you have them on Kealt? It's a large bovine. We raise them for meat."

"You're not from Kealt?" he asked.

"No, I'm from Epsilon II. It's a wonderful place. Have you heard of it?"

"The name sounds familiar…"

"A while ago we learned the zon were coming. King what's-his-name agreed to let us come to Kealt. He said we can stay as long as we like, although I really hope we can go home soon!"

Aden shivered. Now he remembered Epsilon II. Half its inhabitants refused to be evacuated. Before Kealt could send a force sufficient to defend them, the zon conquered them and dug in so deep Kealt couldn't help them. Those that were still alive were undoubtedly food or drones.

"Dursa…"

"No silly, it's Drusa! My real name is Drusilla, but my older brother always called me Drusa and the name just stuck."

"Yes, I'm sorry, Drusa. Do you have any relatives?"

"Yes," she replied brightly, "my parents and brother; that's why I'm so eager to go home. They stayed behind."

Aden felt sick. Either she didn't know they were doomed, or was in deep denial. He suddenly felt very sorry for her. "Come on," he said, offering her his arm, "let's get something to eat."

To his great surprise dinner was fun. Drusa wasn't bright, but she was vibrant, funny, and a good listener. For once, he felt he could have an honest, open conversation with a woman who didn't want something from him. It was very refreshing.

When he finally told her who he was, she responded no differently than if he'd said he was a used hover car salesman. It was truly all the same to her. Every once in a while she'd ask a question that seemed odd for her, but he never even noticed. By the end of the evening, she probably knew nearly as many of Kealt's secrets as Tock, but Aden was convinced she would forget them before they even got to the door.

When it was time to leave, he asked if he could escort her home. She thanked him enthusiastically, and directed his hover car driver to a refugee camp on the edge of Rilan. Kealt had hastily erected the camp to take in refugees from Epsilon II and other colonies until they could make long-term arrangements for them. It looked dirty, dark, and dangerous. When the door opened and Drusa stepped out, Aden grabbed her arm.

"Yes Aden?"

"Would you…would you like to come home with me tonight?"

She gave him a chastising look and said, "We just met! On Epsilon we move a little slower!"

Aden suppressed a smile. "I'm sorry Drusa, that's not what I meant. I have very large quarters, and if you like you could have a room of your own…at least temporarily…until you find a better place to stay."

"Well, that is very kind of you, but my belongings are here. If I leave them, someone may take them. There are people here far worse off than I am."

Aden stepped out of the car himself. "Come on. Let's get your stuff."

"Are you sure?" replied Drusa. "I mean it—you'll get nothing from me."

"I'm sure. Please lead the way."

Drusa took his hand and led him through a rabbit warren of canvas dwellings. In addition to being dark and dangerous, the place reeked of vomit, feces, urine, and other smells Aden couldn't identify and was thankful for it. "How long have you lived here?" he asked.

"Oh, not long—a few weeks," she replied brightly.

"Has anything…bad…ever happened to you here?"

"What do you mean?"

"Never mind," he answered.

Momentarily they turned a corner and came upon two men in the act of mugging an old woman. Aden immediately intervened, throwing one man through a rickety wooden latrine, and pummeling the second man. As he delivered a knockout blow, the first man recovered, rushed him from behind and thrust a homemade knife into his shoulder. Aden wheeled around as the man drew his arm back for a second thrust. Before he could deliver it, Drusa struck him in the back of the head with a board from the ruined latrine, and he crumpled to the ground.

With the two men out of the way, Aden staggered over to the old woman who was now sitting on the ground crying and helped her up.

"Come with us," he said. "We'll get you some help."

Just then, a younger woman came up to them and said she was the woman's daughter. After a brief consultation, the old woman advised that while she was shaken up, she was otherwise uninjured and wished to stay.

As the women were leaving, the two men who had caused the commotion lurched to their feet and slunk off into the darkness. When they were gone, Drusa moved behind Aden and said softly, "Please, take off your shirt and let me look at your injury." When the pain made it difficult for him to comply, she helped him strip it off, then she gently probed the wound with her fingers. When he winced she said, "I don't think it's too bad, but it's bleeding and we need to patch you up until we can get you to a medunit." Then she tore off her blouse and used it to administer surprisingly skillful first aid. As she was finishing up, she said, almost whispering, "Do you want me to get help?"

Aden didn't answer her directly, but gingerly pulled his shirt back on and asked her gruffly if she had anything that was worth dying for. Now wearing only a thin, virtually transparent bra, she grinned and assured him that she *would* die if she couldn't retrieve her favorite shoes.

Fortunately, they had almost reached her tent when the attack occurred. When they got to it, she threw back the flap and startled a man and woman. It was too dark for Aden to make out their features, but he could see that the woman was holding something bright in her hand. When she saw Aden, she turned and quickly shoved it under a towel sitting on top of a small wooden crate in the back of the tent. Other than three cots that took up most of the room, the crate was the only other piece of "furniture" in the makeshift dwelling. Drusa invited him in, and asked the other two if they would join her outside. From the tone of the discussion, they weren't happy she was leaving.

While they were talking, Aden walked back to the crate, made sure they were still arguing, then flipped up the towel to see what the woman was hiding. It was small, silvery, and appeared to be some kind of hand scanner, although it was unlike any he had ever seen. A strange thing for desperate refugees to be in possession of, he thought.

It had a screen, but it was blank. He tried to turn it on, hoping to find a clue to its origin. He quickly gave up—it had no knobs, buttons, switches, or any other obvious controls, and didn't respond to his handling. He guessed it was energized by some unique characteristic of its owner, like a fingerprint or DNA.

He had barely thrown the towel back over it when Drusa returned, grabbed a bag from under one of the cots, and threw her sparse possessions into it. She said brightly, "I don't have much, but when you see my shoes, you'll know it was worth it!" Aden told the other two they also could come with him, but they refused and glowered at them mutely as he took Drusa's bag, slung it over his good shoulder, and led her away.

As they were weaving their way back through the tents, Aden asked, "Drusa, how well do you know those two? Did they come with you from Epsilon?"

"No they didn't," she replied. "I met them when I arrived here. They saw I didn't have anyone to help me and they took me in. They're brother and sister. To tell the truth, Abner, that's the brother's name, has a little bit of a crush on me. That's why he wasn't happy when I agreed to go with you—he was worried I wouldn't be safe. Can you imagine anything so ridiculous?" Just then she tripped over a guy wire and would have fallen if Aden hadn't been there to catch her. "My, I can be so clumsy," she said cheerfully.

When they were again on their way, Aden, still curious about her roommates, asked, "What is his sister's name? Do you know their last names? Or where they're from?"

"His sister is Molly. I don't know their last names or where they came from. Would you like to go back and ask?"

Aden suppressed a smile at her earnest response. "No," he replied. "I was just curious. When we entered the tent, the girl…Molly…had something shiny in her hand I'd never seen before. I'm just curious—do you know what it was?"

"I'm sure I don't. I've never seen her with anything like that. It was very dark. Are you sure it wasn't the light on her time piece?"

"That's probably it," he answered.

When they got back to the hover car, he had his driver take them to the nearest medunit. The doctors quickly pulled the wound together, applied some derma-grow, and, after confirming Drusa's diagnosis that he had suffered no serious injuries, sent him on his way.

When they finally arrived at his quarters, he was exhausted and sore. He led Drusa, now wearing a green medical gown borrowed from the medunit, past several highly concerned and curious servants, and up the stairs to his guest quarters. It was a large room, sparsely furnished, with a window overlooking the palace courtyard.

He had a servant fetch Drusa some fresh nightclothes. When she had come and gone he said, "I hope you like it, there's a bathroom behind that door. It should have everything you need, but if you want anything else, press that red button on the headboard and someone will be here directly. I've instructed one of the servants to take you shopping in the morning. I'm sure you could do with some proper clothing."

He reached into his pocket and pulled out a card. "Here," he said, as he handed it to her, "this will let you come and go as you wish, and buy what you need. You are welcome to stay until you can find a safer, more permanent arrangement. Just, please, don't make a mess, my servants are easily upset." When she didn't immediately answer, he turned to leave.

As he began to pull the door shut she said, "Thank you Aden, you are very kind. I promise I won't abuse your hospitality."

"Drusa, that is no way for someone to live."

"Perhaps not, but what is to be done? War is war and always leaves too little to go around."

"Maybe, but not this time," he said, as he walked out and shut the door behind him.

When he arose the next day, somewhat later than usual, a servant informed him that Drusa had already left with another servant. He wasn't sure she'd come back until the servant confirmed that her meager belongings were still in the room. "God forbid she lose those fine shoes," he muttered sarcastically.

That day he didn't go back to the palace. He commandeered a large construction crew, requisitioned the needed building materials, and ordered them to go to the refugee camp. He stayed with them for two weeks, personally overseeing the construction of more suitable barracks, the installation of electricity, running water, and better lighting, and the implementation of a security force sufficient to maintain order. It wouldn't be perfect, but it would be humane.

When he decided the project was far enough along he could again enjoy the comforts of his own quarters, he left someone in charge he trusted and went home. He had almost forgotten about Drusa, and was surprised to see she was still there. She was again concerned he was avoiding her and offered to leave.

When he told her where he had been he saw a look in her eyes that belied her otherwise blissfully ignorant exterior. As quickly as it came, it was gone.

She hugged him tightly and said, "Electricity? That is so nice! Everyone will be so happy now that they can iron their clothes!"

To his surprise, he again asked her out to dinner and again had a good time. In fact, he took her out every night that week. They talked about everything, from past lovers, to the state of Kealt technology, to the zon. Drusa knew very little about most things, and comprehended less, but enjoyed hearing him talk about them. She was the least self-centered woman he'd ever met. She rarely talked about herself, and he did not push her. He was sure she would get around to Epsilon II when she was ready to face it. Once she did, he sensed that he'd meet the real Drusa.

Curious about her background, Aden studied the refugee registry and found very little on her beyond the names of her immediate family members. This was not unexpected, since the zon had advanced quickly and the refugees had fled with little more than the clothes on their backs. Moreover, there was little in the records on Epsilon II itself. It was a small agricultural colony of less than 20,000 people on the edge of Kealt space. It fell quickly and was given up for lost. He was unable to find any records on refugees named Abner and Molly, who were brother and sister.

True to his word, as the days went by he remained a perfect gentleman, giving Drusa the space he had promised her. It wasn't easy. After all he was a man, and lonely—and she was well built.

Things changed one night when a massive electrical storm rocked the palace. The booms were so loud Aden almost fell out of bed. When he realized what it was, he rolled over and tried to fall back to sleep. Then he saw the figure of a woman in a thin nightgown standing in the doorway, illuminated by each lightning bolt. He didn't say anything as she walked over to the bed, removed her gown, and climbed in next to him.

"I'm scared," Drusa said, holding him tightly.

Aden returned her embrace and felt her warm, naked body trembling. "Under these circumstances," he responded gently, "you could hardly blame me for not being a perfect gentleman."

"*Please don't be*," she whispered.

Aden had been consumed with matters of state for so long, he'd almost forgotten how much he'd missed the pleasure of a woman, and for the next few days he actually looked forward to coming home.

Then, with his wedding just two months away, Drusa informed him she'd found a job and a safe place to stay. He didn't try to talk her out of it. While he had grown to like her, he knew he would never feel more strongly toward her than that; besides, he would be married soon, and as unpleasant as it promised to be, he would not have a mistress. Perhaps, he thought, Glyn and Celesta were right—if he gave Sia a chance she might eventually come around.

Regardless of his pending matrimony, he wanted to put some space between Drusa and himself. He didn't want to lead her on. She needed to find her own way, and he didn't want to be an obstacle.

The day she left, Edris summoned him to his chambers. He had not seen much of his father since he'd returned—they had both been busy. With Drusa leaving, he remembered how lonely he'd been. He could only imagine how Edris felt. When he arrived, Edris embraced him heartily. "Son," he said, "I understand you've made a new friend from among our refugees!"

"How do you know about that?" he asked, wearing a poorly concealed smirk.

"Do you really think the servants, some of whom we share, would keep this to themselves? Regardless, I hope you are being careful with her, you know our intelligence service believes Ardala has planted spies among our refugees; it would be very easy for them to do so, considering the lack of detailed records we have on many of our distant colonies."

"Father, do you really believe Ivege or Polis would do such a thing?"

"I do not," responded Edris, "but Ivege's grip on his government is as tenuous as mine is on ours. No telling what's going on behind his back."

"Well," responded Aden wryly, "she's not particularly well-brained or clever. I don't believe she has the wherewithal to be a very good spy."

"And yet within days of meeting you, she finds herself living in the very quarters of the heir to the throne of Kealt. Not bad for a simpleton."

"Hmm," snorted Aden. "She did at that! She was an Epsilon II refugee. When I took her home and saw where she lived, I couldn't leave her there. It was I who insisted she stay with me. Anyway, she's gone now."

"Yes, I've also heard what you've done with that camp. I'm proud of you, despite the fact that you stopped two politically important projects to do it. You will indeed make a fine leader one day."

"Perhaps," he replied. "I'm sure you're busy father. What is it you wished to see me about?"

"Very well then; I know you have just returned home, but we have an opportunity that will allow us to work with the Ardalans and convince them we are serious about forming a real alliance. Are you interested?"

Of course he was. He would have volunteered to command a garbage barge to escape life as a bureaucrat.

Chapter V

As their first formal act of mutual defense, Ardala and Kealt agreed to send their combined forces to intercept a large zon fleet that was one of several bearing down on Ardalan colonies being evacuated to Dacat V. With the intelligence leaks they'd been experiencing, Aden fully expected the zon to be long gone when the fleet exited hyperspace. After all, they'd been en route for weeks and it was anyone's guess how old the intelligence was to begin with. He and Polis decided not to send advance scouts or probes. If the zon were there, they didn't want to risk tipping them off if they hadn't been already.

The fleet dropped out of hyperspace a half day from the designated coordinates, because Aden and Polis thought it prudent to submit each ship to a full inspection before risking a battle with the zon. They also used the time to plan meticulously their entry into the solar system believed to be sheltering the zon.

Neither Kealt nor Ardala knew much about this region of space; however, they were now close enough to perform long-range scans, which revealed significant fields of radiation and several large asteroid fields. In addition to being dangerous to organic life forms, the radiation would make it impossible to maintain a stable cloak. To Aden's surprise, the scans also confirmed zon energy emanations.

The readings indicated more than 200 ships, but the natural background radiation made it impossible to know for sure. He had hoped to lead Kealt's cloaked ships into the system undetected, with the fleet's uncloaked ships quickly following; however, with the ability to cloak compromised that was now impossible. If they didn't plan their approach carefully, ships could be damaged or even destroyed by the dangerous phenomena, or be easy targets for the zon. The ambient conditions meant it would take time to assemble the fleet safely, and that might be time they didn't have.

Once Polis and Aden agreed on a plan, the fleet was ready to go. After 12 tense hours, the ships reached the zon's purported location. When they jumped into normal space, the reason for the inconsistent energy readings quickly became clear: Orbiting the fourth planet was the wreckage of the zon fleet. Many ships still burned, others were lifeless hulks. A survey of the destruction eventually revealed the remains of 250 zon ships, including 25 of their most advanced battle cruisers and motherships. Too shocked for words, Aden continued to stare at the vidscreen until Gris interrupted him.

"Sir, Admiral Polis is hailing us."

"What?" Aden replied distractedly. "Oh yes, of course, put him on."

When the image of Polis replaced that of the zon wreckage, Aden said, "So much for our preparations. It looks like something has done our work for us."

Speaking in a measured tone Polis replied, "Yes it does; permission to come aboard to discuss this further."

Aden's lips curled up slightly in a grim smile. "Of course admiral; however, before you leave your ship I believe it would be prudent to complete a survey of the wreckage and insure no surprises remain." Aden sensed Polis's concern and shared it. A terrible force had destroyed the zon's massive fleet, apparently without leaving a trace. Such power was almost unfathomable.

The survey took longer than expected. It was ten hours before Aden decided it was safe for Polis to come aboard; when he did, Aden's men immediately escorted him and his entourage to the *Garm's* stateroom, where a sumptuous feast was waiting. Aden embraced him heartily and said, "It is always good to live another day!"

Polis laughed. "It is indeed my good friend. Let's hope we have many more!"

Once seated, attendants hovered over the table ensuring that the needs of Aden, his officers, and his guests were immediately met. Almost a day had passed since their last repast. They were ravenous, too ravenous to talk. Food and drink flew about the table, with nothing more intelligible than a grunt uttered. Twenty minutes later Aden leaned back in his chair, fully stated. Polis soon followed suit. Aden nodded to an orderly who quickly refilled his glass and Polis's. He took a long drink, then carefully set down his glass. Looking grimly at Polis, he said, "I assume you've had a chance to review the results of the survey of what remains of the zon fleet?"

"I have," replied Polis.

"So, what do you make of it?"

"Eh?"

"You know of what I speak."

"Ah, you mean the organic residue we found floating among the debris."

Aden smiled humorlessly. "I do indeed. Have your people ever seen anything like it before?"

Polis furrowed his brow. "No," he answered pensively, "we have not."

"I ask again, what do you make of it?"

"Well," he replied, "it had been alive. In fact, our initial analysis indicates that space is probably its natural habitat."

"Yes, our scientists came to the same conclusion. Where do you think it came from?"

"It's hard to say. Our best guess is that it is battle damage suffered by the forces that did this, most likely the tayron."

"Battle damage?" asked Aden incredulously. "You mean this stuff came off their ships?"

"Perhaps," answered Polis. "Our scientists believe that organic ships are theoretically possible."

"Polis, if this new species is hostile…"

"Yes!" he snorted grimly, without waiting for Aden to finish.

They paused their conversation while orderlies began to distribute dessert. When they were finished Polis leaned over, put his forearms on the table, and whispered, "We're barely holding our own with the zon. Even united we don't have the power to deal with the zon *and* this new threat!"

Aden tapped Polis on the forearm and said, "Well then, let's hope they are friend and *not* foe!"

Polis laughed mirthlessly. "Very good," he replied. "You are a hopeless optimist! I can see why you and Sia clash." When Aden didn't answer he added, "She is my sister and I love her; unfortunately she seems to have heaped on you all sins ever committed against women by men. If she ever gave you a chance…"

A faint smile creased Aden's face. He held up his glass and said, "Here's to Sia, one of God's greatest and most enigmatic creations!"

Polis raised his own glass, tapped Aden's, and said, "Here's to Celesta, who shares those same qualities."

"Indeed," replied Aden.

"So what do we do now?" asked Polis, placing his empty glass back on the table.

Aden finished his own ale and said, "We've programmed the DNA of the organic substance into our sensors."

"And?"

"We're tracking a group of these…life forms…about four light years from here."

"Let me guess..."

"Admiral Selarney," replied Aden dramatically, "we would be most honored if the flagship of the mighty Ardalan fleet would join us as we try to make first contact with what promises to be a most impressive new species!"

Polis stood up and said, "It has been a most interesting repast, Admiral Cade. Thank you for the hospitality you have shown my men and I! I will consider your offer, but I cannot commit this fleet to such an undertaking without talking to my king. May I get back to you in the morning?"

Aden stood up and grasped Polis's hand. "Of course admiral; truth be told I must do the same. I will respect whatever decision you and your government make." They received their mutual blessings the next day and shortly after the fleet set off in search of the zons' destroyers.

Chapter VI

Within a few days, the alien fleet disappeared from their sensors. As Aden prepared his own ships for the journey home, Edris sent new orders: Ardala had a small archaeological colony on a planet referred to as XR564. It was within the evacuation zone Sia was overseeing, and was dead in the path of advancing zon forces. With no defenses, they would be helpless when the zon reached them sometime in the next few days. Ardala could not spare any more ships to rescue such a small group so far off the beaten path.

Fortuitously, Aden and Polis's pursuit of the zon and then the tayron had put them within striking distance of the colony. With any luck, they would be able to reach it and pick up the colonists before the zon arrived. Aden eagerly accepted the assignment, thinking a little excitement would be good for his men after their recent false starts.

Later Polis hailed him on a private channel to provide additional details.

As Aden got comfortable in a soft chair in his quarters, Polis said, "I'm sorry you're getting drawn into this. You're probably wondering why we can't handle this on our own."

"I assumed it was to provide greater strength in the event the zon fleet turned out to be bigger than anticipated."

"Even if that were true, Ardala would never seek your assistance with the number of ships I have at my disposal, any more than Kealt would seek ours under similar circumstances."

Aden picked up the cup of tea that was resting on a small table in front of him, took a sip and said, "Well then, to what do we owe this honor? It's not every day we're called on to help a force as mighty as yours evacuate an Ardalan colony."

Polis smiled joylessly. "To call this little group a 'colony' greatly overstates the matter. They are in fact just a small expedition, twelve scientists in all. For the past year, they have been studying the ruins of a long-dead civilization discovered during a routine planetary survey.

"Four weeks ago, they discovered something they believe to be of critical importance. Unfortunately, it's encased in some kind of crystal matrix, and they've had to extract it slowly or risk damaging it. We did attempt to remove them two weeks ago, but they refused. They said they were too close to retrieving their prize, whatever it is.

"We left them an interplanetary shuttle, hoping that if they changed their minds they could be gone before the zon got there, or at least buy time until we could get to them. Anyway, the zon are almost upon them and the shuttle now seems like a futile gesture."

Now it was Aden's turn to smile. "I see," he said, "but you still haven't told me why you need our assistance."

"Yes, I'm getting to it!" responded Polis. "The expedition has said they will refuse any assistance until they secure the artifact."

"Can't you forcibly repatriate them?"

"No," replied Polis tersely. "Ardalan law is quite clear on these matters. Except under very limited circumstances, none of which apply here, we cannot forcibly remove civilians, regardless of the consequences to them."

"Ah," said Aden, as Polis's meaning became clear, "and I don't suppose Ardala has properly registered XR564 per the Agilare Treaty."

Ardala and Kealt had signed the Agilare Treaty decades earlier. It was an attempt to stop the bloodshed that frequently occurred when one side or the other discovered a resource-rich celestial body, and the other side decided they wanted it more.

Per the terms of the treaty, once registered, a body belongs to the side that registered it, and they would rule it unmolested. While the framers of the treaty meant well, the reality was that the rules of registration were arcane and complicated, and left plenty of room for interpretation. Therefore, instead of protecting planetary rights, the attempt to register an asset was more likely to lead to an attack, since the act of registration required the asset's coordinates as well as a list of its valuable properties.

It didn't take long for Ardala and Kealt to ignore the treaty, and take their chances that the other side would never learn of their valuable discoveries. After all it was a big galaxy, and it was unlikely one side would stumble onto the other's possessions.

"No again," replied Polis, a smile playing on his lips. "Somehow we have failed to get around to registering our claim."

"So, under the treaty, XR564 is essentially fair game. You may not be able to force your people off it, but we can. Is that it?"

"As always, you are very astute."

"Polis, that's dirty business; since my father ascended to the throne, Kealt has never forcibly obtained any celestial body claimed by Ardala or any other species."

"I know," replied Polis, "I'm sorry to say that at times we have not been so considerate. At any rate, we're not asking you to remove the scientists by force. We're hoping that your mere appearance will intimidate them into leaving before the zon arrive."

Aden finished his tea and sat back in his chair. "So," he said, "do you know any of these scientists?"

"Yes. The head of the expedition is Dr. Willa Beltran. She is an old friend of the family's, a distant relative in fact, and well connected. She can be most stubborn at times, especially where her discoveries are concerned. And she believes this is a big one."

"Are they armed?"

"I don't believe so. They're scientists, not fighters. Even if they had weapons, I can't imagine any of them could actually get up the nerve to use one."

"So you say!" Aden snickered. "Have you forgotten Celesta is a scientist too?" When Polis didn't reply he said, "Very well then, it will be done as you say. Now my friend, I must get some sleep. I've been up a long time."

When they reached XR564 several days later, the zon were only hours behind. The size of their fleet was unknown, but it was believed to be a large one. Even though Polis would never admit it, he was glad that Aden had agreed to commit his fleet as well.

Aden had Gris pick out ten of his most proven soldiers, and he met them on the hanger deck. XR564 was a grim world, in some ways more dangerous even than Seti. It was a rocky, lifeless place, filled with active volcanoes, covered with a perpetual cloud of wind-blown dust, and prone to earthquakes and massive, unpredictable climate changes caused by the pull of its three moons. It had very little water and even without the dust, the atmosphere was unsafe to breath for more than a few minutes at a time. What's more, the ionization of the atmosphere severely compromised beaming and cloaking technology.

How twelve people had managed to survive in such an inhospitable environment was a mystery. Perhaps, thought Aden, they were tougher than Polis believed.

He began to pull on his body armor. It felt little different from his regular uniform, which was made from the undercoat of a mammal that lived on the frozen tundra near Kealt's northern pole. There the similarity ended, however.

It was a technical material that instantly took on the color and pattern of its surroundings. In the event the wearer was fired on by either kinetic or energy weapons, the material would stiffen instantly and dissipate the force of the attack. It also could protect the wearer from temperature extremes and toxic chemicals. All in all, a most effective garment. Before he was finished, Gris approached him with a stern look.

"My dear first officer," said Aden, "you look quite disturbed by…something."

"I should say so! This plan of Polis's does not require the Prime Admiral of the Kealt Fleet, who is also Kealt's high prince, to take such a personal risk with the zon hot on our heels!"

"Perhaps not," replied Aden cheerfully, "but you know how I like the unknown, and this world is certainly unknown!"

"Then I will accompany you!" insisted Gris.

Aden rested his hand on his shoulder. He said, "My good friend, as you say, the zon are hot on our heels. If you come with me, to whom should I trust my life up here? You must stay with the fleet and be ready to defend it."

Gris looked at him doubtfully. "Very well then, but only if you promise not to take any unnecessary chances; you know how cross Glyn would be with me if anything happened to you."

Aden finished securing his body armor and picked up his gear. He smiled ironically and said, "What's the worst that could happen?" When Gris merely shook his head disapprovingly, he nodded, then turned and boarded the shuttle.

Aden did not have a weak stomach, but he was queasy when the shuttle finally landed. The atmospheric turbulence had been even worse than anticipated, and it took all of his piloting skills to land safely. Once they had secured the ship, and his squad members had overcome their own queasiness, he asked Major Alba Tarkis for a status report.

"While most of us are feeling a little green, the ship is fine sir," he replied. He studied a panel and said, "As we anticipated the sensors are a little iffy in this radiation, but as best I can tell we've landed about ten kilometers east of the settlement. That's about the closest we can safely get in the shuttle. The terrain between here and there is a little rough. It's going to be slow going. Fortunately the ambient temperature is around 65°—currently."

"All right then," replied Aden. "By now, Polis should have contacted the colony and let them know we're coming. Let's not keep them waiting!"

Tarkis ordered two of his men to stay behind and look after their only means of transportation, and told the remainder of the squad to don their respirators, check their weapons, and grab their gear. Then they stepped out of the shuttle into…hell! The wind was blowing hard against them, and the air was filled with so much dust it was difficult to see more than a meter or two ahead. Without their respirators, they would have been dead within minutes. While the temperature was presently comfortable, Aden knew that it could easily go up or down by 50° without warning. Their armor provided some protection against the elements, but it had limits.

Although they couldn't see it very well, the desolate terrain undulated severely, and was strewn with large rocks, gravel piles, and sand dunes that made it impossible to take a straight line to the colonists. To make matters worse numerous fissures, some impossibly deep, could easily swallow a careless explorer, and it would be just as easy to fall off a cliff. It was hard to imagine anything ever could have lived in such a hostile and unyielding environment.

As the team trudged forward Aden's concern grew. It was going to take them hours to reach the colony, and hours more back to the shuttle. The zon could easily reach the fleet by then. Tarkis periodically consulted a hand- scanner, which held the expedition's coordinates, to ensure the group continued in the right direction. When they reached a cliff face with no way around or over, Aden asked him how much further they needed to go.

"I don't know, sir," he replied. "According to the scanner we're here."

As they were pondering their next move, a figure wearing an environmental suit appeared from seemingly out of nowhere. He—or she—gestured for them to follow. Aden took his weapon off his shoulder and the squad followed suit. When the figure turned and walked away Aden and the squad followed. They traveled through a natural rock labyrinth, finally coming to a stop in front of a large metal door. The figure opened it by waving a hand over an invisible sensor. Aden and the others followed the figure inside until they reached an airlock.

The figure stood patiently as the airlock pressurized. When the cycle was complete, they emerged into a large, pressurized cavern filled with supply crates, scientific instruments, industrial tools, and what appeared to be artifacts. The figure faced the squad and removed her respirator and head gear.

"I am Dr. Willa Beltran," she said, "the leader of this expedition. Admiral Polis told me you were coming."

Dr. Beltran was short and squat, with long gray hair and a naturally stern expression. She reminded Aden of a most unpleasant teacher he'd once had in primary school. When he and his men had removed their own respirators, he said, "This is an unregistered planet. We are here to claim it for Kealt. Under the terms of the treaty governing such matters, we will escort you and your fellow scientists back to Ardala."

"Kealts?" she replied in alarm. "When Polis contacted me, I assumed Ardalans were coming. What trickery is this?"

"There is no trick. We're part of a joint force sent to oversee this sector's evacuation."

"Why did Polis send *you*? Are Kealts now the lapdogs of the Ardalan Government, sent to do their dirty work?"

Aden bit his tongue before responding. He knew she was baiting him, but the insult stung nonetheless. When he felt sufficiently confident that he could respond civilly he said, "We're here to save your lives. As you well know, Ardalan law prevents your own people from forcing you off this rock; since this is an unregistered world we have no such restrictions."

"I see," she replied. With a hand signal armed figures emerged from behind the various crates and pieces of equipment. "We will resist you if you try to remove us by force."

At the sight of armed figures emerging from the clutter, Aden's men raised their own weapons.

"At ease!" he ordered. "We're here to help these people!" When his soldiers had reluctantly shouldered their weapons he said, "No one is going to remove you by force. Polis hoped our presence alone would intimidate you in to leaving. I can see that's not going to happen."

Dr. Beltran studied Aden's face, her gaze coming to rest on his scar. "You look familiar," she said. "Who are you?"

"Admiral Aden Cade."

"Aden…Cade? *High Prince* Aden Cade?"

"Yes."

"Why would Kealt allow Ardala to send its future king to such an insignificant, obscure world, especially with the zon bearing down on us? Does your father wish to see you dead?"

Aden failed to suppress a snicker. "No," he replied, "at least I hope not! As I started to explain earlier, we were part of a joint Ardalan-Kealt fleet investigating zon movements. We happened to be the nearest friendly forces. When King Ivege requested our assistance, we gladly agreed."

"So you have no interest in our discovery?"

"I can't say that definitively, since we have no idea what your discovery is. Neither, apparently, does anyone else. I am, however, most curious!"

Dr. Beltran's stony face broke into a half smile. "If I tell you, will you promise you will not try to force us off this rock?" she asked.

"I already told you we wouldn't."

"So you did. Are all Kealt negotiators as bad as you?"

"I surely hope not!"

One of the other scientists stepped forwarded and protested. "Don't tell him anything!" he insisted. "I don't believe for a second Ardala would cooperate with Kealt on such an important matter!"

Dr. Beltran replied, "Under other circumstances I would agree, but I know Polis well. If he trusts this man, we can too."

The scientist looked unconvinced, but lowered his weapon and made no further objections.

Dr. Beltran shook her head. "These are indeed strange times, when such collaboration is possible."

"Well then," said Aden, "will you and your fellow scientists leave with us now, willingly? If we hurry it may not be too late to avoid the zon."

"We cannot. It's no mistake that the zon are committing their forces to such an insignificant speck in the galaxy. Undoubtedly their sources among our people have told them of what we've found."

"What *have* you found?"

"We don't know exactly. When a previous survey team discovered an energy emanation that couldn't be natural, we came to investigate. It eventually led to this cavern." She waved to a tunnel at the back of the cavern and said, "Through that tunnel lies what we believe is a repository of knowledge left behind by a highly sophisticated race of silicon based life forms. Long before we even existed, they either became extinct, or for reasons unknown, abandoned this planet.

"The signal is emanating from a device encased in a block of crystal in a manner we can't comprehend. We've had no luck moving the crystal itself. Based on other evidence we've uncovered in this and other caverns, we believe it was intentionally left here to document their existence. We think it contains the knowledge of a wonderful, long gone race."

"Indeed," replied Aden, "may we see it?"

Dr. Beltran and the other scientists led them to the back of the cavern and into the tunnel. fifty meters later, they emerged into another even larger cavern. The walls were covered in inscriptions that defied description.

The room was otherwise empty except for what remained of an eight square meter transparent cube resting in the middle of the cavern. In the center of the cube, Aden could see the device the Ardalans were so eager to liberate. Using the most advanced technology available, they had painstakingly removed most of the crystal that covered the artifact, and it was now tantalizingly close.

Aden walked around the cube, fascinated by its undeniable elegance. When he was finished he said, "How much longer?"

"I'm sorry?" replied Dr. Beltran.

"Before you're able to free it from the crystal?"

"Oh, of course! We're very close—perhaps a half a day."

"Why don't you just remove the entire crystal and free the device at your leisure?"

"That's a good idea, the problem is, it's affixed to the cavern floor in a way we don't understand."

"In that case, let's hope the zon are farther away than we think."

"What are you going to do?" asked Dr. Beltran.

"Everything in our power to give you that half a day; can we help you expedite the process?"

"Thanks for the offer Admiral Cade, but it is a delicate operation better left to our scientists. You must be hungry."

"What?"

"It was quite a grueling walk from where you landed your shuttle to here, and you have a long vigil ahead. Would you and your men like to eat?"

Taken aback by her sudden and unexpected hospitality, he replied, "Thank you, but we have our own rations, and we don't want to distract you from your work."

"Please, I insist. Only a couple of us can work on it at a time. The Ardalan Government spared no expense for this expedition, and that includes ensuring its scientists didn't get nostalgic for home cooking. We are quite well supplied—it would be a waste to leave it all to the zon."

"As you wish," he replied.

She took them down another tunnel that appeared to be lined with living quarters hewn out of the rock. The tunnel opened into yet another cavern, which served as a mess hall. She invited them to sit at a long table while she and her fellow scientists prepared the meal. When it was ready a half hour later, Aden and his men devoured it. As he paused to catch a breath, she noted good naturedly, "I see you do like our cuisine!"

"I'm sorry," replied Aden, sitting back in his chair. "I guess we were hungrier than I thought. And as you promised, it was excellent!"

"I apologize for the rude greeting. It's not every day we're visited by the high prince of Kealt. Congratulations on your upcoming wedding. I'm actually a distant relative of Polis and Sia. They are both wonderful, kind people. She will make you a good wife."

Eager to change the subject, Aden said, "I'm sorry you won't be able to see this project through, at least not in the near term."

"What if we insist on staying even after we free the artifact?"

"We will stay and defend you as best we can; but surely once you've liberated your treasure you will want to get it far away from here as quickly as you can."

Dr. Beltran smiled wanly. "Quite so, my dear admiral, I may be stubborn, but I'm not stupid. While I regret we won't be able to take back much of what we've found here, I doubt the zon will take interest in it once they realize there is nothing left of use to them. So as you hinted, we may indeed return one day."

She furrowed her brow. "You know, I met your cousin Celesta when she came to Ardala to participate on a joint deep space science expedition. Once I got past her quite considerable beauty, I found her to be a fascinating person, especially considering her tender age. It's a shame what happened to her out there. How is she?"

"She's had a rough time of it, but she's going to be OK," replied Aden, who then pushed back his chair, stood up, and said, "I don't wish to be rude, but my men and I have overindulged ourselves. We need to be ready to evacuate you and your colleagues as soon as you are ready."

A short time later Dr. Beltran's colleagues announced excitedly that they had freed the artifact. Almost immediately, Gris advised that the zon had arrived in force. While he and Polis did what they could to keep them from sending forces to the planet, there were too many ships and some got through.

With their shuttle hours away, Aden decided the best strategy would be to defend the cavern and hope the fleet's combined forces prevailed before the zon pinpointed their location. With that in mind, he ordered his men to take the high ground around the airlock and form a defensive perimeter. Then he ordered the men remaining with the shuttle to leave, hoping they would divert the zon's attention. As they lifted off, they reported that a large zon force was already less than a kilometer away and moving toward them through the air.

Aden had forgotten they could fly, which negated the natural protection provided by the rough terrain. He approached Dr. Beltran and asked her if her people were actually proficient in the use of the weapons they had brandished at his men earlier. When she assured him they were, he asked them to remain in the cavern and protect the artifact in the event they were overrun.

Just as Aden and his men took their positions, the zon began firing at them from all directions. Tarkis reported that they were close enough to register on the hand-scanner and that there were already over a hundred of them, with more joining the fray every second.

Aden was unable to contact Gris to get an update on the battle and request assistance. Regardless, there was no way he and Polis could provide reinforcements before the zon would overrun his little force. His men fought valiantly, but he knew defeat was just a matter of time. He stood up to fire and a zon particle beam slammed into his shoulder, propelling him back into the rocks. Groggy and bruised, he stood up, found his weapon, and bellowed for Tarkis to give him a status on the zon forces.

"Sir," he bellowed back, "there are now about 150 of them out there, and five more just appeared between the main body and us…wait a minute, this isn't right!"

"What isn't?" demanded Aden.

"These are different life forms. Something we've never seen before."

Aden crouched down beside a large boulder and leaned out cautiously, hoping to get a glimpse of the newcomers. "I can't see anything through this damned dust! Are you sure?"

"I am," he replied, "and there's something else—their weapon signatures are different."

"We know the zon have alien and human allies."

"I don't think so sir, they're firing on the zon. They're gone!"

"The newcomers?"

"No, the zon. They're all gone!"

"How is that possible!" exclaimed Aden.

"I don't know sir, but the new aliens are heading toward our position. Should we prepare to fire?"

"No!" he responded. "If they can destroy that many zon so easily we wouldn't have a chance. Are they still coming our way?"

"No sir. They appear to be waiting in an open area about thirty meters to our west." He pointed and added, "Just over those rocks."

Aden contacted Dr. Beltran and asked if their shuttle was nearby. She told him it was a few hundred meters to the north.

"I wouldn't recommend it sir," advised Tarkis. "A whole lot more zon are coming from that direction, and the south and west as well. They'll probably get there before we can."

"OK," replied Aden, "wait here."

"Where are you going?"

"To meet our new friends; don't fire on anything until I get back."

Aden set off in the direction Tarkis had indicated. When he came to a small open area, he could vaguely make out the outlines of several figures standing on the far side. They seemed to glow, as though their bodies were reacting to the ambient radiation. Although he couldn't see them very well through the blowing dust and low light, he could see well enough to know they weren't human. He moved toward them, but stopped when one of them said in a deep, guttural voice, "Admiral Cade, please don't come any closer."

Aden paused. "Who are you?" he responded. "Are you the tayron?"

""Yes, we are who you call the tayron."

"Why are you here?" he asked.

The creature said, "We're here to warn you. The zon have infiltrated both your worlds. They are attempting to create an alliance with you in the futile belief that, with your help, they might still prevail against us. They must not succeed—the fate of both your planets depends on it."

As the tayron's meaning sank in Aden replied, "There are hundreds of millions of people on Kealt and Ardala. Most would rather die than help the zon."

The tayron sounded sad when he answered, "I know; but not all zon collaborators are unwilling. You and you alone must decide what kind of society you will be—free or slave."

"Can you help us?"

"No. We can't change hearts; you have to do that yourselves."

"I mean here, now!"

"Sorry, can't help here either. We have a rule against interfering."

"Yet you came all this way to warn me. What good will it do if we never get off this rock!"

Before the tayron could respond, one of his companions grabbed his arm and in a female sounding voice similar to his said, "He's right. It's ridiculous to warn him and then leave him here knowing that he and his men will die! All we've been doing is interfering! These humans were holding their own until we forced the zon out of our galaxy and back to theirs." She pointed to Aden and said, "He'll be the king of Kealt one day—if he survives. He's a good man. Is it really in our best interest to stand by and let him die needlessly because we must honor some arbitrary code? To let entire civilizations fall to these monsters? Could we *be* more hypocritical?"

The other tayron let her words sink in, then said, "We'll help you this time, high prince; but you must win your own wars! We will take care of the zon down here and ensure you and your people make it safely back to your ship."

"There are only five of you," said Aden.

"More than enough," replied the creature haughtily. "Unfortunately the bulk of our forces are occupied elsewhere and we have only a small, lightly armed scout ship, which would not make much difference in the battle above. We will return you and your colleagues to your ship, but you must defeat the zon fleet yourselves. Heed our warning!"

In the time it took Aden to blink, he found himself on the bridge of the *Garm*.

"Aden!" exclaimed Gris. "How did you get here? And who are these others?"

"They're scientists, I'll explain later. Get them out of here! What's our status?"

"The fleet is holding its own, but our weapons are down and the mothership is firing on us!" An explosion rocked the *Garm* as if to emphasize the point.

"Have our fighters distract it!"

"They're trying, but there aren't enough of them and they're too small. We need a capital ship, but they're all occupied."

"How are our shields?"

Gris looked at a gauge and shouted, "They're down to 60% and falling!"

"Any ideas?" exclaimed Aden, as another impact nearly knocked him off his feet.

"Just one and you won't like it!"

"Quickly Gris, we're running out of time!"

"Our shields have enough juice left to protect us if we collide with her."

"What?" asked Aden incredulously.

"You heard me, ram the *Garm* right into her bridge. That will cripple her."

While zon weapons fire continued to pummel the ship's hull, a young ensign shouted, "Sir, if we're going to do it, we better do it fast—shields are down to 50%!"

"Do it ensign!" commanded Aden. "And put it on the vidscreen!"

Slowly the huge ship came about and picked up momentum as it closed on the even larger zon ship.

"Sir," bellowed the ensign, "shields are down to 35%. Not enough to get us through the mothership's shields in one piece!"

"Evasive maneuvers!" commanded Gris.

"We're too close sir," he responded.

Another officer shouted, "There is a small ship decloaking between us and the mothership! It's similar in design to those organic ships we've been following. I'm reading a massive power surge. They're firing!"

"Well?" demanded Aden. "Any damage to the zon ship?"

In a stunned voice the ensign reported, "I don't know how this is possible sir—they've knocked out their shields. We're going to make it!"

The zon mothership grew larger on their vidscreen. By the time they guessed what the *Garm* was up to, it was too late. They were now so close Aden and Gris could see the expressionless faces of the zon commanders as they looked up through the transparent covering of their bridge, and then watched helplessly as the *Garm* plowed through it. It was fully halfway into the mothership when Aden gave the order to reverse engines.

"Sir!" exclaimed the ensign. "I'm detecting huge power surges. The ship is going to explode!"

"Get us out of here Gris!" bellowed Aden. The *Garm* surged backwards in a desperate attempt to put distance between it and the doomed ship. Seconds later a huge shockwave belted it. Consoles exploded all over the bridge, lights flickered on and off, and a low gravity alarm rang out. "Damage report!" exclaimed Aden, holding on to a railing

Gris found one of the few working consoles left and shouted, "Main power is off line, we have minimal life support, our shields are down, artificial gravity is failing, and we may have structural damage!"

"Any good news?"

"Yes sir," he replied. "The xanide matrix is stable, we're not losing atmosphere, and most systems are coming back on line on emergency power."

"And the zon?"

"What's left of them is fleeing back into hyperspace."

"How about the organic ship?"

"Gone as well."

When Aden was confident that the zon were gone and the ship was stable enough he could leave the repairs to others, he contacted Polis and updated him on his experience on the planet. It turned out that, not only had the tayron saved his men and the science team, they also beamed all of the team's equipment and other property, including artifacts they had uncovered, into a large cargo bay on the *Garm*. Apparently the hostile conditions on the planet were no match for their technology.

Subsequent scans of the planet were inconclusive, but revealed no evidence that any of the zon sent to the surface had survived. As for Aden himself, his injuries were painful, but not life threatening. As soon as it was safe to do so, he had the science team and their effects transferred to the *Kreg*, which had suffered considerably less damage than the *Garm*.

While it was too early to know, he hoped the supposed database the science team had recovered was worth the trouble it had caused. With the rescue mission concluded successfully and the *Garm* patched up enough to limp home, Aden's dread returned—Sia was waiting for him.

Chapter VII

By the time the *Garm* reached Kealt the wedding was just days away. Before Aden even stepped off the gangplank, Edris summoned him to the royal gardens. He barely had time to clean himself up and change into appropriate clothes before he had to make his way to the gardens, which was a sprawling, two square kilometer expanse that separated the royal palace from the Kealt Capital Cathedral. The cathedral was the seat of the largest religion on Kealt, and the one to which the royal family traditionally belonged. It also was where the royal wedding would take place.

He wasn't surprised that Edris had asked to meet him in the gardens. They both hated the formality of palace life, and used every excuse to avoid it. The gardens served as a welcome respite. It was easy to get lost among its fields of carefully manicured flowers, trees, bushes, and other plant life, separated by meticulously maintained paths.

Despite the park's size it didn't take Aden long to find his father; he almost always found his way to the huge goliathan tree near the center, and today was no different.

Edris was beaming as he approached. He held out his arms and said, "Welcome home my son. We've seen far too little of each other lately."

Aden embraced his father and replied, "It's true; but it is good to see you too."

Edris put a hand on his shoulder and led him to a nearby bench. "You know," he said, as they both sat down, "I never get tired of this place. I thank God war never found its way here." When Aden nodded his head in agreement, but said nothing, Edris wrinkled his brow. "So, you and Polis had quite an adventure—a mysteriously destroyed zon fleet, the discovery of ancient artifacts, and meeting an equally mysterious new race that just happens to be intent on killing the zon. I find it most interesting."

"'Disturbing' is probably a better description," noted Aden wryly.

"I've read and re-read your reports son," replied Edris somberly, as he leaned back on the bench. "Nice work on XR564. Do you think Ardala really discovered anything of significance?"

"*They* certainly do, or at least, one of them does. At any rate, they promised to share their findings with us once they have a chance to study the artifact in depth."

Edris shook his head sagely. "It's still hard to imagine that the zon fleet was merely debris when you reached it, with no sign of the agent of its demise."

"Even seeing it in person, it was hard to believe. Some of their most advanced ships were in so many pieces it was difficult even to identify them."

"So, you believe the tayron did it?"

"Based on what I saw them do on XR564, and to that mothership, I'd say it's pretty clear it was them. At least I hope there isn't yet another all-powerful, vengeful species wandering around the galaxy."

Edris snorted in grim amusement. Then he frowned and said, "The reports say that you discovered some form of organic residue?"

"Yes. We speculate that it came off tayron ships during their battle with the zon, if you could call it a battle. As you know, we reconfigured our sensors to scan for it and discovered what appeared to be a sizable fleet several light years away. It was heading toward zon space. We tracked them, but could never get close. It was as though they were intentionally avoiding us."

Edris stroked his chin thoughtfully. "We can barely fend off the zon. This new visitor is mighty beyond our comprehension. I doubt even the combined forces of Kealt and Ardala could slow down such a power, let alone defeat them."

"Are they our enemy than?"

"Based on your meeting with them it is an open question, but I pray they are not. It seems they are prepared to take drastic action if we cannot weed out the zon sympathizers in our midst."

"That was the warning, and I for one, would not like to call their bluff."

Edris stood up. "I'm sure you have a lot to do. Your wedding is almost upon you. Certainly we can afford to put the concerns of the universe on hold until then. Please, join me for dinner—unless you have other plans? Like spending time with your refugee friend?"

Aden smiled. "You know she moved out. I would like to get an updated status report on the state of my fleet, especially the *Garm*, which I fear has seen her best days."

Edris said, "I know you and Gris are quite fond of her. Fortunately, if the damage to her is severe, her replacement is under construction as we speak. Have you had a chance to review her specifications?"

"I'm afraid I haven't. I'll see you at dinner father."

"Very well; I think I'll stay here just a bit longer. See you at dinner then."

The next few days went by quickly, then the moment Aden had been dreading finally arrived. He paced about the room like a caged animal. He looked so nervous that Glyn laughed. When he stopped moving long enough to ask what was so funny, she said, "You my dear brother—this is not the end of the world!"

"So says you, who are happily married to a man whom you chose and who chose you!"

"I know Aden, but she's beautiful, smart, capable, and all the things you could want in a woman."

"Oh she is all those things to be sure," he agreed, "but I would rather have a troll that loved me than a woman who would wash me away like dirt from her hands if she could."

"You would not and you know it! Believe me, in a short time you'll have her eating out of your hand. A woman hasn't been born who could resist your charm for long!"

In spite of himself Aden laughed.

"Now what do *you* think is so funny?" responded Glyn.

"Stubbornness is one of Sia's qualities that you forgot to mention. I'm sure she'll put forth her best effort."

Before Glyn could answer, Gris entered the room. "Is he still whining about this?" he asked no one in particular. "Does he not realize there is not another unmarried man in the known universe who wouldn't give everything to be in his fine, polished boots today?"

"Don't you start," Aden answered. "One of the benefits of being king is the ability to torture any subject I wish!"

"Ha!" scoffed Gris. "You're not king yet, and even if you were, you don't have that in you any more than your father or Hebrid before him. This will be over in a few hours and a few hours after that you'll be in your royal bed consummating your royal marriage." He looked wistfully at the ceiling, shook his head, and added, "Ah, to be young again with a fresh young thing like her before me!"

"Gris Habaret!" exclaimed Glyn. "Watch your tongue or it will be a long time before you have this 'old thing' before you again!"

Gris stepped smartly to her, embraced her and said, "My dear, simply the musings of an old fool. You are, always have been, and always will be more than enough for me!" Then he tried to kiss her, but she was laughing too hard, as was Aden.

She playfully pushed him away and said, "Shut up before you sour my poor brother on marriage forever!"

Aden shook his head ruefully. "If only I could have what you two have. Truthfully, it's not I that I mourn for, it's Sia. This marriage will crush the life out of her. Even if she does eventually come around to me, it will be as a horse that's been broken; her spirit, that which makes her unique, will be gone!"

Glyn went over to him and caressed his shoulder. "My brother, you are a fine man. You will make a fine husband, and one day, king. I've grown to know Sia over these many months and she also is a fine person. She understands the need for this union, and I have no doubt she'll make you a good wife once all this settles out. She will survive this and so will you."

Before he could reply, King Edris entered the room trailed by an army of aides and bureaucrats, including Tock Horat. "Son," he said, "I tried to hold off these fine fellows as long as I could, but they insist on ensuring that you understand how this is to unfold and all the petty little protocol matters that must be followed."

"Have we not rehearsed this wedding multiple times?" he responded indignantly. "I am not a sulva slug!"

"Na na no, of ca ca course you're not!" responded Tock nervously. "But these affairs are such da da delicate matters. They are recorded for posterity and, well, you know how they still talk about the wedding of dear King Hebrid's predecessor. It's my ja ja job to ensure that this wedding is memorable for all the right reasons!"

Aden indulged Tock, not out of any sense of propriety, but because it helped pass the time and take his mind off what was about to happen. An hour later Tock finally proclaimed he was satisfied. Shortly after, it was time for Aden and the other members of the wedding procession to gather at the entrance to the great cathedral.

At the last minute, another aide ran up holding Aden's wedding sash, which he had forgotten to put on. It was dark blue, matching his gold-striped pants, and also trimmed in gold. He lifted it over his head and settled it properly over his red, gold-trimmed, double-breasted military dress tunic.

Glyn stood back and looked him up and down to ensure he hadn't missed anything else. She fussed over a piece of lint on his pants, and then proclaimed he looked passable. When she took his arm, he leaned over and said softly, "Well Glyn, I may be passable, but you look amazing. The gold in your dress highlights your hair very nicely. I surely hope Sia looks as good as you when she reaches her middle age."

Glyn poked him unappreciatively in the ribs with a sharp elbow. "For your information, I am far from middle age. And if you expect this marriage to last more than a week, you better learn how to talk to a woman properly!"

Aden snickered. "You're right," he said, "but you're still beautiful!"

Glyn's attempt to maintain a stern face failed miserably. She couldn't suppress the smile playing on her lips, nor keep herself from blushing at his blatant flattery. Trying to regain the upper hand, she threw her chin in the air haughtily and replied, "Perhaps you have already learned something!" The blowing of the horns signaling the start of the ceremony saved her from further embarrassment.

Edris and Sarin preceded them down the aisle. Edris was dressed like Aden, minus the wedding sash. When they reached the altar, Aden began his slow walk with Glyn on his arm, feeling more as if he were about to be executed than married.

Despite his dread, he couldn't help but be impressed by the pageantry of it all. Musicians with long horns bracketed the wide, purple-carpeted path that split ornate wooden pews and led to the old priest who would perform the service in front of the huge altar, which was carved from solid granite. Beautiful young girls, dressed in shimmering gold gowns similar to Glyn and Sarin's, threw flower petals at him, which symbolized gentleness and good luck.

As he made his way further down the aisle, Kealt's famed and dreaded Ku Assa soldiers stepped out of nothingness just in front of him, as though showing him the way. They stood at attention along both sides, with their crossed swords held high forming a canopy. With their green, glowing eyes, and shimmering, one piece black uniforms they were an intimidating sight.

When they reached the altar, Glyn took her place off to the side, next to Edris and across from Sarin. Aden stood in front of the priest, bowed slightly, and turned to face the rear of the cathedral. After an excruciating pause, the horns blew again…

At the sound of the horns, Ivege prompted Sia to pull herself together. Despite her best efforts to maintain a stoic demeanor, she had not completely succeeded in preventing tears from seeping out. Her maid of honor fussed over her, trying mostly in vain to repair her exquisitely prepared makeup. When she finally gathered herself, Ivege nodded and Kealt Honor Guardsmen, resplendent in their dress uniforms, threw open the broad doors to the cathedral. Sia, wearing a bright white dress, and Ivege, wearing a dark blue, brass trimmed dress uniform, slowly stepped forward.

Sia had been in the cathedral many times before, but was not prepared for how the Kealts had transformed it for the wedding. It was always awe-inspiring, but today it looked almost otherworldly. Tapestries from both planets covered the balconies, and the large crowd was perfectly attired and seated according their relationship to the bride and groom.

As she continued on, the girls again threw their flower petals. She was so taken by the splendor of the event she didn't notice the Ku Assa until she was almost upon them. They again raised their swords as she passed between them. Even though she knew she was in no danger from them, she suppressed an involuntary shudder. Assassins, murders, saboteurs, bogeymen; they were the stuff of nightmares, something so dreadful Ardalans felt terror at the very mention of them, and rarely did. As she passed through them she was surprised to see that several were obviously women.

Despite her best efforts not to, Sia could not stop herself from stealing glances at the pews, wondering if Celesta or the annoying raven-haired girl Aden had found so interesting at the dance were there. She almost hoped they were, and felt envious that *she* was the one marrying the high prince, even more so knowing she really wanted no part of it. When she finally reached the altar, she faced Aden but could not look at him for fear she would begin weeping openly, and not from joy.

Once she and Ivege had taken their places, the priest began the ritual. As he droned on through the traditional ceremony, Sia's dread increased. She barely heard him when he said, "…and so today we join Sia Selarney of Ardala and Aden Cade of Kealt in holy matrimony. Sia Selarney, daughter of Ardala, do you agree to take Aden Cade, son of Kealt, to be your wedded husband, whom you will cherish and respect for as long as you both shall live, through good times and bad?"

Sia felt detached, almost as though someone else was using her body. A voice that may have sounded like hers, but didn't come from her heart said, "I do."

The priest then turned to Aden and said, "Aden Cade, son of Kealt, do you agree to take Sia Selarney, daughter of Ardala, as your wedded wife, whom you will cherish and respect for as long as you both shall live, through good times and bad?"

Sia gritted her teeth waiting for Aden to seal her fate. When he didn't immediately respond she looked at him for the first time and wondered why he would toy with her so cruelly.

Finally, he said, "No, I will not take this wonderful, most desirable woman, as my spouse. It is past time for Kealt and Ardala to stop hiding behind this primitive and barbaric custom and face our differences openly and candidly. Sia Selarney, you are free to go and pursue your own destiny. I will not force this one upon you!"

When Sia got over her shock she exclaimed, "I will not have blood on my hands because this marriage is inconvenient to me! If it is what it takes to keep us from each other's throats, then I will marry you willingly! Do not be so selfish. I admit this marriage terrifies me, but I…promise…I will be a good wife."

Aden pulled off his wedding sash and threw it to the ground. "I will not marry you under these circumstances, and *I* promise there *will* be peace between us!" He looked from Edris, to Ivege, to Sarin and said, "These three will see to it." Then he stomped off the altar and out of the cathedral.

The crowd exploded in shock. Sia wept uncontrollably. While Sarin put her arms around her and tried to comfort her, Ivege railed at Edris and his now-departed son.

Finally, Edris raised his arms and shouted, "Quiet everyone!" He had to repeat it several times before the crowd took heed. When everyone had settled down he said, “King Ivege, Queen Sarin, and High Princess Sia, I swear I am as shocked as you by my son’s inexcusable behavior. I can assure you I will take the matter up with him directly. In the meantime, I offer my most profound apology to the Ardalan royal family and especially to you, Sia.

"Kealt treasures its good relations with Ardala and prays it will continue. I also can assure you that Kealt remains committed to the joint initiatives we’ve undertaken, including those involving Seti. My son was right about one thing—there will be no hostilities between us over this. I will order Kealt forces to surrender before I allow that to happen. Now please, everyone, go home!”

When the noisy crowd began to file out Edris turned to the Selarneys and said, “I have no idea what happened here today. My son’s actions have shamed and humiliated us all. Please forgive him.” With that, he turned and left.

Chapter VIII

Borg Hassan, Chief Engineer of Seti mining operations, reread the most recent xanide production summary to be sure his eyes weren't deceiving him. "Something wrong?" asked Chief Logistics Officer Arvid Denk, who had just entered the room clutching a sheaf of documents.

"Quite the opposite—according to this report xanide production has increased 25% over the past month alone. We're up 75% over the past six months. As far as I know, that's by far the largest increase in such a short time in the history of this place."

"Wow!" answered Arvid. "I guess those new veins you opened up were richer than you expected."

"I'll say!" responded Borg enthusiastically. "By a factor of ten!" He put the report back on his desk, smiled, and added, "You know, it's funny. Those veins were right under our noses, but if Cale hadn't had that dream I doubt it ever would have occurred to us to look there."

Arvid chuckled. "Guess not; it is funny though, because I never pictured Cale as the dreaming type."

"Me neither. He's usually so serious and matter of fact. If it had been anyone else who came stomping into my office that day I would have told him to take some time off, but he was so sure. It took me a while to convince the big bosses on Kealt. They told me we didn't have the resources to pursue 'visions.' They finally agreed when I threatened to resign."

Arvid shook his head and smiled wryly. "Now that doesn't sound like you boss."

"Nope," he agreed. "You can't survive on a place like Seti if you let yourself get blown about by whims. For reasons even I don't understand, I did, and what do you know? We hit some of the richest xanide deposits ever found."

"Well it turned out OK, so I guess there's no reason to dwell on it."

"Yeah," agreed Borg. He pointed at the sheaf of papers Arvid was carrying. "What do you have there?"

"What? Oh these!" replied Arvid, waving the papers. "I was so impressed by the increase in production I almost forgot to tell you! We just got a lengthy communication from Kealt. We've agreed to share Seti with the Ardalans. They are going to hold the negotiations here on Seti."

"What!" roared Borg, shooting up out of his chair. "We did what?"

"You heard correctly boss."

With his arm outstretched, he exclaimed, "Let me see those." Arvid handed him the papers and watched as a frowning Borg shuffled through them. When he was done, he dropped them on his desk and said, "We're a mining colony! We don't have proper accommodations for a group of pampered bureaucrats, nor do we have the people to babysit them!"

"As you might have read, Kealt agrees—in the next couple of weeks they're going to send an advance team to make all the arrangements."

"Great! Anything else Arvid?"

Arvid laughed. "Xanide production is going through the roof, Kealt is agreeing to share Seti, bureaucrats coming here…personally I think that's quite enough!" He paused in the doorway. "Hey, do you think they'll send Aden…uh…I mean the high prince?" he asked.

Borg grinned warmly at the thought. "I was just a fresh mine grunt the last time he was here, but it seems like yesterday! He shook his head and added, "His marriage is coming up, I doubt the king will send him."

"You know, when I first met him I hadn't been here long either," replied Arvid nostalgically. "I'll never forget the look on King Edris's face when we told him Aden had gone into the jungle alone. He was on the other end of a vidscreen, but I thought we were all going to burst into flames!"

"Wicked cut the boy got," recalled Borg grimly. "Supposedly he got it from some 'unknown life form.'"

"Yeah," nodded Arvid knowingly, "I think we all know what that was."

"We do?" replied a bemused Borg.

"Sure. It was a taal!"

Borg had picked his coffee up off his desk and just taken a sip. He nearly choked on it. "A what!" he exclaimed incredulously. "A taal you say?"

"Aden said he was injured by an unknown, large life form. You know the legends about the taal, how hard they are to find. I'll bet that's what he was hunting for. Why else would he have snuck onto Seti to hunt in such a dangerous area?"

Borg futilely attempted to wipe the coffee off his shirt. "This planet has been surveyed so thoroughly over the millennia it's hard to imagine that anything as large as a taal is supposed to be wouldn't have been seen and cataloged at some point. Anyway, most people these days don't believe they ever existed. If Aden found a taal, why wouldn't he have told anyone?"

"I don't know," replied Arvid shrugging his shoulders, "he doesn't answer to me."

Borg walked over to him, clapped him on the shoulder as he walked him out the door, and said, "That's an interesting theory; but unless you want to be confined to a mental institution you might want to keep it to yourself!"

"Good point boss," answered Arvid cheerfully. "I'll say this though—I wouldn't be surprised by anything around here. One day a whole herd of taal might come marching right up our front doorstep!"

Borg smirked. "We've wasted enough time on mythological creatures! Right now I'm much more concerned about how we're going to make this place livable for dozens of spoiled bureaucrats."

"On that note I'll leave." Arvid stepped into the hallway and then stopped. "Oh boss, one more thing?"

"Uh oh!"

"No, nothing like that; have you met the new cook?"

"The new cook?" replied Borg, raising an eyebrow. "I don't think so, why?"

"Well," said Arvid, "he's not like any cook I've ever met. For one thing, he was able to restart the #5 processing unit."

"He did what? Varley and Jacobs have been working on that thing for six months! They said it can't be fixed without a new trionic inverter, which has to be custom ordered."

"I know. Overbye—that's his name, Byron Overbye—was bored and asked if he could have a crack at it. He claims to have had some past experience in repairing mine equipment." Arvid shook his head and added, "Took him ten minutes. Said it was a glitch in the software. He went over it five times with Varley and Jacobs trying to explain it, but they finally gave up."

"Overbye you say? I'll make it a point to meet him next time I'm at the mess hall."

"He helps me out too. He knows a lot about everything. He's real polished, uses a lot of big words, and catches on faster than anyone I've ever known. And he's a helluva cook to boot!"

"Like I said, I look forward to meeting him. We can always use more brain power around here!" Borg walked back to his desk, picked the documents up, waved them at Arvid and added, "Anything else you need to tell me about, or can I get to this stuff?"

"No boss, I think I've shook you up enough!"

When Arvid left, Borg sat in his large leather chair, quickly glanced at the documents he was holding, and then put them down. He leaned back, put his hands behind his head, and pondered the day's events. He considered himself a student of Seti history, but he couldn't recall ever reading about a day quite like this one.

Anthropologists on Kealt and Ardala agreed that humans originally came to this solar system around 10,000 years ago. Due to wars, the passage of time, and general entropy the only information that remained from that distant period was couched in legends, many of which were contradictory and slanted to support the respective primacy of Kealt or Ardala. Legends on both planets agreed that humans arrived from another galaxy in great generational ships that had somehow veered far off course. They also agreed that Seti was the original landfall, although no solid evidence supporting that theory existed. From that point, the legends diverged greatly.

Some claimed mysterious, godlike creatures native to Seti called taal by Kealt and set la by Ardala had grown tired of human squabbling and expelled them. Others employed a more mundane, but practical explanation for why humans essentially abandoned Seti: Life was too hard here compared to Kealt and Ardala.

Scientists had studied Seti closely for centuries. Despite the difficult conditions, they were a tough, resourceful, and persistent lot, and had mostly cataloged the larger flora and fauna, and their interaction with their native environment. Life on Seti was far more intertwined with the planet it evolved on than anywhere else in the known galaxy.

The xanide formed a foundation for most life forms on Seti, and when removed from it for any length of time they almost invariably died. The xanide itself formed a matrix with other more common minerals that gave it properties it did not have in its natural, raw form.

Over the millennia, Kealt and Ardala had fought many bloody wars over Seti. During the last all out war two centuries earlier, Kealt wrested Seti from Ardalan control. When the war ended, one of the terms in the peace treaty documenting the cessation of hostilities was a clause requiring Kealt to share Seti with Ardala, and avoid interfering with Ardala's existing mining operations.

Kealt initially abided by the terms of the treaty, but over time began to encroach on Ardala's interests. Eventually Kealt forcibly expelled Ardala's remaining minors, in exchange for guaranteeing Ardala a percentage of all xanide mined. Being too weak from centuries of conflict to confront Kealt militarily, Ardala capitulated to Kealt's new arrangement.

Even though they were now technically at peace, smaller armed conflicts periodically occurred. One such conflagration took place 35 years ago. At the time, the Ardalans were insistent that Kealt was holding back their agreed upon share of xanide. They demanded that Kealt allow them to return to Seti to review the books directly, and not have to take Kealt's word for it.

When they sent a small fleet to make a point, Kealt sent its own fleet to intercept them; however, because Kealt ships had the ability to cloak, Ardala quickly lost track of them after they left Kealt. When they materialized right on top of their fleet, the Ardalans believed they were being ambushed and opened fire. Kealt, not willing to start a war over a misunderstanding at least partly instigated by their own poorly chosen strategy, promptly ordered its ships to retreat.

The aftermath of the battle caused political upheaval on Kealt. Among those killed were the only sons of High Prince Edris Cade. The only child of Kealt's reigning king, Olnius Hebrid, was a daughter, Sarin, who, under the rules of royal succession, would one day be queen of Ardala.

Applying arcane rules known only to them, the Council of Elders had selected Edris as the high prince who would one day succeed Hebrid. However, to be a viable high prince they required Edris to have a legitimate heir born of him and his spouse, High Princess Calista Fallon of Ardala. If the aging and ailing Hebrid died before Edris and Calista produced another heir, the crown would go to Abeg Mar of the Mar clan.

Abeg's marriage to an Ardalan high princess also had been arranged and, unlike Edris, he had several eligible heirs. Kealt was at a crossroads. If Edris succeeded King Hebrid, he was determined to continue Hebrid's path to democracy, with full voting rights for all citizens, as well as a true and fair peace with Ardala.

Abeg, on the other hand, was a traditionalist. If he became king, he most likely would dismantle all of Kealt's fledgling democratic institutions and return absolute power to the monarchy. Furthermore, he would use Kealt's still superior military might to crush Ardala before it could complete its latest military buildup.

There was so much animosity between the two high houses, many believed that Abeg himself had falsely told the Ardalans that Kealt intended to attack their fleet with the hope of killing Edris's sons. Eventually Edris secured the monarchy for himself when Calista, who was nearing middle age at the time, was able to conceive one more son.

When Hebrid eventually died, Edris took the throne. He immediately held out an olive branch to the Ardalans, offering them the opportunity to visit Seti any time they wished in order to review xanide production reports, and to establish a permanent presence. Over time he allowed Ardala even greater access to Seti, more in accordance with the actual terms of the existing peace treaty.

However, the Mar clan was still very powerful and had much support among certain segments of Kealt society. King Edris was forced to move forward slowly with his reforms, both on Kealt and Seti. Now, with the zon threat looming over the entire galaxy like a voracious bolba tree, he no longer had the luxury of time.

Finished with his musings, Borg took the last sip of his now cold coffee, then got up and stepped out onto the large balcony outside his second story office. He put his hands on the railing and slowly took in the jungle that bordered the complex. "What are you hiding," he mumbled to himself.

With no answers forthcoming, he shook his head and went back inside. He went over to his desk and picked up a fist-sized piece of raw xanide crystal from its holder. It was the first piece of crystal he saw on his first day as chief engineer well over a decade ago.

He held it up to the light to get a better look. It was opaque and pale blue in color, and surprisingly light. In its present state it was inert, no different from a piece of ordinary rock. However, when properly processed and combined with a number of common minerals, the chunk he was holding in his hand could produce enough energy to power three Vortoc class warships for over five years. And when its fragments became too fissured and burned to power the ships efficiently, they could be recycled and further processed for use in industrial equipment.

Borg carefully placed the crystal back in its holder. He made a mental note to send it to a residence he kept on Kealt, but hadn't visited in years. More production managed by two sovereign worlds meant a lot more oversight than he was used to, and a lot more rules. He suspected that in the near future every piece of crystal would be weighed, cataloged, and accounted for. A valuable crystal like the one on his desk was worth far too much for a lowly chief engineer to hold on to for a keepsake.

For that matter, he wondered how much longer he'd even be chief engineer. Increased production would require increased corporate and political involvement. He imagined that it wouldn't be long before he would be replaced by a slick company man—but that would be a worry for another day. Today he had to begin planning for the various delegations that soon would descend on Seti like rifis bugs...

Chapter IX

As punishment for stranding Sia at the altar, Edris sent Aden directly to Seti to lead the negotiations with Ardala, which had somehow survived his humiliation of the Ardalan royal family. The assignment had a twofold benefit: Edris knew Aden despised few things more than diplomacy and would suffer accordingly, and it would give him a chance to rehabilitate himself in the eyes of the Ardalans, since he would essentially be handing half of Seti to them with no quid pro quo.

To make the best of what, for him, was a bad situation, Aden arrived a week early hoping to reacquaint himself with Seti's vast wilderness. Much to his displeasure Kealt security demanded that he stay close to Kuste, which was what passed for the only city on Seti. If he wanted to see the planet, he would have to do so through the air following specific routes deemed safe from xanide interference. He thought about sneaking out as he had years before; however, realizing what a stir that would cause, he decided it would be best to take his responsibilities seriously.

Now with little to do until the Ardalans arrived, he quickly became bored. He never thought he could ever get excited over mind-numbing discussions on mineral rights, free air corridors, and waste disposal. However, when the ship carrying the Ardalan negotiators finally arrived, he had to restrain himself from sprinting to the spaceport.

As he stood by the gate waiting for the Ardalans to disembark, he wondered idly if he would know any of them. For security and political reasons, the identities of all parties to the negotiations were a closely held secret.

He was disappointed he didn't recognize any of the mostly older men and women who shuffled into the reception area. He went up to the person who appeared to be in charge and said, "Welcome to Seti! I am High Prince Aden Cade. Do I have the privilege of speaking to the leader of the Ardalan delegation?"

The old man laughed and shook his head. "You most certainly do not high prince!" He glanced over his shoulder and said, "Here she comes now."

Aden turned to follow his glance. Of course—it was Sia! When the old man saw his shocked look he cracked an ironic grin. "Oh yes. Good luck to you!"

Sia's face registered similar shock when she spied Aden. For a moment, he thought she would literally turn and run. Instead, she gathered herself, walked over to him, and held out her hand for him to kiss.

"High Prince Aden Cade," she said evenly, "so nice to see you again, even if it is sooner than I expected."

"You mean like never?" he said, before taking her hand and kissing it.

When Sia didn't answer, but smiled at him condescendingly, he added, "I can assure you the pleasure is all mine, although both our parents must be having a good laugh at the thought of us working together on this treaty."

"Perhaps," she replied. "I can assure you, this isn't my idea! I haven't set foot on Ardala in nine months and I miss it. When it was time for me to leave Kealt the first time, my father insisted that I oversee a refuge problem we were having on some of our colonies. I believe you played some small role in that event? I went straight from that back to Kealt for the...the wedding. And now here I am. I am convinced my father will never let me go home again."

"I'm very sorry Your Highness, really I am. I suppose such travails don't do much to improve your mood, at least where I'm concerned!"

Sia smiled sarcastically. "Why Aden Cade, is that what passes for humor on Kealt? Don't worry, I won't bite, if that's what you're afraid of."

He smiled back and said, "I suppose that's true." Then he held out his arm. "High Princess Sia Selarney, I have no idea what clock you're operating on, but I suspect you would like to see your quarters."

She took his arm and said, "I would indeed. Please lead the way."

When they reached the enclave of temporary quarters Kealt had set up for visiting diplomats unaccustomed to rustic living, Aden paused at Sia's door. "Yes?" she queried, holding the door, but not inviting him in.

"Your bags should be here directly, Your Highness. Sia, it is good to see you again, despite the circumstances." Before she could respond, he grinned, bowed slightly, and walked away.

A week later the negotiations were almost complete, having gone far smoother than anyone could have anticipated. To celebrate Aden decided to visit what passed for a pub on Seti. He found Gris and dragged him along. Seti, being primarily a mining operation, boasted few amenities. The "pub," such as it was, was nothing more than a reclaimed storage room filled with mismatched furniture, tables made from empty barrels, and a bar that consisted of large wooden packing crates bolted together and covered with plywood.

Despite its bare walls and ramshackle construction, when Aden and Gris arrived they found it packed with members of both delegations, young and old. That night Kealt had arranged for live entertainment and the loud music and raucous patrons created a carnival atmosphere, which Gris pointed out as they entered the normally restrained establishment. They quickly settled into a rickety booth someone had cobbled together from scrap lumber. Several ales later Aden asked, "Well old friend, tell me you haven't grown tired of these negotiations as well?"

"Indeed," replied the older man. "How I wish for days of old when a man could come here and risk his life on a real hunt. Now it carries the musty smell of bureaucrats, and treaties, and talk, talk, talk!"

Aden laughed. "I agree. Fortunately, if we are successful in negotiating this treaty, the 'good old days' may be back. Opening up more areas for resource exploitation and recreation is high on the list for Ardala and Kealt."

Gris lifted his glass. "Well then," he toasted, "here's to successful negotiations!"

When Aden clanked his glass so hard he spilled ale on both of them, they both guffawed.

"Easy lad!" exclaimed Gris. "This ale is too good to wear!" Then he tossed down what was left of his drink and slammed his glass down onto the table. "Aden, Glyn and I are very proud of you. You are a fine leader, and one day you'll make a fine king!"

"Not if my father succeeds in turning Kealt into a democracy."

"Well if he does, then you'll make a fine president, or prime minister, or chancellor, or whatever it will be!"

"Gris, if it comes to that I'd rather start another war with Ardala!"

"Are you two war mongering? I thought these negotiations were supposed to encourage peace, not foment more conflict!"

Aden and Gris stared up at Sia, open-mouthed.

"Your Highness," responded Aden, as he and Gris lurched to their feet, "I was making a bad joke, a very bad joke. I can assure you, Kealt would rather be drawn into the sun than fight Ardala!"

"Yes," agreed Gris, "we would rather suffer a plague of blaque pox than go to war with you!"

"Or be eaten by slime ants," continued Aden with an exaggerated wink.

At the last, he and Gris raised their glasses and slammed them together, guffawing heartily when each was again soaked with ale.

"Very funny," replied Sia. She narrowed her eyes, glared at Gris and said, "Glyn would be so disappointed to see you carousing like this. Now, if you two have had enough to drink I have some business with the high prince."

"Your Highness!" protested Aden. "We've been at this for days; could this not wait until morning?"

Gris bowed to Sia. "I'm sorry Your Highness, we have been very rude. I will leave you with Aden…ah…the high prince." Before Aden could protest he was stumbling toward the door, laughing as he went.

Sia slid onto the bench Gris had vacated. "Could a lady have something to drink around here?" she asked.

"Oh, of course Your Highness. Gris is correct, I have been insufferably rude this evening." He waved at a nearby server. "What would you like?"

"A glass of Kealt wine would be nice."

"Kealt wine, is it? Easily done," he replied. When the server arrived he said, "A bottle of your finest Kag wine please. I believe we have a bottle or two from the Alacava region?"

"Why yes we do," replied the server, "but we've been told to save it for the celebration marking the conclusion of the negotiations." The look on Aden's face convinced her to reconsider. "What I mean is, of course Your Highness, I will have a bottle here directly."

As she scurried off, Aden took his seat. Sia said, "Used to getting your way I see."

"For you, Your Highness, I would move mountains."

Not sure if he was teasing her, she ignored his response. "I believe the negotiations are going very well, don't you?" she asked.

Aden grimaced. "I expect you would, since Kealt is the only party giving anything up."

"You mean full control of Seti, which you wrested from us by force?"

"Your Highness, I am not passing judgment on the legitimacy of Kealt's control of Seti. I am merely stating a fact. By whatever means we got it, we have it. And now we're giving half of it back at no cost to Ardala…except for, perhaps, hopefully, some good will. I'm not saying it isn't the right thing to do, merely that it isn't easy for us to do it."

Sia's face softened. "I'll give you this High Prince Aden Cade, you're not a very good negotiator, but you're honest. Are you always so?"

"Well, I could say yes and still be a liar."

"You could, but you are no liar, that much is certain." She halted their conversation when the wine arrived. The server opened the bottle and once Aden approved it, she poured them both a glass. When she left, Sia said, "I never thanked you for calling off our wedding. That was a brave and risky thing for you to do. I realize you had your own reasons for doing so, but I still appreciate it."

"My own reasons?" asked Aden, furrowing his brow.

"Of course; are you going to deny you and Celesta are lovers?"

Aden had picked up his glass to take a sip and nearly spat out his wine. "Lovers?" he sputtered.

"We're very close, to be sure, but we are not, never have been, and never will be lovers! She's my sister's daughter! I helped raise her! I once changed her diapers!"

"Does she prefer women then? Or do you prefer men?"

"Your Highness!" protested Aden, "This is a most inappropriate line of questioning! Surely you did not come here just to torment me!"

"I'm sorry," she replied, "now I'm the one being rude; whom you copulate with is none of my business." When Aden opened his mouth to protest again, she held up her hand. "I'm here for an entirely different matter. I wish to see Seti."

"You do?" he replied sarcastically. "You do know that until the negotiations are complete the planet is off limits. Neither side wants its diplomats wandering off. This place is too dangerous."

"That's not true. I know parts of it are open to air traffic."

"Technically you're right, but the approved routes are so high, and over such desolate areas, it's pointless."

"Nonetheless, I would like to see it tomorrow."

"You would? Tomorrow you say?"

"Yes. It is a day of rest from negotiations."

"Very well, if that's what you wish; I'll find out what aircraft and pilots are available and get back to you later tonight."

"I already have my pilot."

"Oh, and who would that be?"

"You."

"Me?" sputtered Aden. "Why me?"

"I've asked other pilots and to a person they agree that you are the second best pilot on the planet."

"Really? Then why do you want me?"

"They all claimed *they* were the best."

"Your Highness!" protested Aden. "So you, of all people, want to be stuck on an aircraft, alone with me, flying over land you won't even be able to see? I see no sense in this!"

She stood up to leave. "Thank you for the wine, high prince. I look forward to flying with you tomorrow."

Aden left the pub shortly after Sia, most disturbed by her request. It was not logical coming from her. She was not the kind of person who would enjoy sightseeing from 10,000 meters, nor would she be even mildly interested in spending time alone with him. Something else was at work here, and he resolved to be prepared. He woke up Arvid Denk and provided him a list of supplies he wanted for the flight.

Arvid took the list and without looking at it headed to the supply depot. He lifted his other hand and stared at the fistful of currency Aden had stuffed in it for the inconvenience.

As he left, Aden looked at his chronometer and saw that it was earlier then he thought—

plenty of time to catch up with Drusa, who had traveled with him to Seti. Not long after he called off the wedding he had sought her out and they were again seeing each other regularly, despite Edris's reservations. She had come to Seti at his request, ostensibly to assist Tock with his research relative to the negotiations. In reality, she could do little more than file papers and perform basic administrative functions. As luck would have it, she found him.

"Oh there you are, Aden Cade!" she said brightly as they nearly passed each other on what amounted to Kuste's main street. When he stopped she said, "I was hoping I'd find you at the pub, but when I got there they said you'd just left."

"Well you're in luck," Aden replied with a smile. "I was looking for you as well." He held out his arm, and together they began walking down the street. "How was work?" he asked.

"Very boring. Mr. Horat is kind of mean."

Aden suppressed a smile imagining Tock's frustration. "Well, I'll make a note to talk to him."

She was wearing a revealing blouse and form fitting slacks that flattered her. As they walked on, he stared at her ample cleavage, and suddenly felt a great desire to be alone with her. He thought of taking her to the royal hunting lodge, but quickly decided that would be indiscreet; besides, his father was there. So instead they returned to his small, one-room guest quarters. As he hoped, she quickly made him forget about the unpleasantness that came with being a bureaucrat in charge of a boring negotiation. When he finally began to drift off to sleep, she snuggled up to him.

"Aden," she whispered.

"Yes," he replied sleepily.

"I will never forget what you did for me. You are the kindest, most selfless man I've ever met."

Aden turned to face her. He gently caressed her face and said, "I'm very sorry for what happened to you and your family. I wish there were more I could do."

"Am I here for pity's sake, then?"

"Drusa…"

"It's all right," she said. "That was unfair. Just…whatever happens, please know I will never betray you—or forget you."

"Or I you," he replied.

Drusa kissed him, said goodnight, then turned away so he couldn't see the tears seeping from her eyes.

When Aden tried to get up the next day, her soft hands pulled him back to bed. "Not yet," she whined, back to her normal temperament. "It's too early!"

Aden looked at the chronometer on the nightstand and was startled to see it was already past the time he had agreed to meet Sia at the airfield. Before he could get out of bed, there was a knock on the door. "Be right there!" he shouted.

He jumped up and quickly pulled on his pants from the night before. "I'm sorry sweetie," he said, while throwing the covers over Drusa's head. "If Sia finds out you're the reason I was late I'll never hear the end of it." When he finally opened the door, Sia greeted him with a particularly cross expression.

"I'm the Ardalan high princess! I will not be kept waiting. You were supposed to be at the spaceport 30 minutes ago!" As she was chastising him, she glanced over at the bed and saw a pair of naked feet sticking out from beneath the covers. "Really Aden! I would expect someone in your position to be more discreet!"

Just then, a muffled voice whined, "Aden it's stuffy in here!"

Wearing a smirk, Sia said, "Well, and just when I feared I might never meet a pair of talking feet! Please hurry, will you? I have to be back in time for a meeting with our ministers."

Aden quickly grabbed the rest of his clothes and ushered her outside. He finished dressing as they rode in the hover car to the airfield. When they arrived, Sia was not impressed with their mode of transportation.

"What is that?" she asked, pointing to the dilapidated old ship. "Surely you don't expect me to fly in that?"

"I'm sorry," replied Aden. "It's the best I could do on such short notice."

"What...what is it?"

"It's an old cargo freighter. I know it doesn't look like much, but it will suit our purpose."

While they were talking, Arvid and another man rolled a pallet up to the ship. Before he loaded it on board, he walked over to Aden and said, "Hello Your Highness. I didn't get to tell you last night that it is good to see you again. You've been away from Seti too long." He lifted up a clipboard and added, "I have the supplies you ordered. I have to ask, are you expecting to fight a war during the three hours you're scheduled to be gone?"

Aden laughed and slapped him on the shoulder. "Arvid old friend, I hope not; but you well know that on Seti you can never be too prepared."

"Very well—may I go over the manifest with you to ensure we've packed everything you wanted?"

"Please do."

"OK—we have one M87 plasma rifle with two spare power packs; one G45 plasma sidearm, also with two spare power packs; one HJ35 fully automatic gas powered projectile rifle with 1000 rounds; one X26 semiautomatic gas powered projectile sidearm with 500 rounds; one WS450 crossbow with 25 explosive tipped bolts; one TR51 survival knife; two emergency extraction beacons; two EXT105 backpacks; a week's worth of emergency rations for two people; a tent and two sleeping bags. I see you are already wearing your combat sword. Does that cover it?"

Aden took the clipboard from the logistics officer and flipped through the pages. "I also requested three YT5 force field emitters, 20 HE82 hand grenades; a class II, xanide shielded, hand-held two way communicator; and 30 ZSG24 grenade rounds for the HJ35."

Arvid scowled and took back the clipboard. When he couldn't find the missing cargo either he said, "Byron, I thought I asked you to double check this!"

Byron Overbye walked over, took the clipboard from Arvid and flipped through it. When he got to the last page he said, "I'm sorry sir, it's here as well. For some reason the last page printed double sided. The stuff's here on the back."

Satisfied everything was in order, the men began loading the aircraft.

"Why all the hardware?" asked Sia. "The logistics officer is right—you've brought enough weaponry to take on a zon infantry battalion."

"Not quite, but Seti is a dangerous place. I've learned it's best to never take her for granted."

Once the gear was stowed and the ship fueled, they climbed onboard. Aden secured himself in the pilot seat and began the preflight checklist. When he was finished, he looked over and saw that Sia was still standing.

"Your Highness, do you intend to stand the entire trip?"

"Oh…no…I mean, I've never flown on such a craft before."

"I'm sure you haven't," he replied, suppressing a smirk. "I know it doesn't look like much, but I'm sure you'll be much more comfortable if you sit in the copilot chair."

"Yes of course," she agreed, before settling in next to Aden.

When she had trouble securing herself, he leaned over and attached her harness. "Ready?" he asked, once they were settled in.

"Yes."

"I doubt it," he replied, then punched the throttle. Sia screamed as the G forces shoved her back into her chair. Once they reached altitude he asked, "Did you survive the ascent, Your Highness?"

"I...I think so," she replied shakily. When she regained her composure, she craned her neck from side to side in a vain effort to get a look at the Seti wilderness. An hour later she complained, "Am I ever going to be able to see anything down there?"

"I warned you," chastised Aden. "We're too high up."

"Then take me closer!"

"I can't. Besides being prohibited, it isn't safe."

"I thought you were the best pilot on Seti?"

"Perhaps in the universe," he joked, "but even I can't fly through xanide radiation."

"Then this is a waste of time, please take me back!"

"Gladly Your Highness," he replied, as he punched the new coordinates into the autonav. "We'll be home in no time."

Almost immediately alarm bells filled the cockpit.

"What is that?" exclaimed Sia above the din.

"We are being bombarded by waves of xanide radiation. I'm losing control of the ship!"

"Is this your idea of a joke?"

"I can assure you it isn't!" he responded tensely. "If I can't get out of this field soon we're going to crash. Go back into the cargo hold and secure yourself. You'll be safer there."

"I most certainly will not! I will not allow you to frighten me like some adolescent schoolgirl!"

"Damn it Sia, now! I don't have time to pick you up and carry you back there!"

His tone convinced her that they were indeed in trouble. Without another word, she unbuckled her harness and staggered back to the cargo hold. Once inside she secured herself in one of several passenger seats. Aden pushed a button on his console, which closed and secured the bulkhead.

As his efforts to avoid the radiation slammed Sia about in her chair, she could not appreciate the skill it took for him to identify new xanide field formations and weave in and out of them before the ship's systems failed. He had flown on Seti before, but had never experienced anything like this. The xanide fields seemed to be forming and moving with deliberate purpose, as though they were driving the ship toward…something.

It wasn't long before he could no longer outmaneuver the disruptive radiation. When his sensors picked up a large clearing thirty kilometers distant, he gave up trying to escape the field and devoted his efforts to reaching the clearing.

With fourteen kilometers to go, the ship's systems failed. Aden attempted to glide it in manually, but it wasn't designed for that purpose. It began losing altitude rapidly, too rapidly to reach the clearing safely.

As the ship sank to tree top level, Sia could hear and feel large tree boughs scraping and jostling the ship. One especially large tree limb peeled the canopy from the cockpit and struck Aden in the head, rendering him unconscious. The ship continued through the trees unguided, clearing a path with its hull.

When it crash-landed Sia waited for him to come back to tell her it was safe to get out of her seat. When he didn't she took stock of her condition, and, after concluding that she was uninjured, released herself from her restraints. She hurried to the cockpit hatch and tried to open it, but discovered the controls were no longer functioning. Even more ominously, Aden didn't answer when she banged on it.

Chapter X

Despite being unable to open the hatch, and with no word from Aden, Sia refused to panic. She methodically studied the hatch, and when she saw "*manual operation*" stenciled on a metal plate, she peeled it off, revealing a lever and instructions for its use.

As directed, she pulled down on it and the hatch opened slightly. Encouraged, she lifted it and pulled down again. When she did it a third time, the hatch jammed with the opening still too small for her to slip through. She peered into the cockpit and could see Aden's arm hanging limply from the pilot's chair, with blood collecting in a pool beneath it.

"Aden!" she exclaimed. "Aden, can you hear me!" When he didn't respond, she looked about the cargo bay for something she could use to force the hatch open.

She found a crowbar in a tool locker, then returned to the hatch and positioned it in a way that maximized her leverage. Using all her weight against it, she could feel the hatch giving way. She repositioned herself and tried again, further increasing the gap. By the third try, it was wide enough for her to squeeze through. She dropped the crowbar and forced her way into the cockpit, afraid of what she would find.

Aden was still strapped in his chair. He was alive, but unconscious and bloody. Sia undid his restraints and with great difficulty eased him onto the deck. She shook him gently.

"Aden," she said softly, "Aden, can you hear me?"

Although he didn't answer, he seemed to be uninjured except for a bleeding head wound, but that had largely stopped on its own. She found some water and a clean towel and began to clean the blood from his head and face. Whatever had knocked him unconscious apparently glanced off him, leaving a small cut at his hairline and a large knot on his skull.

While Sia was able to tend to his external wounds, she was more concerned that he could have significant internal injuries. Realizing there was nothing she could do about that, she did what she could to make him comfortable. She covered him with a cargo blanket to keep him warm and placed a rolled up towel under his head.

With nothing to do now but wait, Sia went back to the cargo bay, opened the escape hatch, and left the ship in order to take stock of their situation. They had landed—crashed—in a large, grass-covered clearing. The air was hot and oppressive, and it took her a moment to catch her breath.

At the far end of the clearing, about forty meters away, squatted the ugliest, most obscene looking tree Sia had ever seen. It was dark crimson in color, thick around the trunk, about 20 meters high, and instead of leaves it was covered in windblown vines. At least she thought they were windblown until she realized how still the air was. In fact, they were moving independently in some kind of grotesque dance.

The base of the tree was littered with groups of sticks projecting into the air. Sia recoiled in horror when she realized that the "sticks" were actually the remains of animal carcasses. The tree was carnivorous, and from the looks of it liked large prey.

Remembering that with the canopy gone Aden was essentially lying out in the open, she turned and hurried back into the ship. She secured the emergency hatch before going into the cockpit to check on him. He was still out, but the color was returning to his face.

As she tended to him a long shadow slowly slid over the cockpit—night was coming. She had been reluctant to move him without a better sense of his injuries, but her fear of what other dangers might be lurking nearby, waiting for the night, quickly overruled her caution.

She noticed that the air, which had been still and quiet, was now beginning to stir. With each passing minute it carried an increasing cacophony of cries, screams, growls, chirps, and other more malevolent sounds.

She picked up the crowbar and with it slowly forced the hatch open wider. When it was wide enough to admit Aden, she went over to him and worked the blanket under him in a way that would make it easier for her to drag his massive, deadweight across the floor and through the hatch.

As she bent down to grasp the ends of the blanket, movement near the grotesque tree caught her eye. Looking up she saw that the vines were no longer hanging from the tree, but had dropped off and were slithering across the clearing, heading directly for the ship. A sense of urgency gripped her as she strained to pull Aden's bulk through the hatch.

The vines were moving faster the closer they got to the ship, and she feared she wouldn't be able to drag him to safety before they breached the cockpit. She halted her efforts long enough to retrieve his sword, which he had removed prior to takeoff and hung on the back of his chair. She slung it over her shoulder and hurried back to her task.

Just as his feet cleared the hatchway, Sia heard the vines slam into the hull. She ran to the hatch and reversed the direction of the manual door control, pumping the lever furiously. She said a silent prayer of thanks as the hatch closed more easily than it had opened. However, with just one more cycle to seal it, the vines burst over the edge of the cockpit and slithered ravenously toward the small gap that remained.

Before she could pull down the lever to complete the last cycle, the first of the vines burst through the opening and began wrapping themselves around Aden's leg. Sia stepped back from the lever and pulled the sword from its scabbard.

It was heavy, far heavier than she should have been able to handle; however, fueled by adrenaline and the desperation of knowing their lives depended on it, she wielded it with surprising ease. She swung down on the vines, severing them with one blow. They let out a howl that froze her blood and then withdrew through the hatch to lick their wounds.

She dropped the sword, ran back to the lever, and pulled it down with all her might. As the door banged shut, she could hear the angry vines slamming into it, hissing furiously that she had denied them such an easy meal.

Sia returned to Aden, picked up the sword, and carefully used its tip to pull the lifeless remains of the vines off his leg, which was now bleeding through his pants. She found a medkit and was pleased to find that, in contrast to the ship, it was fresh and well stocked. Aden had said it was good to be prepared on Seti, and it appeared that he included a good medkit in that assessment.

She ripped open a bag of sterile bandages, grabbed a tube of healing ointment, and brought them back to Aden. Then she used his knife to cut off his pant leg and saw that he was bleeding from numerous red welts left by the vines. She packed the wounds with ointment and began wrapping the bandage around his leg. It tightened on the wounds, as it was designed to do, and quickly staunched the flow of blood.

Without power the cargo bay was now almost dark, lighted only by the faint glow of the sliver of Seti's rising quarter moon, which had begun filtering in through the observation portals.

Throughout the night strange and violent sounds rent the air, and the ship periodically rocked as creatures banged on the hull trying to find a way in. The few times Sia was brave enough to look outside she saw that the clearing was no longer empty.

There were things that walked on six legs and stood two stories tall; packs of creatures that looked like large, slavering mice; and a giant, fanged, centipede-like creature that took an hour to force itself across the clearing by paddling its ungainly legs, its belly bulging from a recent meal.

She witnessed many other frightening creatures, eating and being eaten, most so horrible she couldn't even begin to describe them. Although she was terrified, she soon became too exhausted to care; she curled up next to Aden, covered them with a blanket, and went to sleep.

The next morning she reached over to check on him and was startled to find he was gone. When she jumped up to see where he was, he laughed.

"Ah, Your Highness has finally arisen. I take it I have you to thank for the tender care my injuries have received?"

"How are you feeling?"

"Much better, thanks to you. I have a little bit of a headache, and my leg hurts like Xanta's fire, but I believe my wounds will heal." He had also packed extra clothing, because he was wearing a fresh pair of black, military style pants.

"Good," she replied tersely. "Maybe now that you're feeling better you can explain why the best pilot on Seti, and maybe the universe, found himself unable to safely fly a simple, well defined, air route?"

Aden walked over to one of the passenger seats and sat down heavily. He pointed to another seat and said, "You might want to sit as well, Your Highness, this could take a while."

"I prefer to stand," she replied. "And please make this quick; I bore easily, and this promises to be very boring!"

"If feeling better means you're back to your usual, wonderful temper, I think I'd rather you left me in that chair."

"My question is a valid one."

Aden sighed. "It is indeed. Before I answer you, could I ask you a question or two?"

"Oh, very well if you must," she responded gruffly.

"Why did you even want to take this journey?"

"I have no idea. There was nothing to see and I would die before I'd allow myself to go anywhere with you."

"Undoubtedly correct on both points, and yet here we are."

"I assume you're trying to make a point?" she answered crossly.

"I am," he said. "To answer your question: As a youth I flew many hours on Seti. My experience has been that Xanide field formation is very predictable and easy to navigate around. Even a novice can avoid them with minimal training."

"Yes? And your point is…?"

"I'm getting there Your Highness. The xanide fields we ran into yesterday were different from any I have ever encountered, or even heard of. It was almost as though they were alive and trying to drive us to this place."

"That is ridiculous," replied Sia, as she sat down next to him, apparently tired of standing. "Is there no story too tall to justify your juvenile efforts to force me to be alone with you? Really high prince, radiation fields with a life of their own? Don't insult my intelligence!"

"If you recall Your Highness, I didn't even want to go. You insisted."

"So I did, for reasons I can't now fathom—are you ever going to get to the point?"

"I am about to tell you something I've never told anyone. You need to promise to keep it to yourself."

Her curiosity piqued, she agreed.

"Have you ever heard of a creature called a taal? I believe the Ardalans call it, set la?"

"I have never heard of a taal, except as an epithet to describe me," she replied gruffly. "I have, however, heard of the set la; it is a mythical creature that can control men's minds."

"An epithet? 'Taal' is not an epithet, it's…"

"Please spare me your tortured explanation," interrupted Sia impatiently. "I don't really care. You were saying?"

"I believe it—the taal—can manipulate minds, not control them. And it is not mythical; it…they…live on Seti."

"I think you suffered a more serious head injury than you realize," she replied.

"I'm dead serious," he said. He raised a hand to his cheek and touched the scar. "You see this scar? I received it from a taal I once captured."

"*You* captured a taal? You *are* delusional!"

Aden laughed. "These creatures do exist and they have been manipulating both our worlds for millennia."

"And I suppose you have proof, other than your scar, that is?"

"Let me ask you this: Why do you think our peoples have fought so many wars over this place?"

"No mystery there," she replied, "it's the richest source of xanide in the known galaxy."

"So it is. And yet, no matter how many lives are lost fighting over it, whichever side controls it hardly mines it at all. We currently have fewer than 300 miners here, and are mining the least productive veins on the planet. Before you blame it on Kealt stupidity, I can assure you that when Ardala ran the place, you did no better. That I *can* prove!"

Sia shifted uncomfortably in her seat. "I think you've conveniently forgotten that for the first time ever, Ardala and Kealt are on the verge of agreeing to work together to increase recreational use and mineral exploitation."

"I haven't forgotten. I have to admit it's taken me a while to figure out why, after so many millennia, they're finally allowing us to take more from this place. What upset such a neat little fruit cart?"

Now positively curious, Sia answered, "And your conclusion is?"

"You know as well as I: the zon. I think the taal are concerned that if we don't work together, the zon will destroy us both. They're afraid they may not be able to manipulate them as easily as they can us. And without the power to manipulate, they are essentially helpless before a ruthless, technologically advanced adversary. So, as much as it probably pains them to bring our peoples together, for them it may truly be the least of two evils."

Sia shook her head in disbelief and laughed at him. "That is one incredible tale. I doubt even crazy Celesta could have come up with something so bizarre. And finally, we crashed because...?"

"I don't know for sure; but I believe the taal manipulated you to get you on this ship, and to demand that I be your pilot. I also believe that somehow they are capable of manipulating xanide, and used it to bring us down here. Why they want the high princess of Ardala and the high prince of Kealt I can't guess, but I'm sure we'll find out soon enough."

"For the record, I don't believe anything you said," Sia replied, "but even if *you* do, we can't sit here and wait for them to contact us. It's just a matter of time before those…those things find a way into this ship."

"You're right," he agreed. "Nor can we expect a quick rescue from the mining colony. They would only have a rough idea of where we went down, and no efficient means of getting to us.

We've never been able to shield a ship or any other vehicle sufficiently enough to allow it to function for very long in xanide radiation. A survey ship is designed to fly in quickly, land at a designated spot, drop its cargo and leave again. But without knowing where we are, they couldn't use one of those either."

"How do you mine the stuff if it drains power so?" asked Sia.

"Xanide is only energized in the presence of certain other minerals. The stuff we mine is not located near these minerals, and is essentially inert." He stood up, walked over to a wall of charts, and began flipping through them. "Thankfully, whomever manages this rust bucket knows enough not to trust computers."

He flipped through several more, before ripping one out and laying it on the floor in front of Sia. He found a marker and a compass and kneeled down next to the chart. He aligned it with the compass and then marked two spots.

"You see this mark?" he asked, pointing to it. "Based on our last heading this is where we are now." He pointed to the other mark. "This is the closest area free from xanide interference. We need to get there in order to use our extraction beacons. It's about thirty kilometers west of here. That might not seem like much, but in this jungle we'll be hard pressed to cover much more than five or six kilometers a day."

"Will they still work by the time we get there?"

"Good question. I honestly don't know, but it's the only chance we have of getting out of here quickly."

"I heard you say we only packed six days worth of food!"

"We'll be dead from something else long before we starve to death. I'm much more concerned about the water. We have plenty of it, but it weighs so much we'll be limited in what we can carry. I have purifying equipment, but I'd rather not have to trust it on Seti's water."

With Sia's help, Aden spent the next three hours attempting to retrieve supplies and equipment from the cargo hold, which had been crushed in the crash. When they were finished he laid everything on the floor that hadn't been destroyed or damaged and took inventory.

The plasma rifle was ruined, as was the projectile sidearm. The projectile rifle survived, along with 200 rounds of ammunition. He could only find three days worth of food.

Only one box of grenades remained. Thankfully the crossbow was intact, but with only 20 explosive bolts. Somehow, the three portable force field generators were in one piece, although, without testing them, he didn't know how effective they'd be. The hand-held communicator had disappeared, but he recovered both extraction beacons, which appeared to be in operating order. He also found some rope.

He picked up one of the two backpacks and filled it with half the food, some water, and a sleeping bag. He handed it to Sia and asked her if she could take more. She hefted it, handed it back and said, "I can take double that."

Aden raised an eyebrow, and stuffed it with more water and the bolts for the crossbow. He put the remainder of their supplies into the second backpack. He strapped on the plasma sidearm and extra power packs, but doubted they'd be of much use. They were shielded against xanide radiation, but he knew from experience they would be depleted quickly.

He folded the map and put it into his vest pocket, and secured the compass to his belt. When he was finished he said, "Well Your Highness, it's now the afternoon. We could start out now and possibly make a kilometer or two, or we could spend another night here and give ourselves an entire day. What say you?"

"While I want to spend as few nights out here as possible," Sia replied, "I suggest we stay here tonight and start off fresh in the morning."

"Good choice Your Highness!" answered Aden brightly.

Then he reached into a duffel bag he had also retrieved from the hold and pulled out a pair of black, military style pants similar to what he was wearing, as a well as a black t-shirt, boots, and other accessories. He left the pile of clothing at his feet and said, "That dress you're wearing is quite flattering, but it's not well suited for a trek through the jungles of this planet. I suggest you exchange it for these clothes."

"They are horrible looking!" she whined. "Besides, they won't fit me!"

"They will if I'm any judge of female anatomy," he replied. "I packed them for you myself. As for its tastefulness, this attire is quite popular among the youth on Kealt. You'll also find it comfortable, roomy, and dirt repellent. I think once you put it on you'll find it acceptable."

Reluctantly Sia walked over to him, picked up the gear and said, "Very well. Now please leave so I can change without you leering at me!"

"By all means," he replied with a smirk. "With your permission I'd like to spend what daylight remains hunting for fresh meat. I'd like to save our emergency rations for the journey. They are awful tasting, but lighter and easier to transport than real food."

"You *eat* the animals here?" she asked incredulously.

"Actually, there are game animals here that are quite tasty. We need to survive Your Highness. I suggest you adopt an open mind."

"Fine by me. I have no desire to starve to death."

Aden picked up the projectile rifle and slammed a clip into it. He said, "I've only got 200 rounds for this, I hope it's enough. The plasma sidearm was designed to work here, but even shielded the radiation will leach it dry in a very short time."

He left Sia in the ship with orders to secure the hatch and not venture outside until he came back. After what she'd seen the night before she needed no convincing. He returned less than an hour later with a small mammalian-like creature slung over his shoulder. He banged on the hatch and Sia emerged wearing her new clothes.

"Your Highness," he said, gawking at her as she walked past him, "how do you find your new attire?"

"As you said, it is...acceptable."

"More than acceptable! Those clothes actually look quite flattering on you; the pants especially favor your well-made backside!"

"Are you always so relentlessly crude?" she harrumphed in reply.

"I admit I can be crude on occasion," he admitted with a smirk, "but not relentlessly so."

Sia huffed at him again, then, driven by her growing hunger, followed him to where he would prepare the creature for eating. She pointed toward the tree that had attacked Aden and asked, "Is this safe with that thing over there?"

"As long as we don't disturb it we're safe for now. It's typically dormant during the day, as are many of Seti's 'children.'"

He gathered some rocks and created a makeshift hearth, then collected several armfuls of dead wood. When everything was ready, he set the wood on fire with the plasma sidearm, drove a steel rod through the carcass he had already cleaned, and suspended it over the fire.

Sia was impressed at the speed with which dinner was ready. When he handed her a well-muscled leg bone she wrinkled her nose and asked, "What is this? You aren't trying to kill me now, are you?"

"We call it a tamalok," he replied. Then he smiled, lifted the bone to his mouth, and ripped off a big piece of meat. He swallowed the mouthful, then smiled again and said, "It…is …delicious! Once you taste this I doubt you'll ever settle for what goes for meat on your planet!"

A doubtful Sia took the bone from him and nibbled off a dainty bite. Her eyes opened wide. "I hate to admit it," she said, "but you're right, this *is* delicious!"

"I'm sorry I can't offer you any wine, I neglected to provision it."

"It seems that is the only thing you forgot!"

When they were finished, he wrapped up what remained of the tamalok and threw it off into the jungle. One less thing to attract dangerous fauna he thought, although there seemed to be no shortage of it anyway.

As the sun began to settle, they retreated to the relative safety of the ship. With little to do except wait for bedtime, they quickly became bored. Aden suggested they could pass the time by making love, and laughed uncontrollably when it elicited the expected response. When Sia realized he was teasing her she became even angrier.

Later, when he stood up to look out one of the portals, she noticed he was favoring his injured leg. She put aside her anger and said, "Come over here and let me look at your wound. You shouldn't be limping like that."

"Really Your Highness," he replied, "I'm touched by your concern, but I assure you, I'm fine."

"I insist."

"Oh very well," he groused, and lurched over to her.

She knelt in front of him and said, "Lower your pants, and for the love of God I hope you have shorts on!"

"Let's get this over with," he replied gruffly, as he undid his belt and dropped his pants. Looking down at Sia kneeling in front of his crotch he said, "You do realize how ridiculous you look?"

She didn't answer, but gently unwound the wound. When the sodden bandage dropped away, she almost gagged at the smell. Using a small chemical torch she found in the medkit that still worked, she was able to confirm her fears: His leg was infected, and from the looks of it badly, the result of a digestive enzyme the vines had injected into him before she was able to remove them.

She carefully cleaned and repacked the wound, then covered it with a fresh dressing. While he pulled up his pants, she took a bottle of antibiotic pills from the medkit, shook two pills into her hand, gave them to him. "I don't like the looks of it," she said. "You need help and quickly."

"Is that concern, Your Highness?" he replied. When he saw she was too worried to offer a rebuttal, he added, "We call it a bolba tree."

"A what? What's a bolba tree?"

He patted his wounded leg gingerly and said, "The thing that did this. The bolba tree is just one of a thousand ways a man—or a woman—can die on this planet. It might be the most unpleasant though. Those vines would have dragged me back to what passes for a mouth on that thing. Slowly it would have sucked on me until my body was almost devoid of fluids. Then it would have pulled me inside to digest what was left.

"When it was finished it would force my remains out its equivalent of an anus, and I would join the pile of bones that reside in its shade. Oh, and the worst of it is, I'd be alive almost until the end."

"What a truly disgusting life form! I don't care if it is dormant during the day, we must be sure to grant it wide berth when we leave in the morning."

"We will indeed!" agreed Aden heartily. He rolled out a thin air mattress and placed a sleeping bag on top of it. When he was finished he threw Sia the other set. While she was preparing her bedding, he said, "We'll need to be up early if we want to make any distance. We'll be heading through some pretty tough stuff; best to call it a night."

They both slept fitfully that night, dreading what the day would bring.

Chapter XI

When morning came, Sia was relieved to see that Aden was moving more freely, and hoped the worst had passed. They set out an hour after sun-up, just long enough for the creatures of the night to retreat to their lairs. They skirted the bolba tree, which, based on the fresh piles of bones shaded by its twisted branches, had enjoyed a banner night.

Not long after they left the clearing, the path they were following led them past the entrance to a large cave. When Aden moved toward it, Sia protested that it wasn't safe and insisted they keep moving. He heeded her warning, but not before peering into it and observing that its walls were lined with xanide, more xanide than any human being had ever seen before in one place.

As he promised, the trek was tough going. In addition to the rough terrain, it was hot, humid, and rained frequently. By the end of the day, he estimated they had covered less than four kilometers. As it got closer to nightfall, he found a small clearing and set out the force field generators.

"Will those work here?" asked Sia.

"They're heavily shielded so they should work, at least for a little while. The problem is, for them to work effectively in this environment, I'll have to boost the power consumption. I don't know how long they'll last." He pulled a remote controller out of a vest pocket and activated the field. While Sia saw nothing, Aden seemed pleased. He pitched the tent he was carrying, and as they laid out the sleeping bags said, "We can't trust these generators. We're going to have to take turns standing watch. You want first or second?"

"First I guess."

"When the force field is on we can still be seen, but it'll contain our scent. Since many of the creatures out there rely primarily on smell, as long as we don't move around too much most of them probably won't even notice us." He pulled out a bottle and shook out two pills.

"Are those the antibiotics?"

"Ah, yeah," he answered.

Once Aden turned in, Sia tried to make herself comfortable by sitting on the most accommodating object she could find. It had rained heavily for much of the day, and she was damp, hungry, and tired. She didn't know whether she should be angry at Aden for crashing their ship, or grateful for being so resourceful. Either way, she thought, when this was over she would leave Seti as fast as she could and never look back, negotiations be damned.

As the evening progressed she was pleased that the force field seemed to be working. Several times hungry monsters ambled up to the campsite only to be violently repelled by an invisible wall. In order to conserve power, Aden had set the edge of the force field uncomfortably close; so close that at times she thought she could feel the breath of the things on the other side.

She noticed that when something hit the force field it lit brightly, but each time a little less so. When it was time for Aden's watch, she wondered if it still worked. She went into the tent and shook him. When he merely groaned she shook him again and said, "Are you going to take your watch or not?"

He sat up slowly and squinted at her. "What?" he asked.

"You heard me, your turn!"

"Oh, yes of course," he replied, and crawled out of his sleeping bag.

When Sia saw he was naked except for the bandage on his leg she said, "You might be more comfortable if you put some clothes on. I certainly will be!"

When morning came, she crawled out of the tent and found him asleep. She shook him and demanded that he wake up. "What's wrong with you?" she complained.

"I'm sorry Your Highness," he replied groggily, rising to his feet. He began patting his vest, disappointed he couldn't find whatever he was looking for.

"Are you looking for these?" she asked, waving a bottle of pills.

"Yes, my antibiotics, please give them to me."

"These are painkillers. I found them in the tent. Your leg isn't getting any better is it?" She put her hands on his face. "You're burning up. You need to rest."

"Look, Sia, we don't have a lot of time. I got you into this, I have to get you out. I can't do that sleeping or dragging a bad leg."

"*I* got us into this," she insisted. "You tried to talk me out of it, remember? If you didn't come as prepared as you did, we'd probably be dead already!"

"Like I said, without those pills I won't be able to move. If I can't move we die. At this point, I don't see many alternatives."

Reluctantly she agreed. She handed him the pills and said, "You're right. I'm very sorry. I've been awful to you and all you've ever been to me is kind."

"Uh oh, I'm in worse shape than I thought," he joked.

"You are," she replied grimly.

That day they covered eight kilometers by taking advantage of several large open areas and following paths plowed through the underbrush by large creatures Sia tried not to imagine. The day's journey was mostly uneventful; however, on a several occasions Aden signaled for her to be quiet and pulled her off the path in order let a monstrosity pass.

The first time, she peered curiously through the brush. What she saw froze her: It was a huge, ambling three-legged creature that looked like a giant pear, with vicious, toothy jaws that hung open revealing a spiny tongue that was at least three meters long when fully extended. As it moved down the path it looked about with its one, large, bulbous eye set on a fleshy stalk protruding from its head. As she watched it, the eye turned a full 360°. It had one long, two jointed, clawed arm that hung from what in most animals would be the stomach region. The claw was wrapped around a piece of a smaller version of the 'millipede' creature she'd seen her first night on Seti. Most grotesquely, its legs were still paddling uselessly. After that, whenever they had to step off the path she closed her eyes and buried her head in Aden's chest.

That evening they were celebrating their good fortune in surviving another day when the force field generators died. "Quick!" exclaimed Aden. "We need to get as high up in one of these sickus trees as we can!"

He pulled the rope out of the backpack, put the backpack on, and tossed the rope over the lowest branch. He pulled himself up first, and then helped Sia. The branches were close together which, Sia noted, made climbing easier. Aden didn't tell her it also made it easier for predators to reach them.

That night he nearly exhausted the plasma weapon's power supplies defending their position. As he feared, its shielding was only marginally effective. They were less than halfway to their destination and he had almost exhausted their most effective weapon.

The next day he could no longer keep pace with her. They had covered less than two kilometers when nightfall came. They climbed another sickus tree and by morning they were down to the crossbow and five bolts. A kilometer into the fourth day, Aden collapsed near the center of a small clearing. Even the pain pills offered no relief.

Sia half carried, half dragged him to a nearby stump. He offered no resistance when she pulled down his pants to check his bandage. He was so far gone he remained mute when she gasped at the condition of his leg.

She kneeled down next to him, wrapped her arms around him and cried. He revived briefly and croaked, "Take the supplies that are left and get out of here. The map and compass are in my vest pocket. I believe the terrain ahead is easier. If you're lucky you can get to the extraction point in one more day."

"I'm not going anywhere without you," she replied. "I know you'd never leave *me* here."

When he passed out again she didn't know what to do. Nightfall was coming and he was too heavy for her to drag up a sickus tree.

When the forest began to shake in all directions, she was terrified. She still had the crossbow, but no idea how to use it. In desperation, she pulled the sword from Aden's sheath and stood up.

The weight of whatever was coming was so great the ground began to vibrate. Just when she thought she'd had as much as she could endure, huge feline-like creatures emerged from the jungle in all directions. They stopped about 15 meters from the two humans and formed a circle around them. All but one turned and faced outward. Sia didn't know how she knew, but the creature that continued to face them was a female. Furthermore, she was familiar with Aden, even fond of him.

As she lumbered closer, Sia held up his sword in a futile attempt to ward her off. The creature ignored her, approached Aden, then leaned down and sniffed him. At first Sia thought she was going to eat him, but instead she began licking his leg.

After what seemed an eternity the creature raised its huge head, turned around and came face to face with her. "I am not afraid of you," Sia exclaimed. "I know what you are, set la…taal!"

The creature leaned in so close to her, its heavy breath threatened to knock her over. Still she held her ground, brandishing the sword pathetically. She felt, rather than heard, the creature's response.

"We are as you say," its "voice" echoed in her mind. "The one you call Aden has proven himself brave and honorable. We have come to trust him. We will tend to him and protect him. Why should we allow you to live?"

Before Sia could answer, a voice behind the taal croaked, "Because I ask it of you, my old friend! I have no doubt she also possesses the qualities you appreciate in me in equal or greater abundance!"

"Aden!" exclaimed Sia, as she ran to him and helped him to his feet. She threw her arms around him and cried, "How is this possible?"

"I'm not sure," he replied, taking his sword back from her and returning it to its sheath. "Apparently taal saliva is the antidote to whatever those vines left in me." When she continued to embrace him, he pushed her away with some difficulty. "Easy Your Highness, you're going to hate yourself in the morning." With his admonishment, she reluctantly regained her decorum and stepped, sheepishly, to his side.

"Well said, high prince!" answered the taal. "We have been watching your struggles. She is indeed of commendable character. We have no doubt she will bear you many fine children, if you are ever able to crack the stone exterior that protects her heart."

"Ah, yes," he replied, glancing awkwardly at Sia. "In the meantime, I'm sure there is a reason you've finally revealed yourselves to us."

"There is indeed. As you have correctly guessed, we have been manipulating your worlds for centuries. We did so in self-defense. Many thousands of years ago, the first humans came to Seti. They had been traveling in generational ships for hundreds of years when they encountered something they called a 'wormhole,' which deposited their ships in this galaxy. By the time they found their way to this solar system their ships were failing and their society was on the brink of collapse. We helped them rebuild their society, and, for a time, things were good between us.

"Eventually the humans were able to repair some of their ships, adapting xanide crystals, as you call them, as power sources. Those that had landed outside the xanide fields headed back into space to explore the two habitable planets you call Ardala and Kealt. These planets were much better suited for human life, and before long few humans remained on Seti save for the xanide minors.

"As your race replenished itself, dependence on xanide grew quickly. Unfortunately neither

Kealt nor Ardala had it in abundance. At first, we agreed to allow increased mining, but then the humans began fighting each other over mining allocations and eventually turned on us.

"With no technology to defend ourselves, we turned to our only defense, our ability to manipulate pliant human minds. With surprising ease, we kept Kealt and Ardala at each other's throats. We allowed just enough mining to avoid drawing attention to ourselves, and for your societies to prosper. We didn't care which side 'controlled' Seti, so long as the other remained determined to win it back. And, over time, we were even able to make most humans forget about us, except as creatures of myth and legend."

"So you are the reason we've fought so many wars!" exclaimed Aden. "How many lives have been lost because of you? You are as bad as the zon!"

Sia expected the taal to be angry. Instead she could feel the shame in her response.

"You are correct high prince. We have much to account for. We acted out of fear, not prudence. And you also are correct in that we fear the zon. If left unchecked they will destroy us all!"

"So," responded Aden, "now you're hoping Kealt and Ardala will put aside our differences long enough to defeat the zon. Once that's done, you'll restore the status quo. Is that it?"

"You are partly correct, high prince. We wish to form an alliance with your two worlds. It is time for us to come out of the shadows and become citizens of this solar system. We now agree that too many have suffered under the 'status quo,' as you call it, to go back to it."

"How can we trust you?"

"We trusted you those many years ago. Do you really think it was that easy to capture a taal?"

"It *was* you, wasn't it? You *let* me do it?"

"Of course—we were testing your character. Had you faltered we would have slaughtered you."

Aden turned to Sia, shrugged his shoulders and said, "At least they're honest!"

"They are not," she replied testily. "You were right to ask how much blood has been spilled because of them. And we wouldn't even be here if they hadn't forced me to insist that you take me up in that ship!"

"You also are partly correct, high princess," replied the taal. "While we encouraged you, we couldn't force you to kill each other. Nor could we make you come here. We played on your attraction to the high prince. Human emotions are so near the surface; you make it easy for us."

Ignoring the fact that Sia was rapidly turning red, Aden asked, "So what do you want from us?"

"One day you will be king and queen. As leaders on your respective worlds, we have decided that we want you to bring the message back to your peoples that we are ready to take our place as the third great society in this solar system.

We want to be party to the treaty between Kealt and Ardala regarding Seti."

"If that's the case," answered Aden, "why did you let us risk our lives for so long? For that matter, was it you who caused my ship to crash in the first place?"

The taal said, "That wasn't always our plan. We did bring down your ship, but not on purpose. We intended to manipulate the xanide radiation in a way that would allow you to land your ship safely.

"Once you realized you couldn't leave, we would guide you to something of great importance to both your worlds, again, assuring as best we could, that you got there safely. Then we would guide you back to your ship and allow you to leave. Unfortunately you were a more skilled and determined pilot than we anticipated, making it impossible for us to bring your ship down in one piece, or close to where we wanted."

"What made you decide to reveal yourselves to us?" asked Sia.

"That was a decision we debated until just recently. When we realized the seriousness of the high prince's physical condition and our role in causing it, and the fact that we had unwittingly destroyed your only means of getting home, we agreed we had no other choice but to step forward. Once we did, to use a human cliché, 'in for a little, in for a lot.'"

Aden sensed that she was holding something back. "I'm not telepathic," he replied, "but there is something you're not telling us."

The taal didn't answer at first, and Aden got the distinct impression she was consulting with the others. Finally, she said, "You are right. The zon are coming."

"To where?" asked Sia.

"To Ardala."

"Why Ardala?"

"The zon have more deeply penetrated the Ardalan Government. They believe it to be the easier target."

"Liars!" exclaimed Sia. "We would never capitulate to those monsters!"

"Nonetheless," replied the taal calmly, "they are coming; we have been exposed to minds harboring this information. You can deny it, or you can prepare."

Aden put his hand on Sia's shoulder and said, "Assuming you are correct, why now?"

"Several years ago the zon made the mistake of attacking several small colonies belonging to a species you call the tayron. The colonies were on the edge of tayron space and lightly defended. Emboldened by their success and seduced by the potential richness of their new feeding grounds, the zon penetrated deeper into their territory. By the time they realized the might of their new adversary dwarfed their own it was too late.

"The tayron now are like a mad bull pursuing the zon across the universe. They will only rest when they are obliterated from existence. Unfortunately, the zon have chosen to consolidate their forces here due to the availability of a satisfactory food supply, abundant resources, and compatible worlds.

"With their hands already full with the tayron, they are desperate to prevent an alliance between Kealt and Ardala. Once they have gained control of Ardala, they will move on Kealt. They hope that with the forces of your two planets at their disposal the tayron will hesitate to press their attack."

Aden finally understood the taal's true fear. He stepped closer to it. "And if the tayron arrive to find our worlds collaborating with the zon…"

"You know. They told you."

"They will destroy us. All of us."

"What?" exclaimed Sia. "You know these aliens?"

"I met them once, briefly, when we evacuated your scientists from XR564. They warned me they would not tolerate it if they found either of us collaborating with the zon."

"And you kept this to yourself?"

"No, I briefed Polis; didn't he tell you?"

"No, but it wouldn't be the first time. He feels he needs to protect me. He can be quite annoying at times."

Aden turned his attention back to the taal. "So what now?" he asked.

The taal kneeled down and said, "If you climb on I will take you to something of great importance to both your peoples."

Aden could sense her distaste as he walked up to her and tried unsuccessfully to pull himself up onto her back. In order to assist him, she reluctantly agreed to let him use his rope to create a makeshift harness. After he finally succeeded in mounting her, he reached down to offer Sia his hand. When she stayed where she was, he said, "Don't be frightened. They're trying to help."

"I don't trust them," she replied. "I believe they still haven't told us everything."

"Perhaps not," answered Aden, "but right now there isn't much else we can do."

Reluctantly she put aside her fears and allowed him to help her up onto the gargantuan creature. As it stood up and lurched into motion, she wrapped her arms around him and said, "Don't get excited, I just don't want to fall off!"

For the most part the taal stuck to well-traveled trails, but at times she used her great bulk to break new trails through the thick underbrush. Sia was not surprised that, even though it was now night, none of planet's horrors got in their way. She wondered if there was any creature in the universe that could physically threaten a taal.

As they moved on, the path became narrower, the brush thicker, and a thick fog settled over the jungle, making it impossible to see more than a few meters. Aden reached back and touched the hilt of his sword as if to assure himself it was still there. Death could come from any direction on Seti, and he wanted to be prepared. His action further unnerved Sia, who hugged him tighter.

To make things worse, they both could sense the taal's growing unease. In the event they met a larger creature, she would have very little room to maneuver, especially with the two of them on her back. They made her vulnerable, and, on Seti, that was not a good state. When, just after daybreak, the fog began to lift and the trail opened into a small clearing, they felt her relief. Almost immediately, an immense reptilian-like creature burst out of its hiding place and exploded into her.

The force of the impact knocked her over, spilling Sia and Aden to the ground. The taal tried to get up, but the creature had her pinned to the ground, her neck clamped in its long, toothed snout. She continued to struggle, but the creature was crushing her windpipe, making it difficult for her to breathe. She was fading quickly.

Sia grabbed Aden's hand. "Come on," she exclaimed, "let's get out of here! You can't help her!"

As she tried to pull him away, they both sensed a faint plea for help. It was the taal, clearly on her last breath.

"I've got to try!" he responded, and rushed toward the behemoths.

"Of course you do!" she muttered unhappily.

By the time he reached the taal she was barely moving. He grabbed the makeshift harness, pulled himself up onto her side, and found himself face to face with one of Seti's most malevolent monsters. Fortunately the creature ignored him, intent on finishing off its huge prize. On Seti size mattered, and compared to the main combatants he was more than puny.

Aden reached over his back and pulled out his sword. He walked over to the monster and calmly thrust it into its eye socket as far as it would go. It immediately released the fallen taal and bellowed loudly. Then it turned toward Aden and with its snout swept him off his perch.

Now fully focused on him, it crawled over the taal in order to reach him. Aden began backing up, but there was nowhere to go. The foliage bordering the trail was too thick for him to run through and the open part of the trail led right to Sia, who stood transfixed by the horror unfolding before her.

Aden knew it was a futile gesture, but he yanked out his knife and held it in front of him. Predictably, the creature ignored it and gathered itself to spring. Just as it leapt forward, something blasted it sideways. The taal had revived! And she was angry. Without the element of surprise, the monster was no match for her. She clamped her jaws onto its side and tore off a huge chunk of meat and bone. Then she reached into the wound with her paws and with frightening ease rendered it in two.

When she was satisfied there were no other immediate dangers, she bade Aden and Sia to climb back onto her. First, Aden walked over to the fallen monster and yanked his sword from its eye socket. He wiped it off on the grass as best he could, then returned it to its sheath. When they remounted the taal, Sia asked her if she was OK. When she didn't answer, and even though Sia hadn't asked him, Aden assured her with a touch of sarcasm that he was fine too.

"What was that?" she asked, ignoring him. "And why didn't she know it was there?"

Aden shrugged. "I don't know, I've never seen one of those before. Maybe they can't read the mind of all of Seti's creatures? Perhaps one day she'll tell us, but I wouldn't hold your breath."

Not much further down the trail, the taal came to a stop. They were at the edge of a large mound hundreds of meters high that extended off into the jungle in both directions as far as they could see. Aden didn't believe it was a natural formation.

At his request, the taal knelt down and they dismounted. He began walking along it as though he was looking for something. When he came to an area bare of vegetation, he picked up a large stick and began scraping at the dirt. When the end of the stick hit something hard, he jabbed into it. To Sia's surprise, it made a hollow, metallic sound.

"What have you found?" she asked.

"As I suspected, this isn't a natural formation."

Her curiosity aroused, she replied impatiently, "Well then, what is it?"

"Mostly likely a ship of some sort—from the looks of it, a very big one. Bigger than any ever built by our two worlds." Speaking to the taal, he said, "Do you know what this is? Why have you brought us here?"

"You are correct high prince. This is a ship. It was from your original home world. It carried tens of thousands of your kind across the stars before crashing here. Initially it served as a source of shelter, technology, and raw materials. Eventually your ancestors made it a shrine of sorts. As they migrated from this planet they eventually forgot it."

"You mean you *made* us forget it!" exclaimed Sia.

"Yes," she replied.

"I must ask again," said Aden, "why have you brought us here?"

"Inside there are archives that your ancestors left behind. They tell of your original home world, the journey across space, and the early days of settlement. Before there was a Kealt and Ardala, you were one people, united in the struggle to survive. We believe the information this ship holds will remind you of that and help reunite your peoples."

"This happened a long time ago," noted Sia. "How do you know this?"

"Our telepathic nature makes us natural historians; by reading each other's thoughts, we are constantly transferring knowledge. As a result, our collective memory is vast, if imperfect at times."

"What Celesta wouldn't give to have a crack at this!" said Aden to no one in particular.

Sia silently agreed.

Chapter XII

Ardalans and Kealts alike were shocked when Aden and Sia returned to Kuste on the back of a taal. As they rode down the center of the settlement, Arvid reminded Borg of his prediction. News of the rediscovery of the solar system's second sentient species spread fast.

Considering the importance of Seti and the taals' reemergence, the kings of Ardala and Kealt agreed to handle the new treaty negotiations personally. However, instead of negotiating with each other, they would now negotiate with the taal as rightful monarchs of their own world.

It had been months since Sia last saw Gabo. With her father now handling the negotiations for Ardala, she was at last free to return home. The day before her ship was to depart, she decided it would be proper etiquette to say goodbye to Aden, whom she might never see again. When she couldn't locate him, she checked with his aides who advised he'd gone to the pub.

When she got there, she found him sitting with the same raven-haired girl she'd seen him dancing with on Kealt before the wedding. She chastised herself when she felt a twinge of jealousy. She wasn't some smitten schoolgirl, she reminded herself. She was the high princess of Ardala.

Putting her unwelcome emotions aside, she walked up to his table. When he didn't notice her, she touched him gently on the shoulder. As he turned around she said, "Please excuse the interruption high prince, but I'm leaving tomorrow and I thought it proper to say goodbye."

"Aden, I'll catch up with you later," said Drusa, while standing up.

"Please," replied Sia, "don't leave on my account."

"It's quite all right Your Highness."

Aden stood up to protest, but she was already walking away.

"May I sit down?" asked Sia.

Trying his best not to betray his irritation he replied, "Of course." He waved at the table and added curtly, "Please, be my guest."

Sia sat down and smiled at him. "I wonder, why do people always run away when I come? Is it my cheery disposition?"

Disarmed by her rare attempt at humor, Aden put his irritation aside and smiled back at her. "Your Highness, you are a ray of sunshine always."

Ignoring his obvious flattery she said, "Who was she?"

"Who was who?"

"The little Caluthian pastry who just left. I can't be sure since she's clothed now—mostly—but weren't those her bare feet I saw sticking out from under your covers?"

"Caluthian pastry?" repeated Aden. When Sia merely stared at him mutely, he said, "Ah, if you mean the young woman you just scared away, her name is Drusa Prine. She's a refugee from Epsilon II. I invited her to be part of the Kealt delegation."

"She looks familiar. Didn't I see you dancing with her at the ball your father threw to celebrate my return to Ardala, which, unfortunately, never actually happened?"

"You are most observant. I can't believe you remember her."

"I think most women would remember their future husband dancing the night away with someone who looked like her."

"Well that never happened either. Anyway, you are being most unfair! You would have nothing to do with me! I was merely trying to enjoy myself like everyone else."

"You don't need to justify yourself to me—it was just an observation. Does she have a real reason for being on Seti?"

"Well," he replied hesitantly, "she's not, actually, technically, a part of the formal negotiating staff if that's what you mean. I asked her to come and help with any research that might be needed."

Sia smiled condescendingly. "Oh yes, of course. I'm sure her research ability, and other skills, are unparalleled and much appreciated."

"Please remind me why you came here?" replied Aden sharply, his good will quickly fading.

"I've made you angry!" she said, frowning. "Honestly, we're like fire and wood. Believe it or not, I didn't come here to provoke you. Do you have any more of that fine Kealt wine we had before?"

Aden hailed a server, who advised he still had some bottles left. When he scurried off to retrieve one, Sia said, "How is your leg?"

"Healing magnificently," he replied, "along with the rest of me."

She smiled. "I'm glad you're feeling better. As I mentioned, today is my last day. With my father taking over the negotiations, I'm free to leave. I've been away from home for months. I miss it terribly!" What she didn't say was that she missed Gabo even more.

Before Aden could answer, the server returned with the wine. When he departed, she said, "I expect you also will be leaving. I imagine anyone would after what we've been through!"

"I'm staying!" he replied enthusiastically. "I wouldn't miss these negotiations for the world. All my life I've been fascinated by the taal, and now to actually meet them a second time…you couldn't drag me from this place!"

Sia looked at Aden as though through new eyes. With his long, black, unruly hair, uneven whiskers, scarred face, strong cheekbones and thick chin, he looked like he'd been carved from the Seti wilderness itself.

As much as she disliked the thought of it, she was beginning to understand him. Despite his royal birth and heavy responsibilities, he was a simple man at heart and a dreamer. Who else would venture into one of the most inhospitable landscapes in the universe and attempt to capture a creature everyone else had stopped believing in centuries before—and then actually do it? The more she stared at him, the more she also realized he was every bit as handsome as his father.

"Uh, Sia?"

"Yes?" she replied with a start.

"You're staring at me."

"I am not!"

"Yes you are!"

Embarrassed, she looked away. "I just realized how much you look like your father."

"Well then, I'll take that as a compliment!"

She finished her second glass of wine. When she attempted to refill her glass, she expressed disappointment that the bottle was empty. She demanded that Aden order another one. When the server had again come and gone she asked, "Are you and Drusa close?"

"We're friends, more or less," he replied. When Sia smirked in response, he said, "Actually, she's fun to be around, but we don't have a lot in common. Eventually we'll tire of each other and go our separate ways."

"Oh, why do you say that?"

"I don't want to sound unkind. She has a good heart and she's been through a lot, but truthfully, between you and me, she's as dumb as a sulva slug, or at least pretends to be."

"I have no idea what that is, but she can't be that bad!"

"Oh yes she can!"

His exaggerated expression made Sia laugh, and that made Aden laugh. They were still laughing when the server returned with their third bottle of wine. When he advised Aden there was only one bottle left, he told him he had better get it before someone else ordered it. Aden laughed at his own ironic humor, which caused Sia to laugh even harder.

"Did you see the look on his face?" he gasped between breaths. "He thinks he's going to be in so much trouble when my father walks in here and asks for a bottle of that wine!"

"Oh, then we shouldn't drink it!" replied Sia, who could barely breathe she was laughing so hard. "We mustn't get the poor man in trouble!"

"He'll be fine. I'll tell my father we finished it—if I remember!"

Before they knew it, the fourth bottle was empty. When Sia insisted he order yet another, Aden was equally insistent she'd had enough. Kealt wine was stronger than typical Ardalan wines and she wasn't used to it. She was obviously quite drunk and he wasn't feeling bad either.

She resigned herself to the fact that no more wine was coming, and, after a while, asked Aden to escort her back to her ship, where she would wait for tomorrow's liftoff. They left the pub arm and arm. They hadn't gone far when she stopped under a copse of trees.

"What is that," she asked, pointing to the blue glow that had settled over the jungle.

"It's a reaction between the xanide, other native minerals, and the moonlight," he replied.

"Why didn't I notice it before?"

"It only happens during a full moon; tonight, for the first time since we've been here, the moon is full."

Sia stumbled on a rock and would have fallen if Aden hadn't caught her. She put her arms around him and said breathlessly, "So, you are good for something!"

Impulsively he leaned down and kissed her. To his surprise, she kissed him back. Intoxicated by the feel of her body, her scent, and the lion's share of four bottles of Kag wine, he put his hand on her perfect breast and squeezed it gently. She erupted like a supernova, pushing him away and slapping him.

"You uncouth ugak boar!" she screamed. "You Kealt beast! I'm not a simple farm girl smitten by the smell of dirt and tree sap! I am Sia Selarney, high princess of Ardala! I would rather die than let you embrace me!"

When Aden got over his shock, he grabbed her wrists and stopped her assault. Or so he thought until she began kicking him. "Let me go you brute!" she demanded.

"I will if you stop hitting me!"

She stopped struggling and repeated, "LET…ME…GO!"

Aden released her and braced himself for a renewed onslaught. Instead, she began crying. "I trusted you!" she exclaimed, before running away.

The next day he tried to say goodbye, but she wouldn't see him. He felt guilty for taking advantage of her, but only a little. As her ship was lifting off, Edris stood next to him. He put a hand on his shoulder and said, "There goes a beautiful woman, eh?"

Aden grinned sardonically. "Yes, and as hard to figure out as a malarian puzzle."

"You mean that?"

"I do."

"She's not that complicated."

"Please then, father, would you be so kind and enlighten me with your vast wisdom on the opposite sex!"

Edris chuckled. "Isn't it obvious?" he replied. "You intimidate her, and she is not one to be intimidated."

"I…intimidate…her?"

As the ship faded into the sky, they turned and walked toward the hover car that would take them back to town. Edris shook his massive head. "She agreed to marry you before you set her free. I have no doubt she would have made you a fine wife. Deep down I think you impressed her by your willingness to forgo such a great prize with everything that was at stake—no other hot-blooded male could have done that! You are as strong willed as she, and that is what intimidates her."

Now it was Aden's turn to shake his head. "There may be wisdom in what you say father, but there is also the matter of Celesta. She was as much a wedge between us as anything. Isn't it past time, for all our sakes, to reveal the truth?"

Edris stopped, put his hands on Aden's shoulders, and looked him solidly in the eye. "And so we will, soon, but not today. We are so close to achieving the political reforms Kealt deserves. Unfortunately, there are still powerful forces that would keep us caged in the past. The truth about Celesta could be the thing to tip the balance toward the Mar clan. You know what that would mean for Kealt."

"I do," Aden sighed, "but I don't know how much more she can take."

"She is strong, stronger than you give her credit for. For now she will have to sustain herself on the knowledge that we love her."

They walked on in silence. When they got to the hover car, Edris changed his mind about spending the night in his temporary quarters and asked Aden to join him in the royal hunting lodge, which was located far from the settlement, deep in the Seti wilderness. Aden quickly agreed.

The lodge was large by Seti standards, but simple and rustic. It was unguarded at Edris's insistence. As a compromise, his security officers had installed a security perimeter that would neutralize energy weapons and deny entry to anyone without an authorized security crystal. As an additional precaution, his staff monitored the lodge remotely.

When Aden stepped inside, he went over to a wall where his old hunting gear and a large selection of swords, knives, and other weapons and tools still hung from pegs on the wall. He pulled a large knife from its sheath, turned it over in his hand, ran his thumb along the blade and winced. "Still sharp!" he said. "I'd forgotten about this. You gave it to me for my thirteenth birthday. I put it to much use. Do you remember?"

"I remember my son," replied Edris, placing four bottles of ale and two glasses on the large, cracked, rectangular wooden table that dominated the great room. He motioned for Aden to take a seat across from him. Aden knew his father well enough to know something was on his mind. Edris filled his glass and drained it in two swallows. His face took on a dreamy expression as he refilled his glass. When he was done, he looked up and said, "I missed this place. Before these negotiations, I believe the last time I was here was…"

"…when I came here to catch the taal?"

"I believe you're right!" agreed Edris. "It has been a long time." He leaned forward, put his hands on the table and said, "I miss the hunt, my son. I've never felt as alive as I have in the jungles of this place!" He scowled and added, "It's good to be king, but sometimes I think I'd rather be here with a crossbow on my shoulder than anywhere else in the universe."

"I miss it too," replied Aden, "although a bolba tree was almost the end of me."

Edris snorted. "I heard. Getting soft are we?"

"Well I was unconscious at the time, having been knocked out while courageously trying to navigate my dead ship to a safe landing!"

Edris reached across the table and grabbed Aden's hand. "We haven't had much chance to talk about it, but I'm worried about the zon. We don't yet have the forces to repel them if they do indeed decide to make our neighborhood their home."

"Will the taal help?"

"It is too early to tell. If they permit us to increase xanide production, we'll be able to build up our forces faster; but who knows if that will be enough?" Edris's expression had again taken on a faraway look.

A knock on the door startled him back to the present. "Come," he commanded. He and Aden stood up when King Ivege and Polis entered. "To what do we owe this pleasure?" queried Edris evenly.

"We need your help," replied Ivege. "We have intercepted disturbing information from the source you alerted us to: Sia is in grave danger and so is Ardala!"

Chapter XIII

Gabo Sin had a secret. Secrets were nothing new to him. After all, as Ardala's Minister of Intelligence he had many secrets, secrets he had kept well.

They involved everything from military affairs and politics, to xanide production, crop yields, petty squabbles among Ardalan bureaucrats, and even salacious rumors involving members of the extended royal family.

He knew secrets about the Kealts. He even knew the secret to making a perfect soufflé and a flaming Dfulo cocktail.

There were secrets that embarrassed him, humored him, and that he wasn't proud of. In the wrong hands the secrets he knew could destroy corporations, end marriages, and even bring down the government of Ardala. These secrets had one thing in common: They were safe with him, until two months ago, anyway, and that was his new secret.

He hadn't asked for it, hadn't sought it out, and didn't want it. It was the one secret he was dying to tell, and would tell if he were physically able. It was the secret that had ended his life as he'd known it, and, barring a miracle, could quite possibly bring about the end of Ardalan Civilization.

He thought back to the day when the secret was thrust upon him. He should have been suspicious when the minister of antiquities, Quagar Mull, invited him to participate in a survey of the ruins of the Great Crystal Palace of Ornithar.

The two men had never liked each other and did their best to avoid each other's company. However, if there was anything Gabo cared about as much as he cared about Sia Selarney, it was Ardalan history. The promise of seeing parts of the ruins that were off limits even to the royal family was too much to resist, and, he thought, might even help him get his mind off Sia, at least for a little while. In fact, he was so glad to be going he did something he almost never did: Put aside his caution.

When the day came, he eagerly stepped into one of the two hover cars that would take the party to the ruins. He thought it was a rather small group for such an undertaking, but not being a scientist himself, Gabo assumed they knew what they were doing.

He was briefly concerned when he learned that among the team were four security officers. They seemed out of place on a scientific survey so close to the heart of Ardalan strength. When he asked Quagar about it, he claimed that Defense Minister Lucas Frock had insisted they accompany senior ministers whenever they left the palace.

While the Ardalan Government publically refuted allegations it had been penetrated by the zon, the truth was, it was greatly concerned. Since Minister Frock was as naturally cautious as Gabo was, he accepted the explanation.

Once they set down well inside the ruins, Gabo eagerly stepped out of the hover car. He patted the weapon he had lately begun carrying to assure himself it was still there. Then he enthusiastically hefted the small backpack he was carrying onto his broad shoulders, looked up at the perfect blue sky and proclaimed, "What a beautiful day, eh Quagar?" However, instead of moving out, Mull and the others stayed where they were, looking about nervously.

"Something wrong?" queried Gabo.

"Oh no, no, not really," replied Quagar distractedly.

"Then why are we standing here?"

Quagar appeared to be listening for something. When a low, almost indiscernible hum rose to the west of their position, he replied, "Be patient, they'll be here very shortly."

"Who will?" asked Gabo, his initial puzzlement giving way to concern.

The hum grew increasingly louder and then it stopped. Gabo was about to insist that Quagar tell him what was going on when zon started appearing all around them, as if they were stepping through invisible doors. He reached for his weapon, but two burly security officers grabbed his arms and stopped him.

"What are you doing Quagar? Whatever it is, you won't get away with it!" exclaimed Gabo.

"Oh yes I will," Quagar assured him. "And what's more, you'll help me."

Gabo struggled unsuccessfully to free himself from his captors. He retorted, "You're crazy if you believe I'll ever have anything to do with these monsters!"

"That's almost exactly what I said!" replied a grinning Quagar. "Still, I think you'll find my new friends can be quite persuasive."

Then he nodded to the zon closest to him. The creature unsheathed its stinger as it approached Gabo. When it was standing in front of him, it paused briefly before plunging it into his neck.

He screamed as it began to draw blood from him, and watched helplessly as the light pink fluid coursing through the almost transparent zon began to turn a darker shade of red. Gabo felt his consciousness fading; however, just before he blacked out the zon reversed the process and began to force the blood back into his body.

Gabo didn't know it at the time, but it also was transferring neural fluid. Over the next hour, the creature repeatedly drained and replenished him, each time leaving behind a little more neural fluid. As the level of fluid increased, Gabo felt himself slipping away. He knew he was helpless to stop it, but refused to give in completely.

He wouldn't have been able to explain how he did it, but through force of will, he was able to hide away a piece of his remaining individuality. He hoped there was enough left to influence the zon plan for him, if not overcome it.

When the zon and Minister Mull eventually returned him to the palace, he went about his duties as though nothing had changed; and for the most part, nothing had. The zon controlled him with a light hand. They allowed him to do everything he did before, and at times he almost forgot they were in the background manipulating him.

He dutifully reported everything he knew to them and followed their commands. He'd tried suicide and he'd attempted to reveal his secret, but the zon were too strong. So he fought back when he could, not directly of course, but in subtle ways.

Using his hidden consciousness, he would occasionally guide himself to send out communications to the zon and their allies over an unencrypted frequency, or use an old code that the Kealt had broken long ago. He didn't do it often out of fear of being discovered, but it was something.

Shortly before Sia was to return from the negotiations on Seti, he learned that Kealt had chosen Celesta Mar to be its new ambassador to Ardala. He knew one of her secrets, the one about the "black hole." He knew her other secrets as well.

In the hidden part of his brain where he was able to think without zon interference, he began to formulate a plan. On the surface, it would seem to dovetail nicely with the zons' plan for Ardala. He counted on them underestimating Celesta's inner strength. If anyone was capable of beating them, it was her. If he could only hold on to a portion of his sanity just a little bit longer, he was convinced she would save them.

Gabo knew his plan would hurt Sia badly, which was the last thing he wanted to do. He comforted himself with the thought that she would be better off without him, since the Gabo she'd known had died weeks ago. That Gabo was tall even for a Kealt; he also was blond, blue-eyed, athletic, and handsome. He was fun to be around and easygoing.

Sia had loved the old Gabo, or at least thought she did. Gabo also was very fond of her, but he was 20 years older and a confirmed bachelor. He knew that Sia was more in love with the idea of Gabo than Gabo himself. He also knew that one day she would have to do her duty as high princess and marry a man she wouldn't choose and might never love. If she had him to cling to it would be even harder on her, so, he tried to push her away gradually.

It was a hard thing for him to do—he loved women and Sia was a woman above all others. Still, Gabo was a decent man. He had known her since she was a child. Nothing was more important to him than her happiness. Therefore, even before his unwanted secret was thrust upon him, he had tried hard to separate himself from her. That was why he suggested that King Ivege send her to manage the refugee issue on Dacat V.

Once he was infected, he comforted himself with the thought that she would not have time to return to Ardala before her marriage, and that once married, the indomitable Aden Cade would keep her safe from the zon.

His plan to protect her would have worked except that Aden turned out to be as decent as Gabo himself, and refused to marry her. Fortunately he was again able to delay her return to Ardala by convincing Ivege that she should be Ardala's representative to the Seti negotiations. Now that they were over, he was out of pretenses. She was on her way back to Ardala, eager to meet a man who was now dead, at least in all things that made a man a man.

He had to form a new plan, this one involving Celesta. He had done his best to leave breadcrumbs for others to follow. In the part of his mind that was still his, he was sure she had followed them here.

On the day Celesta was to arrive on Ardala, Gabo went to the spaceport to greet her. As the Chief of Ardalan Intelligence, he used his influence to convince spaceport security to allow him to walk out onto the tarmac and meet her.

When she stepped onto the gangplank to exit the ship he waved to her. She smiled, waved back, and walked over to him. As she approached, Gabo remembered the first time he saw her. She was young, fresh, serious, and self-assured. She also was incredibly beautiful. She knew he was smitten by her from the beginning, and constantly teased him good-naturedly. He had tried to forget the last time he saw her: Strapped to a gurney, soaked in urine and covered with feces, alternately crying, screaming, and gibbering incoherently.

When Celesta reached him, she hugged him. Not a perfunctory hug, but an emotional, lingering hug. Gabo was startled. She had never hugged him before, and now she was embracing him like an old lover. It was then that he knew she had found the breadcrumbs. When she finally released him, he could see tears welling up in her eyes.

"Gabo," she said, "it is so nice to see you!"

"Ambassador Celesta Mar!" he replied cheerily. "The title fits you well, although I'm not sure Ardala is ready for you!" He held out his arm for her. "Welcome to Ardala! How was your trip?"

Quickly putting on a more stolid exterior, she took his arm and answered, "Long and boring at commercial speeds. I thought I'd never get here!" When he didn't answer she added, "We have a lot of catching up to do. I've been told that my quarters aren't quite ready for me. Would you mind terribly if I spent the night at your home?"

"There you go, teasing me again!" he joked.

As they walked away from the tarmac she said, "I promise I'll behave myself—at least a little!"

"Oh, that would be such a shame! Anyway, truth be told, I was aware of your circumstances and intended to invite you to my humble estate."

After a short walk, they reached his private hover car. It was a luxurious affair, covered in chrome and sporting a stylish red on black paint job. Except for a small backpack, she had sent her luggage ahead to her permanent quarters. Gabo took her pack, secured it in the back seat, and helped her into the car. Forty minutes later they turned onto a dirt road that Gabo noted led to his abode.

Eventually they turned onto a long gravel road and off in the distance Celesta could see a massive estate. "Is that yours?" She asked in amazement.

"It certainly is," he replied, not without pride. "I inherited it from my parents. They, in turn, had inherited it from my father's parents, and so on and so forth. The Sin family accumulated its fortune over the course of three centuries. Our good fortune began the last time Ardala controlled Seti, when my ancestors mortgaged everything they had to bid on several new mining claims.

"The claims turned out to be sitting on some of the richest xanide veins ever mined, and my family was set financially for generations to come. Once we were sufficiently wealthy, we did what many bored rich people do: We got into politics." He cocked an eyebrow, shook his head, and added, "I myself hate politics, but I'm not above using it to my advantage. I won't bore you with the whole story, but I pulled in quite a few family favors to get my present job."

As he drove on to the main house, Celesta marveled at the opulence of his estate. They passed perfectly manicured flower gardens, quaint, well-maintained guesthouses, and servant quarters that would make even well to do Kealts envious, as well as perfectly maintained athletic fields, a well-stocked private zoo, and a stable that held a number of exceedingly valuable mounts.

When they pulled up in front of the massive doors of the main house, Celesta gasped at the size of it. She stepped out of the hover car and reached into the back to grab her backpack. When she asked Gabo how many people lived in the house he smiled indulgently.

"Right now just me. There are 30 or 40 full time servants who live on the estate, but in this house there is just me."

"No family?"

"I'm afraid to say I'm the last of the line. And since, at this point, it seems unlikely I'll ever reproduce, the end of the line as well; unless, of course, you would like to volunteer to perpetuate the grand Sin name!"

"Gabo, I could never live up to your standards!" Celesta joked. "After all, I am just a humble orphan, born of modest means and blood."

Gabo grabbed her by the shoulders and locked his eyes onto hers. He exclaimed, "My dear Celesta, you are anything but humble! You are a radiant jewel, a precious stone for the ages. You are unique in the universe. You are sex, beauty, brains, passion and compassion; strength, courage, and perseverance, and a loving soul. You are hope and salvation. You are all good and noble things combined in a way that never will be again. Do not ever—*ever*—underestimate yourself!"

Celesta was taken aback by his unexpected intensity and sincerity. She stared back at him, speechless. When she finally regained her composure she quipped, "And a lot better at chuttleball than you'll ever be!"

As she and Gabo dissolved into laughter, he said, between breaths, "We'll see about that in the morning, if you're willing!"

As they continued toward the house, Celesta said, "Don't you ever feel lonely here? Or overwhelmed?"

"I said I live here by myself, but I didn't say I was alone. I have guests all the time; and during the day, typically a rather large number of servants are running around catering to my every whim! Also, much of the grounds are open to the public. However, today I fear everyone is gone. You arrived during a national holiday—the grounds are closed, I gave the servants the next two days off, and I have no other guests at present."

As he said the last, he suddenly remembered that he hadn't actually had any guests since his secret was imposed on him. He didn't want to risk others becoming food for the zon, or worse, their servants.

Celesta stared up at the massive, six story estate. The walls were made of humult stone, a green igneous rock native to Ardala. It glistened in the sun light, and lent the grand edifice the appearance of substance and permanence. Two large balconies were carved into the stone on each side of the main entrance, and expensive sculptures dotted the facade. Countless windows allowed in a copious amount of sunlight, and flowering plants sat in ornate boxes beneath them.

When Gabo ushered her into the house, she saw that the interior was as elaborate and well done as the exterior. That was, except for Gabo's personal items, which seemingly covered the floor of the large foyer. When he saw her staring at the mess, he sheepishly said, "I'm afraid I'm no housekeeper. Hopefully someone will be here in the morning to clean this up despite the holiday."

Once Celesta had freshened up, Gabo invited her to have a drink with him in the game room, which was located below ground level. It was paneled in dark wood and replete with animal skins, horned trophy heads, hunting implements, and paintings of Gabo's ancestors in various manly poses.

The floor was covered with rough stone, a rustic bar occupied one wall, and hunting murals covered the high, vaulted ceiling. A large, open fireplace dominated the room, and it was blazing even though it was summer in the Ardalan capital. Gabo explained that the fire was necessary to overcome the cold air being pumped into the room for effect. He pulled two large, overstuffed chairs up to the fireplace, then walked over to the bar and prepared them both a drink.

Over the next two hours they had many other drinks and discussed everything from the state of Ardalan technology, to Gabo's most recent lovers, to the weather on Kealt. For a moment, Celesta even made him forget his secret. It seemed she could make a man forget just about anything if she wanted to.

Just when Gabo thought the night would never end, she rubbed her eyes and said, "As much as I'm thoroughly enjoying our reunion, I'm going to pass out in this chair if I don't get up now. Would you mind showing me to my room?"

"Of course not," he replied.

Fortunately her room, which was as outsized as everything else on the estate, was just off the top of the main stairs on the second floor, so she didn't have far to go. Once she changed into her nightclothes she laid down on the huge, four poster bed. Despite her fatigue, she barely slept.

The next morning, as promised, Gabo challenged her to a game of chuttleball. Despite her exhaustion, Celesta felt invigorated as the ball flew back and forth across the net. Gabo marveled that, in addition to her many other talents, Celesta was an excellent athlete. He was no slouch at the game, but she was winning almost every point. The few times he won, he was sure she was trying to humor him. After two hours he was soaked with sweat, but she looked almost as fresh as when she arrived.

"Celesta," he huffed, "haven't you had enough yet?"

"I guess I have!" she replied. "You've worn me out."

Gabo laughed. It was a real laugh, his second in two days, something he hadn't done since, well, since he died. When he caught his breath he said, "Celesta, you can't ever stop teasing me, can you?"

She feigned a hurt expression and answered, "Gabo, it would be easier to stop breathing!"

With that they both laughed. As they walked off the court Celesta took his arm. “I have to leave soon. Would you mind if I freshened up first?”

Gabo stuck out his other hand to take her racket. “No, of course not,” he agreed. Later, as they were climbing the steps to the house, he said, “I’m sorry the place is such a mess, but I wasn’t expecting guests. I asked one of my maids to forgo her day off and come by to clean it while we were playing. Hopefully she’s done by now.”

“For me Gabo?” she replied, feigning breathlessness and batting her long eyelashes.

“For you and no one else!”

When they stepped into the foyer, Gabo was relieved to see that the maid had indeed come and gone. He and Celesta headed up the stairs together. When they got to the top he touched her shoulder and leered at her. He said, “You know there’s a water shortage here—we’ll use less if we shower together.”

“Gabo, you better be careful,” she replied coyly, “one day I might just take you up on that!” Then she walked away in a flirtatious manner, disappeared into the bedroom and closed the door.

Gabo shook his head in amusement and walked down the hall to his own bedroom. Later, as he was soaping himself in the shower, his hand lingered briefly on the spot where the zon had infected him.

Initially the lump where the stinger went in was quite large. Now he could barely feel it. Soon it would be gone altogether. The zon voices also were becoming fainter, which meant the neural fluid in his blood was breaking down.

As the voices diminished he felt himself becoming more and more uneasy. Before long he wouldn't be able to hear them at all. Then he would go mad, stark raving mad, and probably die.

But the zon would never let it get to that point. They always waited until their subjects began to feel the discomfort of withdrawal before injecting fresh fluid—better they knew what was in store for them if they tried to resist. The fact was, except in the most insignificant ways, you couldn't resist even if you wanted to.

When he was finished, he stepped out and dried himself off. He was about to grab some fresh clothes when the door chime pealed. He wrapped the towel around his waist and stepped out into the hallway. The sound of running water and the closed door told him Celesta was still in the shower. He walked down the stairs and through the foyer to his front door, then he peaked through the keyhole—it was Sia!

Chapter XIV

For reasons unknown to Sia, but appreciated nonetheless, her ship landed on Ardala two full days early. The first thing she did after disembarking was close her eyes and inhale deeply. She always fancied that Ardala smelled wonderfully different from anywhere else she'd ever been. Considering that she'd been away longer than she ever had before, she thought the air smelled especially sweet, even on the tarmac.

Her aides quickly hurried her along—even a princess was not allowed to linger long on the tarmac. They escorted her onto a special shuttle that bypassed customs and took her directly to a waiting hover car, which in turn would take her to the palace.

She was dying to see Gabo, but knew her parents would be disappointed if she didn't see them first. She half-expected Gabo to be there to meet her, but it was doubtful he even knew she had come home, since she hadn't warned him of her early arrival. And with Ardalan commercial ships being notoriously punctual, he had no reason to check on her flight. Anyway, she thought, it would be fun to surprise him!

When she reached the palace, Sarin was waiting for her. Sia stepped out of the hover car and Sarin hugged her enthusiastically. "What's that for?" she asked. Her mother was not unaffectionate, but she was typically more reserved.

"Welcome back dear," she said with a tear in her eye. "I know how much you've missed this place and we've missed you too! I'm so happy you're back, and so is your father!"

"He's the one who keeps sending me away!" protested Sia.

"You can't blame him. He has to look after all of Ardala and its colonies. These are very trying and wonderful times, as you well know!" She took Sia's arm and asked, "Are you hungry?"

"I think I could eat a tamalok."

"A what?" asked her bemused mother, as she led her toward the palace steps.

"Oh, I'm sorry; it's a tasty little creature that lives on Seti. I'm afraid I know more about *that* place than I ever wanted."

Sarin smiled. "What a remarkable planet. I can't believe you not only found a set la, you actually befriended one!"

"As much as I would like to take credit for that, I can assure you it was entirely Aden's doing.

If it weren't for him they might have eaten me, and I mean that quite literally! I'm sure that man could befriend a horvis toad if he wanted to!"

"Hmmm, do I sense a change of heart toward him?" teased Sarin.

Not willing to answer her mother directly, Sia said, "I have found him to be far more…complex…than I imagined. He has a good heart. He will lead Kealt well one day."

"Yes, I'm sure he will—whoever his queen is!"

"Mother, please! It wasn't I who walked out on our wedding. I said, 'I do,' remember?"

"Yes, and I'm sure your attitude toward him had nothing to do with it."

Sia stopped, faced her mother, and gestured indignantly. "None of us can change what happened. I've been away a long time. If you don't mind, I would prefer to savor my return home and not dwell on that whole unpleasant business!"

Sarin took her arm and gently led her up the palace steps. "I'm sorry dear," she replied, "I'm being selfish. To be honest, I was looking forward to having him as a son in law; but you are right, it's done, and now is the time to celebrate, not remonstrate. We're happy to have you home. In fact, your father has been almost giddy these last few days."

"Father? You're kidding."

"I know he's very reserved with you, but that's just his way. He's missed you greatly, possibly even more than I."

They continued to talk until they reached the dining hall. Before they went in Sarin paused. "Sia, please, this isn't my idea."

"What isn't?"

Sarin didn't answer, but smiled slightly and stepped into the dining hall. Sia followed and was greeted by a cacophony of cheers.

Embarrassed, Sarin said, "He insisted on a party. I think he's been around too many Kealts."

Sia laughed. "I think I have too. I'm afraid I'm actually I'm going to enjoy this!"

She was right: She did enjoy it, although she was disappointed Gabo wasn't there.

The next day she could barely contain her excitement as she got dressed. She was finally going to see him! She had done some discreet checking and learned that he was off that day, and most likely at home.

When she was ready, she took a last look in the mirror and fussed over a stray lock of hair. Then she called up a royal hover car and directed the driver to take her to Gabo's estate. When it finally pulled up to the front of his mansion she got out of the car, told the driver to wait until she was sure he was there, then walked up the steps to the house and rang the door chime...

Gabo froze on the other side of the peephole wondering what to do. Then he gathered his nerve and hesitantly opened the door partway. "Sia," he said uncertainly, "I thought you weren't going to be here until next week at the earliest!"

When he didn't ask her in, she pushed passed him. "Oh, I'm sorry, is this an inconvenient time?" When she heard the shower running at the top of the stairs she said, "You left the water on. Shouldn't you turn it off?"

"Sia, I can explain…"

"Explain what?" she asked.

Just then the water stopped, and seconds later Celesta stepped out of her room and walked down the stairs. She was holding a skimpy towel over her chest that didn't completely cover her orange crotch.

"Oh, Sia!" she said brightly. "I'm sorry, I forgot my bag." She walked over to the couch where she'd left it and leaned down to pick it up. She giggled when the towel slipped and exposed one of her breasts. Then she smiled seductively at Gabo and added, "I'll be right back."

As she turned around, Sia saw that the towel wasn't wrapped all the way around her body. She and Gabo gawked speechlessly as she retreated up the stairs to her room, flaunting her perfect butt as she went.

When Sia regained her composure she exclaimed, "You and…her? What is wrong with you? Do you know what kind of person she is? Why don't you just put a knife in my heart?"

"Sia," replied Gabo desperately, "you've got to believe me, we're just friends!"

Obviously not convinced she retorted, "Sure she is; and how many other 'friends' do you invite over who walk half-naked through your house?"

They were still arguing when Celesta came back into the foyer. This time she was wearing a short, thin, flowery dress that was clingy and almost sheer. It was obvious she wasn't wearing any underwear. She smiled condescendingly at Sia. "Oh, you're still here! Gabo this is so boring!"

Infuriated, Sia turned and rushed out of the house, slamming the door as she went. Gabo threw it open and watched helplessly as she jumped into her hover car and sped away. When she was gone Celesta went to Gabo, reached up and massaged his shoulders gently. In an innocent voice she asked, "Whatever is wrong with her?"

"I think she was looking for someone who isn't here anymore," he replied sadly, as Sia's car disappeared from view. "He's been gone for a long time."

Chapter XV

The next day Sia woke up thinking for a moment she'd had a bad dream. Gabo and Celesta! In her worst nightmare she couldn't have dreamed that Gabo, her anchor, would betray her for someone as shallow, cloying, and unstable as Celesta.

She was shocked she had misjudged him so badly. For a moment she wished she could go back in time and merely watch as Celesta's life teetered on the edge of that railing. The instant shame she felt made her hate Celesta even more.

Thinking about them together made her physically ill. She needed some air. It was a beautiful day in Dilax, so she decided to go hiking. She walked over to the com station and requested a transport to the ruins of the Great Palace.

Ten minutes later, there was a knock on her door. When she opened it, two security officers greeted her.

"Hello Your Highness," said the senior of the two. "We're here to take you to the ruins, as you requested."

"Ah, Captain Sulok," replied Sia. "A bit below your rank to babysit for a grumpy princess, isn't it?"

"In light of recent events, Minister Frock insists that all members of the royal family have a security escort when leaving the palace grounds," he answered matter of factly. "Minister Sin personally requested that I accompany you."

"I see," she replied coolly. "I hope you're prepared for this."

"Minister Sin briefed us on your…abilities. I can assure you, we will not encumber you in any way."

"Very well then; let's go."

The ruins of the old palace were thirty minutes away by hover car. It had served as the home of the Ardalan royal family until Kealt destroyed it during their last major war.

Even in their current state, the ruins were magnificent. Built 1000 years earlier by a distant ancestor of Sia's family, the remains of the palace complex covered fifty square kilometers. Rather than rebuild the old palace, parts of which were still radioactive, it was decided that a new palace would be built on its current site. The ruins would be left as they were, as a testament to the cruelty and brutality of the Kealts.

The ruins were mostly closed to the public in order to preserve them, as well as for safety reasons, and to preserve the dignity of the dead still entombed within the sundered buildings. However, as a member of the royal family Sia enjoyed greater access. In better times she and Gabo often visited what was left of the old palace, to think, be alone, and enjoy the splendor of the old kingdom. Today she wanted to lose herself in the solitude of the broken walls, or at least try to, considering that she was being shadowed by two hulking security officers.

She directed the captain to dock the car at what had once served as the main entrance to the palace. She stepped out and gazed upward at pillars that had once supported gates seventeen meters high and seventy across. The pillars were now broken and the iron gates long ago dissolved to dust. Still, the scale of what the entrance had been was evident.

She was about to start toward it when she felt something brush her arm. Startled, she turned and saw that the nearest security guard was three meters away. "Must be my imagination," she muttered. Then she turned back and began walking briskly toward the entrance.

An hour later she was impressed that her "babysitters" were not only keeping up, but seemed oblivious to her strenuous pace. She also was disappointed that the ruins did not have the palliative effect on her mood she had anticipated.

To the contrary, she became even more furious at Gabo's betrayal.

Six kilometers into the complex, she found herself standing at the edge of an overgrown plaza that overlooked the forest below. The view was spectacular. As she gazed down at the trees she felt her anger finally begin to ebb. It occurred to her that this was Aden's world. The woods, the wildness, the isolation; these were things he loved. She smiled sardonically. Maybe they were more alike than she was willing to admit.

The sound of weapons being drawn from holsters broke her reverie. Startled, she turned and saw that the guards were pointing their guns at her. With a strained voice, Sulok exclaimed, "Run…Now!"

Before she could react, the younger officer fired. The shot missed her by centimeters. The captain turned his weapon on his subordinate and pulled the trigger. As he fell to the ground with a smoking hole in his chest, Sulok turned back to her and again desperately exclaimed, "RUN! NOW!"

Now terrified, Sia sprinted away from him. She glanced over her shoulder and saw he was pursuing her. When a blue beam lanced over her shoulder, she headed into the ruins hoping to find a place to hide.

To her surprise, the bulky captain was gaining on her quickly. In desperation, she dodged behind a wall hoping to lose him. When his footsteps ran past, she thought she had succeeded. As she turned to head back toward the hover car where she could call for help, she collided into someone standing behind her and fell to the ground. Expecting to see the captain, she found herself staring up at Celesta.

"You!" she exclaimed, as she scrambled to her feet and held up her fists. "I should have known you were behind this, you evil, psychopathic bitch!"

"We can talk about this later; right now you need to follow me!" insisted Celesta.

"What?"

"Please, follow me now if you want to survive this!"

"What are you doing here?" demanded Sia.

"NOW!" she exclaimed.

Sia heard the captain's footsteps return and they were getting closer. "You'll never get away with this!" she replied.

Celesta ignored her and stepped behind a tree. As the captain rushed passed, she stuck out her arm and caught him in the neck, causing his feet to go out from under him. When he crashed to the ground, she pounced on him and twisted his head sharply. After ensuring he was dead, she stood up and said, "I am not your enemy, but if we don't get out of here now, he'll find us soon enough."

Before Sia could reply, she heard a large military transport approaching. Against Celesta's warning, she ran into a nearby clearing and began waving her arms.

As she gesticulated wildly to the descending craft, Celesta caught up to her and said coolly, "You are a fool. I have no idea what Aden sees in you."

"I don't know what's going on here," hissed Sia, "but soon you'll be under arrest where you belong; and even you can't escape from an Ardalan prison!"

"We'll be lucky if either of us lives long enough to see that."

When the transport landed, Sia ran to it. The door to the command cabin swung open and Gabo stepped out. He stuck his arm out as she attempted to embrace him.

"Please!" he said, looking as though he had just bitten into an unripe kaca fruit, "don't make this any more unpleasant than it has to be!"

Sia suddenly realized the soldiers who had accompanied him had their weapons drawn and were pointing them at her and Celesta. Gabo gestured toward his men, two of whom grabbed Sia and secured her wrists.

"Gabo, what are you doing?" she exclaimed.

He ignored her, looked at Celesta and said, "My dear, I have eight of my best men with energy weapons that are set to kill trained on you. I doubt even you could overcome all of them." He nodded toward his officers and said, "Search her. I want to be sure she isn't hiding any of her little toys."

Celesta removed the small backpack she was carrying and dropped it on the ground. She said, "All my 'toys' are in this backpack. If any of your men touch me I may die, but believe me, some of them will too."

As three soldiers approached her warily, Gabo replied, "If you men knew what she was, you'd take more men." When the soldiers paused, he said, "Very well, we won't search you; but you understand we're going to have to secure your wrists."

Celesta nodded her assent and allowed Gabo's men to take her arms and secure them behind her back.

Sia glared at him angrily. "What are you doing?" she asked.

"He's serving his zon friends," replied Celesta, as the soldiers finished binding her. Upon hearing Celesta's claim, several soldiers looked uneasily at each other.

"Celesta," answered Gabo, "you have about the most active imagination of anyone I know, sane or insane. You certainly fall into the latter group. If you must know, I'm leading a vanguard of Ardalan patriots who are sick of your father's concessions to the Kealts and his efforts to undermine the royalty. Because of him, we have become weak and soft. By today's conclusion, I will be leading Ardala and that will end."

"This is treason!" replied Sia. "What happened to you?"

"I got an offer I couldn't refuse, literally," he answered. Then he waved an arm toward the ruins. "I and many others have no desire to make peace with the descendants of the people who did this, or be ruled by an elected rabble. It is time we regained our former glory!"

"This is insane," said Sia. "You of all people know Kealt is not our enemy! Many times they have shed their own blood to protect our people!"

Celesta ignored Gabo's men and walked over to her. She gently nudged her shoulder and said in a low voice, "He's beyond reason. He's not the man you knew. For now we need to go along with these *kangars* and see how this plays out." Sia reluctantly acquiesced and together they boarded the transport.

As they neared the palace, Sia looked out a view port and could see smoke rising from numerous locations. Celesta followed her gaze.

"Gabo and his allies are trying to start a civil war. It remains to be seen if he has the forces to prevail."

Sia replied, "We just left a ruin, and now he's trying to create another?"

"Aden is on the way," said Celesta. "If Polis needs help, he will be here soon."

"Aden?"

"Yes," answered Celesta. "We knew Gabo and his allies were about to make a move, although not this soon. Your decision to visit the ruins was fortuitous for them. They thought it would present an excellent opportunity to kill you and allow them to claim it was an accident. They also tried to kill your parents, but they are out of their reach. Kealt will not interfere in your civil war, but we've agreed to stand by Ardala if the zon decide to show their hand."

"Where are my parents?"

"Safe."

"How do you know about this?" asked Sia. "Did the taal tell you?"

"No. Kealt has sources among the zon's conscripted allies. We know they have infiltrated both our governments, but are more deeply entrenched on Ardala. With our help, Ardala has identified a handful of their minions and has been following their movements, hoping they would lead us to the others. We also have been intercepting transmissions between your planet and the zon."

"How dare you!" exclaimed Sia. "Ardalans would never work with the zon! And to spy on us is a treaty violation!"

"Certainly your people would not help the zon of their own free will," replied Celesta calmly, "but they have power over men's minds; and we have not been spying on you. The transmissions we intercepted were encrypted with a code your government knows was compromised years ago.

When we realized what it was we immediately reported it to your father."

Before Sia could respond, the transport lurched to a halt within the palace grounds. Gabo came back into their compartment and said cheerily, "Last stop! Now, I don't expect any trouble from you two, especially you Celesta! If you behave we might let you live; then again, we might not. It's not all up to me you see. So, I ask that you exit the transport and follow my men peacefully. I will rejoin you shortly."

"Where are you taking us?" demanded Sia.

"Don't be so impatient!" responded Gabo cheerfully, before he turned and walked away.

When Sia and Celesta exited the vehicle, Gabo's men quickly surrounded them, and one said, "Please, follow me."

Sia took Celesta's lead and followed them without protest. Twenty minutes later, they were in the Ardalan throne room. Sia loved this room, with its red carpets, gold trimmed woodwork, dusty displays of Ardalan culture and history, and the throne of Ardala.

The throne was thousands of years old, and had survived the destruction of the old palace. When she was a child and no one was around, her father sometimes allowed her to sit on it. It was made of bone, fur, wood, silver, and triluminum. It had been refurbished repeatedly over the centuries, but still contained many original pieces. Whenever she sat on it, she was sure she could feel the breath of past Ardalan kings breathing on her neck. It sickened her to think that today it would be defiled by a traitor like Gabo.

The longer they waited, the more Sia's anger turned to apprehension. She was worried about her parents and concerned for her own safety. Celesta, on the other hand, didn't seem worried at all. If anything, she appeared relaxed to the point of boredom. Was she actually working with Gabo, or just too crazy to care?

When Gabo himself entered the throne room he was holding Celesta's backpack and wearing his finest dress uniform, which included an ornate sword in a gold scabbard. He strode directly to the throne and dropped Celesta's backpack next to it. When he tried unsuccessfully to sit on the throne, he exclaimed, "Damn sword!" as the weapon made it impossible for him to sit properly.

He stood up and walked past Celesta and Sia to the broadcast equipment that was brought in whenever the king wished to communicate with his subjects. He unbuckled the sword and laid it on a console. Then he pointed to a red button next to it.

"In few minutes, when I am sitting on the throne properly, one of my men will push that button and I will announce to the world the good news. No longer will we be led by a weak, sniveling collaborator, but a man who will remind them of who they are!"

Halfway back to the throne he turned and pointed to Celesta and Sia. "Please make sure they are standing behind the camera, I don't want anyone to see them. It would ruin the shot!"

Gabo's men turned them around and pushed them back toward the console, near the sword. When everyone turned to face Gabo, Sia noticed that Celesta had moved in front of the red button. With her hands still tied behind her back, she extended her arms, felt around with her fingers until she found it, then pushed down.

Gabo took his seat on the throne. He instructed all but two of his men to leave and obtain news on the battle. He told the remaining soldiers to train their weapons on Sia and Celesta. Then he said, "You're right of course, Celesta Mar, about my little friends. I had to be coy in the ruins, because not all of my supporters know whom they are actually supporting yet, but they will soon. I'm sure you will agree that from time to time even great men need the help of others to do the right thing."

"I understand," replied Celesta condescendingly. "And when will we have the honor of meeting these others?"

"As you wish, princess," answered Gabo. He looked right, then left; then he said, "It's all right now, you can all come out. You're safe here. My men are in control, and with your help soon the planet will be too."

Sia was shocked when a large number of man-sized, insect-like creatures stepped seemingly out of thin air into the room. They were zon, and a lot of them.

She had seen pictures of them before, but photographs failed to convey the horror of the things that now stood before her. They were translucent, almost transparent, and filled with a pink fluid that moved through their bodies with the help of multiple beating organs she realized must be their hearts.

She could see other internal organs as well. They had gossamer wings held tightly against their backs, but, unlike real insects, they only had four limbs—two thin, hairy legs that terminated in what bore a loose resemblance to human feet, and two similar looking arms that ended in large, awkward looking pincers.

Their heads—if anything in this world had been created in hell it was their heads—were ringed by three large, multifaceted, yellow eyes arranged in a manner that gave them a 360° degree view. They had saucer-sized membranes where their ears should be. Where there should have been a nose and mouth hung a long, pendulous proboscis that periodically inflated and deflated. On top of their heads sprouted numerous antennae. Even on Seti they would have stood out in their grotesqueness.

As if the hideous tableau could not get any worse, the zon gave off a stench that reminded her of week-old carrion lying under a hot summer sun. She pulled a handkerchief out of her pocket and wretched into it when several of the monsters materialized almost on top of her.

Seemingly unfazed by the zons' sudden appearance, Celesta sounded almost disinterested when she said, "These creatures are all very interesting; but you and I both know they are merely drones. Where is their queen? Surely there is at least one on Ardala?"

Gabo smiled. "I suppose with the end almost upon you there would be no harm in introducing you to our benefactors."

With a nod from Gabo, one of the soldiers walked over to a panel behind the throne and moved several objects on the wall in sequence. When he was finished, he stepped back and watched as the panel swung inward. Ivege had never bothered to tell Sia there was a secret room behind the throne. She wondered if he even knew about it, or if it was something Ardalan Intelligence kept to itself.

When the door opened fully a stench emanated from it that overwhelmed even the smell of the drones. Sia heard a shuffling sound from inside the room and gasped when a zon at least three meters tall eventually shambled into view.

It bore only a vague similarity to the other zon. Its head was disproportionately larger. Its body wasn't translucent, but covered with grayish, hairy scales. It had wings, but they were smaller and more fragile looking than they should be for a creature so large.

Sia didn't know it, but because of these differences it couldn't fly or make itself invisible; in fact, as evidenced by its slow, shuffling gait, it could barely move at all. She could see pinkish fluid pulsing through its huge brain and the nerves feeding its three, malevolent looking eyes, two of which faced forward. It also had a massive proboscis, and its arms were terminated with something more akin to hands than pincers.

As Sia stared at it in horror, the cold, analytical part of her brain noted that the "hands" made the thing look intelligent and even more sinister looking. She never realized how significant hands were, or how evil looking they could be.

"What's the matter?" taunted Gabo as he watched the expression on Sia's face. "You've never seen a zon queen before? Of course, that's not what she calls herself, but it's a most apt description." He pointed in the direction of the smaller zon and added, "Celesta was right, these drones, left to their own devices, are primitive creatures only interested in sucking the blood out of anything they can find. They have no real, independent intelligence."

He then pointed to the towering monster that had moved to his side. "Now this magnificent creation is entirely different. She is supremely intelligent. Not only that, she is telepathic and can control large numbers of drones and weaker queens simultaneously over great distances, even interplanetary distances.

"If her servants feed on other species and inject their fluids into them, she can control them as well, although not as easily, nor at such great distances. They use species captured in this manner to operate the technology they steal or wrest from others, since their drones' bodies sometimes lack the necessary physical and mental dexterity to do so directly.

"The zon also use their abilities to infiltrate the political power structure of worlds they are interested in, such as Ardala." He then began reeling off the names of prominent Ardalan officials, whom he alleged were under zon control.

When he was done, Celesta smiled grimly. She said, "I know you will forgive me for what I am about to do, as I forgive you."

Gabo, who Sia noticed was now twitching as if under a great strain, forced a smile. "I knew you would save us Celesta."

Sia was trying to understand the meaning of their cryptic exchange when Celesta easily freed herself from her bonds and grabbed the sword Gabo's men had carelessly left within her reach. She yanked it out of its scabbard, then, moving faster than Sia thought possible, waded into the zon and began hacking them to pieces.

The angry zon issued a loud, cacophonous buzzing sound that made Sia want to cover her ears. When the two human soldiers aimed their particle weapons and began firing, they missed Celesta, but destroyed a number of zon that wandered into their line of fire. Upon dispatching the last of the drones, she turned her attention to the soldiers, decapitating one and disemboweling the other. The queen let out an angry high-pitched hiss that drove Sia to her knees in pain. Celesta seemed immune to it, as she faced the immense creature and cried, "You have failed! And now you will die!"

The creature waved its long limbs at her futilely as she began to cut it to pieces. First, she sliced off its arms, then its wings, and then she swung the sword across the zon's lower body separating it from its legs.

Now limbless, it crashed to the floor helplessly. While it was lying on its back, Celesta approached its head and said, "I feel you even now trying to take hold of me. You had your chance. Now it's my turn!" The creature angrily waved the stinger protruding from its now erect proboscis at her. Celesta sliced it off, then straddled the queen's thorax and cleaved its head in two.

With the monstrosity silenced, Sia turned her attention to Gabo, who had stood by and watched as Celesta slaughtered his allies. Celesta approached him and said, "It's over now Gabo. You're free."

He smiled wanly. “I tried to stop them," he replied, "but they were too strong.” He walked over to one of the fallen humans and picked up a particle weapon. “I will never be free, not after what I’ve done. Celesta, you of all people should know that.” Without another word, he lifted the weapon up to his head and pulled the trigger.

Chapter XVI

Seemingly unfazed by Gabo's suicide, Celesta ran over to the throne and dug through piles of limbs and viscera until she found her backpack, then she picked up an energy weapon and slung them both over her shoulder. When Sia remained where she was, unmoving and in shock, Celesta grabbed her by the arm and pulled her toward the door. "Come on!" she exclaimed. "We don't have much time before reinforcements arrive!"

Sia numbly followed her out into the hallway. Once outside, Celesta grabbed her by the shoulders and shook her. "Come on Sia, I need you. You can mourn later. I will too. Right now we have to get out of here!"

"I'm…I'm all right," she replied shakily. "I know this place well. By now, Gabo's men have undoubtedly erected force fields at all the exits. There's no way out!"

"I've studied the blueprints of your palace," replied Celesta. She pointed to a door leading to the outside. "That door opens onto an alleyway. Around the corner should be a maintenance hatch for the sewer system. I believe we can make our escape through there."

"Are you sure?" answered Sia doubtfully.

"Yes. Please follow me."

Sia nodded her assent and followed Celesta out the door and into the alley. When she stopped over a sewer grate and used the sword to pry it off, Sia said, "It's dark down there. How will we find our way?"

"I know this goes against your most basic instincts," replied Celesta, "but you're going to have to trust me." She secured the sword to her backpack, then slung it over her shoulder with the energy weapon and descended the ladder into the darkness. After determining that it was safe, she called for Sia, who put aside her fears and followed her down.

When she reached the bottom, Celesta climbed back up and pulled the grate back over the hole. When she was finished she came down, put her hand on her chronometer and said, "You may be the only Ardalan to see what you are about to see and live." Then she touched something on her chronometer and seemed to disappear, except for a pair of glowing green eyes.

Sia gasped. "You're Ku Assa! Of course, I should have known! Who else could do the things I've seen you do!"

"Yes," agreed Celesta gruffly, "you are dim witted. Now, this suit allows me to see in the dark." She handed Sia the end of a rope she had pulled from her backpack. "I will be holding the other end. I'll walk as slowly as I can, but you must trust me. We need to get out of here quickly. I suspect this is where the zon have been living. They're on the surface now, but before long they'll be searching for us down here."

"Where are you taking us?" asked Sia.

"I have emergency extraction beacons. Soon Aden's fleet will be in range. When it is, I'll activate the beacons and he'll retrieve us; but we need to get out from under the city, otherwise the force field protecting it will block our signal."

For the next 30 minutes, Sia held on to the rope and followed Celesta. Fortunately for the two women it was Dilax's dry season—the tunnels had very little water in them and the smell was almost bearable.

Sia said a silent prayer of thanks that they also weren't completely dark—as they passed under grates on the streets above there was enough light for her to see that Celesta was right: the zon had been living below their feet. Sia guessed that the bundles they passed from time to time were husks of bodies they had drained for food.

As they traveled on, Celesta seemed to be slowing. At first Sia thought it was out of consideration for her, but when she stumbled and nearly fell, she realized something was wrong. She pulled on the rope. "Stop!" she commanded.

"We're still too close!" replied Celesta tensely. "I'm bleeding and if we don't get far enough away, the smell will lead them to us."

"If we don't stop you'll collapse!" answered Sia. "We need to treat you. I hope you have a medkit in that bag you're carrying!"

"We don't have time!" insisted Celesta. She turned, took a step, and fell. When she tried to stand, she stumbled and fell again.

Sia put her arm around her and helped her up. "Come on," she said, "let's have a look."

Celesta didn't resist when she helped her sit on one of the narrow shelves that lined both sides of the sewer. Once she was situated, Sia helped her take off her backpack and began rummaging around inside it. When her hand closed on a long cylindrical object she said, "You have a torch! Why didn't you use it?"

"I was afraid it would draw attention to us. Besides, I can see better through my Ku tech eyes."

Sia turned on the light and searched the bag for the medkit. When she found it, she said, "All right then, off with that suit."

Reluctantly Celesta touched her wrist and the suit vanished. She was again clothed in the jumpsuit she had been wearing when Gabo captured them. Sia unzipped the back of the suit and helped her pull it down to her waist, then shined the light on her to see where she was injured. She stifled a gasp when the torch revealed numerous gashes, some of them frighteningly deep. Celesta was good, but there had been too many zon. They had gotten to her repeatedly with their pincers before she ultimately prevailed.

Sia pulled a towel and a bottle of water out of the backpack, then took the cap off the bottle and poured some water onto the towel. As best she could, she cleaned Celesta's wounds. She was obviously in great pain, but accepted her ministrations stoically. After a while, she asked her for the medkit and removed a package containing several pieces of a flesh-colored material.

She handed them to Sia and said, "Place these over the most serious wounds. Press them down until you can feel them adhering to my skin. They'll stop the bleeding and hopefully prevent infection from setting in. Once they're in place I'll have to sit here until the bond is complete."

Sia did as Celesta instructed her. After a few seconds the material pulled the wounds together and stopped the bleeding, as Celesta said it would. When she was finished, Celesta said, "Thank you. I couldn't have gone on much longer. We're not far from where we need to be. Take the torch and the backpack. I'll tell you how to get to a safe beaming point and how to operate the extraction beacon."

"You're badly hurt Celesta. You need medical attention immediately. With these wounds I don't know how you're even alive."

"You won't be for long, either, if you don't leave now!"

"I'm not going anywhere without you," replied Sia. "I saw you turn on the broadcast equipment. Thanks to you, all of Ardala knows about Gabo's treachery and the zon threat. I doubt there will be much of a 'civil war' now."

"If you stay you're as stupid as I thought, but brave. I can see why Aden loves you."

"Loves me? After the way I've treated him?"

Celesta smiled. "You are all he talks about. No other woman has ever made that kind of impression on him."

"Oh, at least one has," replied Sia. "I've seen the way you two look at each other. I thought for sure he'd marry you once he called off our union."

"Marry *me*? We're related!" protested Celesta. "So yes, we're very close, but not lovers."

"You're adopted. On both our worlds such a marriage would be permitted."

"You don't understand."

"Then help me!"

"Shine the light on my face," commanded Celesta. When Sia complied, she said, "Look closely."

"OK," she replied, "What am I looking at?"

"Come on, you can figure it out."

Sia studied her face. Even in her disheveled, bloody state, she was beauty personified, but surely that was not her point. Sia studied her perfect cheekbones, fine nose, full lips, freckled skin, and strong chin. She turned her attention to her eyes, which were cat-like and gray. For the first time she realized they were the same color as Aden's.

Sia gasped when she realized that if it weren't for the orange hair and freckles, Celesta would be a female version of Aden. When she got over her shock she said, "It couldn't be! You're related to him by blood—a cousin?"

"Closer," snickered Celesta.

Sia's eyes widened in astonishment. "You're his sister!" she exclaimed. "His *full* sister! How could I have been so blind?"

"Very good, you're not so slow after all," teased Celesta good-naturedly. "I am indeed."

"How is that possible?" asked Sia.

With some effort, Celesta shifted her position until she could rest her back against the wall of the sewer. When she was comfortable she said, "King Edris's predecessor, King Hebrid, your grandfather, had only one heir, your mother Sarin. Since male heirs always ascend to the throne on their own planet, High Princess Sarin was destined to become queen of Ardala. Without a male heir to succeed Hebrid as king of Kealt, it fell to the

Council of Elders to select an heir from another high house. They chose Edris of the Cade clan.

"In order to be crowned king upon a former king's death, the king in waiting is required to have at least one legitimate heir at the time of his accession. When the council anointed him the future king, Edris had two sons and a daughter.

"As you know, Aden's two older brothers were later killed in a skirmish with your people. By then, Glyn had already married a commoner, leaving Edris with no heirs to the throne. If Hebrid died before Edris produced another legitimate heir, the council had decreed the crown would pass to Abeg Mar, whom you've met.

"Abeg had eligible heirs from his own arranged marriage to an Ardalan princess. Edris's only hope of keeping the crown was to have another child. According to Kealt rules of royal succession, only a legitimate son or daughter can inherit the throne.

"With Calista aging and no longer fertile, this wasn't possible for her. Out of desperation Edris turned to a woman he trusted from the Mar clan, who had once been his lover. She was a childless widow, having lost her much older husband years earlier in another battle with Ardala. She agreed to bear Edris a child, as long as he agreed to father a second child with her, whom she would keep for herself. In neither case would she make the father known…"

“And the queen agreed to this?” interrupted Sia.

“Yes,” replied Celesta. “She was a good woman who loved my father and always put her own needs second. Also, she didn’t like the Mar clan any more than he did, and wanted an heir just as badly.

"In order to protect their secret, she and my mother spent the nine months of her ‘confinement’ on a distant, thinly populated colony known for its discretion. Officially my mother served as Queen Calista’s handmaiden, but in reality it was the other way around.”

Before she could continue, Sia pulled a t-shirt out of the backpack. "Here," she said, "let me help you put this on. I think you’ll be more comfortable if your bare skin isn’t touching the rock.”

With Sia’s help, Celesta pulled the garment over her head. When she was finished, Sia sat down next to her and helped her resume her previous position. When she was again comfortable Sia said, “I’m sorry I interrupted you. I’m dying to hear the rest of the story!”

Celesta smiled. “Yes, I imagine it’s riveting! So, where was I? Oh yes—my mother eventually bore Aden, and, as agreed, handed him over to Edris and Calista. A few years later Edris kept his bargain and I was conceived.

"There was a great scandal when I was born, my mother being unmarried and the widow of a

Kealt military hero. We were outcasts in the Mar clan and lived in poverty. Edris could do little for us; if he tried to help, he would only risk Aden's future, as well as the future of Kealt itself.

"When I was still very young, my mother learned she was dying. Not willing to expose Edris or leave me to indifferent relatives, her only alternative was to approach Glyn, who knew nothing of her arrangement with my father.

"When she told her of her plight, Glyn confronted her parents, who refused to take me in. Many people were already skeptical that Calista had in fact conceived Aden; Edris was afraid that, except for my hair and freckles, I looked too much like him and Aden, and if he took me in the truth would be too obvious."

Celesta smirked and tugged on her long, curly orange locks. "Fortunately I inherited my mother's crazy hair. It's enough of a distinction that, so far, despite the occasional impolite rumor, it has kept our family secret safe. Of course, a simple DNA test would quickly reveal the truth, but without solid evidence to support it, politically it would be too risky to demand one.

"Anyway, ignoring Edris and Calista's concerns, Glyn took me in when my mother died, and raised me as her own. When King Hebrid died, Edris ascended to the throne."

"Does Aden know of this?" asked Sia.

"Of course," replied Celesta. "He's been a wonderful brother. We did everything together. So perhaps now you understand why we're so close."

"Edris is king now. Why do you all continue this charade?"

"Even now, if it became known that my father had no legitimate heirs, the Mar clan could challenge his right to the crown. Although Abeg Mar no longer has any eligible heirs, since his children were married off to other Kealts years ago, the Council of Elders could still choose someone other than Edris. While my father is not without support on the council, it is impossible to predict whether they would side with him or elevate another Mar, or some other high house, to the crown.

"I don't know how Ardala resolves issues regarding royal succession, but the Council of Elders is largely autonomous in these matters. While there are rules of a sort, they have never felt bound by them and in the past have acted capriciously, at least to someone looking in from the outside. We might well have our own civil war."

"I don't envy your family Celesta," answered Sia. "Changing the subject, and I know this is petty, I wish I had known I wasn't competing with you. But what about that odd looking, overly well-endowed girl Aden spends so much time with…Drusa, I believe."

"You're right," replied Celesta. "She is very unusual looking, although in a way many men would probably find attractive." When Sia scowled she quickly added, "To be honest, I don't like her. She acts like a dolt, but I'm convinced she's hiding something. Regardless, you can't seriously believe she holds a candle to you! She showed up at a time when my brother was very lonely. While he certainly enjoys her company, I can assure you, that relationship will quickly run its course, especially if he believes you are the least bit interested in him."

Changing the subject again, Sia said, "Were you following me today?"

"Yes. I was sent to protect you. When we reported the signals we were intercepting to your father, he eventually traced them to Gabo. Your father knew then that he was under zon influence and that you were in danger. He didn't want to tell you for fear you would immediately confront him. Before that happened he hoped he would first lead your security service to others working for the zon.

"In the meantime he needed someone to look after you he could trust, but he didn't know which of his men he could depend on. So, he turned to my father for help from the Ku Assa. Your people have this belief that we are invincible."

"Yes," replied Sia, "but you also terrify us. You are the stuff of nightmares to us."

"I know, but the truth is we're spies, infiltrators, and royal bodyguards, not wanton killers. We gather intelligence and assess the battlefield for weaknesses. We rarely get involved in actual combat."

"Royal bodyguards? How come you're never with Aden when he needs you? Like when we were lost on Seti!"

Celesta smiled grimly. "We are very few and stretched throughout the galaxy. Aden decided we had better things to do than look after him."

"You know, you were quite clumsy. You brushed against me outside the ruins, didn't you?"

"I wasn't clumsy. It's hard to stay close, yet stay out of the way, when people don't know you're there."

Sia laughed. "Well I'll just have to take your word for that." Becoming serious again she said, "Celesta, can I ask you a personal question?"

"Why not?" she replied. "It seems I have few secrets left anyway."

"What really happened to you out there? I never believed that story about you being trapped by a black hole. I'll bet you were never crazy either, were you? Why did you make up such a story?"

"You're right about the black hole, but for a time I was truly insane. A little over a year ago, Polis and Gabo approached Aden with intelligence they had gathered on the zon. It involved a planet they had seized from a primitive alien species. They were using it as a hub from which they coordinated and controlled their forces in that sector.

"The planet was too far inside zon territory to risk a direct military assault. However, Polis and Gabo were confident the intelligence they had received would allow them to infiltrate a small force. This force would attempt to download data from the zon central network and then destroy the base.

"Ardala didn't have the tools to pull off such a feat by itself—it needed Kealt's stealth technology. Aden took the plan to the Edris, who agreed to it, but only if the Ku Assa conducted the actual raid. At that time he wasn't willing to share our stealth technology with you. Ardala agreed, and I was one of ten Ku Assa officers recruited for the mission, based on my military training and scientific background.

"Polis took a small fleet and escorted our team as close to the zon world as he could without being detected. We took a cloaked ship down to the surface and landed near the zon central network. When the zon security codes worked even though they were weeks old, we should have suspected something was wrong. Instead, we put it down to good fortune and proceeded to the target.

"When we got to the data core it was unguarded, but we couldn't access it—the zon were on to us and had changed the security codes!

So, we set our explosives and attempted to leave. We didn't get very far before we became dizzy and disoriented. The zon used some kind of gas that circumvented the bio filters in our suits and quickly rendered us unconscious. Knowing that our target was the data core, they were able to locate our explosives and neutralize them.

"When I revived I was in a cell, naked, and hanging from a chain manacled to my wrist. I could hear my team members screaming as those things sucked the life out of them. Soon a queen came to my cell. She stuck her stinger into my neck and I could feel my life leaving me. But before she had drained me completely, she discovered who I was. Then she began injecting a neural fluid into me. When she was finished, I could hear her thoughts. She was trying to turn me into a drone.

"When we failed to report back as scheduled, Polis was under orders to abandon us. Ardala had no desire to risk precious military resources on a futile rescue attempt. However, Polis being Polis, he refused to leave without at least trying to save us. So, he contacted Aden and asked for his support.

"It took two days for Aden's fleet to reach him. Together they attacked the planet. They were outnumbered three to one, but they broke the zon defenses and destroyed the outpost. I'm sure you're familiar with this event—your people refer to it as *The Battle of Slaglis*. It marked a turning point in relations between our two planets.

"Polis and Gabo led the rescue team that searched for Ku Assa survivors. When they found us, I was the only one left. They later concocted the "black hole" story to give an explanation for why my team was in that part of the galaxy.

"By the time they reached me, I was already addicted to the neural fluid the zon injected into me. The fluid isn't addictive in and of itself; it enables the real addiction, which is the need to be controlled. The zon don't actually have to tell you to do things, their mere presence in your mind has a calming effect. When that presence is removed by distance or because the neural fluid hasn't been replenished, a person can go insane. If you're strong enough, and can hold on until the fluid reaches a blood concentration too low to serve as a conduit, the addiction can be broken.

"By the time I was rescued, I was already addicted, and, without a queen to calm my mind, I fought to stay sane. For the next six months my mind and body burned for the zon to control me.

"After I escaped a second time, I was put under physical restraint 24 hours a day. The doctors tried to treat me with drugs, which ease the symptoms, but inhibit the body's natural ability to fight off the addiction.

"Although I insisted they allow my body to suffer in order to beat it, I was too hard to handle, so they kept pumping me with drugs. When you saw me on the railing that day, I was almost over the addiction. I had run away again when the doctors insisted on more drugs. Glyn took me home after that, and shortly after I finally broke the zon's hold on me."

"I've heard of *The Battle of Slaglis*," said Sia. "So that's what really happened out there. Why is it such a secret?"

"As you mentioned before, even now many of your people harbor a visceral fear of the Ku Assa. Considering Ivege's somewhat shaky position, especially at that time, he and Edris decided it best not to reveal our role in the raid."

"Celesta, I'm so sorry," replied Sia, "I had no idea what you'd been through. I'm afraid I've terribly misjudged you. At least that bastard Gabo got what he had coming to him."

Celesta shook her head and smiled wanly. "Pity Gabo, don't revile him. Senior Ardalans under zon control set him up. I was theirs after just two days. He held them off for weeks. He is the reason we became aware of the plot against your family. He purposely left clues for us to find. Then to save you, he did everything he could to keep you away from him. That is why he kept you away from home for so long, and was so callous toward you: He was trying to protect you by pushing you away.

"And, knowing what I was capable of, do you think he'd really be so careless to leave me with my back to the communication console with a sword in easy reach? For that matter, he could have just as easily killed us in the ruins. He had no real reason to keep us alive at that point. Gabo was beyond saving and knew it, but he was a hero even if he won't be remembered that way."

"Celesta," asked Sia hesitantly, "did you and he…I mean, the two of you…?"

"No," laughed Celesta. "We never had that kind of relationship, and he was probably incapable of that by the time I returned to Ardala. It was all a show, on both our parts, for the benefit of you and the zon. I'm sorry I was so mean to you at his house, but I couldn't miss such a perfect chance to drive a wedge between you."

"Boy you sure did," agreed Sia. "I have to admit, the bare butt was a nice touch!"

"Yes, I guess I went a little overboard."

"I'll say," replied Sia. "Why did you stay with him? Weren't you afraid the zon would try to infect you again?"

"I knew that was a possibility, but after having fallen from grace due to my 'breakdown,' I hoped I was no longer of sufficient value to be interesting to them. I stayed with him because I knew you were coming, and I didn't want you to be alone with him." She smiled and added, "Believe it or not I'm a nice person, and usually modest as well. It wasn't easy for me to be so callous."

"You liked him, didn't you?"

"I did," answered Celesta. "I only knew him for a short time, but he was a good man. In fact, he was a lot like Aden and Polis—honorable, brave, handsome, and decent. He wasn't a fighter, but he wouldn't back down from a fight either. When I met him at the spaceport, I hugged him. I think he knew I was saying goodbye. We both knew there was no way back for him."

"Apparently not," agreed Sia somberly. After a brief pause, she said, "I'm sorry if this isn't the most appropriate time to bring this up, but I know you've become close to my brother. He is quite taken with you."

Celesta looked away and held her hand up to her face. There wasn't much light, but Sia didn't need much to tell she was trying not to cry. She touched her knee gently and asked, "What's wrong?"

When Celesta composed herself, she turned back and said with a sniff, "We were getting too serious. Because of what the zon did to me, I can never have children. He doesn't deserve that. I won't see him anymore."

"I don't understand," replied Sia.

"The neural fluid they inject is very persistent. Over time, and with much suffering, the human immune system can knock it down until we don't notice it anymore. The problem is, it never goes away completely. The doctors believe if I ever became pregnant, I would pass some on to the baby. Without an adult immune system to fight it, it would overwhelm its body."

Sia caressed her back. "I'm so sorry," she said. "I'm so sorry I ever thought ill of you. You are the most remarkable person I've ever met."

Celesta snickered. "You give me too much credit. If you'd ever open your eyes you'd realize Aden is the remarkable one. Who else could wander off in the jungles of Seti, and not only come out alive, but on the back of a creature no one had seen for thousands of years! Did you ever wonder why someone as accomplished as Gris is still his first officer? He could have had his own command years ago, but Glyn wouldn't let him leave Aden's side. She knew Aden would protect him, and all his men, with his life. She'd never trust anyone else to look after her husband."

"I understand," she answered. "I've seen him take on a monster larger than a taal with little more than his bare hands and win. I actually do appreciate him. Unfortunately, we got off on the wrong foot. For one thing, it's hard for me to get over the fact that I was being forced to marry him. Besides that, the one time I let him kiss me he groped me!"

"He what?" asked Celesta, suppressing a giggle.

"We were on Seti and we'd both had a lot to drink. When he was walking me back to my ship, I stopped to look at the sky—it was shimmering blue! Have you ever seen it that way?"

"No," replied Celesta. "I've never been to Seti."

"Well, it was all very romantic. When I tripped on something, he caught me. We were very close and…and I kissed him. And then he groped me!"

"What did you do then?" asked Celesta, trying hard not to laugh at Sia's earnestness.

"I slapped him of course, and ran away."

This time Celesta couldn't help but laugh, and almost collapsed from the pain. When she recovered, she forced herself to her feet despite Sia's protestations.

"I'm fine," she insisted. "We need to get moving. I'm sure the zon are looking for us." She pulled her jumpsuit back on with Sia's help and activated her suit. Ten minutes later, they heard a buzzing sound off in the distance.

"They're on my blood trail!" said Celesta. "From the sound of it, there are too many even for me to handle this time, even with a particle weapon. Fortunately we're almost where we need to be." Off in the distance Sia could literally see the light at the end of the tunnel.

Following her gaze Celesta said, "That light you see up there is the end of this tunnel. It juts out beyond the edge of the cliff on which the palace stands, and should be beyond the force field protecting it. Once we're there, we'll be able to initiate the extraction beacons. If Aden is up there, he'll beam us to safety."

By the time they reached it, Sia thought she could see the zon scrambling toward them. It wouldn't be long before they were upon them. Celesta took a beacon out of her bag and pushed a button. When a small light flashed green, she told Sia it meant Aden's ship was in orbit. When she told her to hold out her arm, she refused.

"Where's yours?" she protested.

"I don't know. It must have fallen out; but Aden can use the signal from one beacon to beam us both out."

"I'm no expert on these things Celesta, but I don't believe you. I'm not going to leave you to face these monsters alone."

Before she could protest further, Celesta grabbed her wrist and forcibly secured the beacon to it. She pushed another button and as Sia dematerialized, the last thing she heard was, "Aden needs you!"

When Sia was gone, Celesta took the energy weapon off her shoulder, aimed it down the tunnel, and pulled the trigger. When it clicked uselessly, apparently damaged during the fight, she threw it down and ran to the edge of the culvert. She looked down at the rocky, unforgiving ground 150 meters below. There were too many zon for her to fight off with just a sword, and she was too weak to even try. She knew if they caught her, they would again try to turn her into a clone or worse.

It occurred to her that she was no different than poor Gabo. In reality, there was no hope for either of them once the zon got their pincers on them. She had survived longer then Gabo, but only delayed the inevitable. Now there was only one more thing to do.

When she reached her decision, she was surprised the only emotion she felt was relief. She put down the sword and backpack; then she held out her arms, closed her eyes, and jumped.

Chapter XVII

Ivege's report alarmed Edris. He ordered Aden to return to Kealt as quickly as possible in order to muster a suitable fleet to help defend Ardala. With the *Garm* out of commission, he was forced to use a standard military transport. Fortunately, it was faster than the *Garm*, allowing Aden and Gris to arrive on Kealt the same day they left Seti.

When they exited the transport, Captain Frune Jasper greeted them effervescently. He saluted them stiffly and after they saluted back said, "Welcome home sirs. If you would follow me, we have a hover car waiting for you. The ministers are dying to hear about your discovery of the taal."

Aden suppressed a smile. "Ah yes, in a moment captain. He pointed to four gleaming ships lined up at the far edge of the spaceport. "Are those them?" he asked.

Jasper said, "Sir, if you are referring to the four newest and most capable warships in the Kealt fleet, than yes, it is indeed 'them.'"

"I think the first officer and I would like to get a closer look at them," said Aden.

"Of course Your Highness," answered Jasper, who waved at a man sitting nearby in a transportation cart.

As the cart approached, Gris said, "Admiral, if it's all the same to you and the captain, I think I'd rather walk. We could use the exercise."

"If you wish," replied Jasper, "but the ships are more than a kilometer away."

"What?" said Gris. "They can't be more than a couple of hundred meters from here."

Not wishing to contradict a superior, especially one as storied as Gris, he reluctantly replied, "Sir, the ships are so large, if you aren't familiar with them it's difficult to put them in the proper perspective. I can assure you, they're over a kilometer distant."

Before Gris could answer, Aden put his hand on his shoulder and said, "Captain, we'll defer to your judgment. We don't want to keep the esteemed ministers waiting for too long!"

Jasper was correct: The ships were a lot further away than they appeared. As they got closer, Aden marveled at their size. Despite their vast bulk, they appeared sleek and graceful. They were low slung and had a roughly triangular configuration, although the three points were rounded off, giving the ships an elegant appearance. Each ship sat on three massive, retractable pylons. He asked the captain how big they were.

Happy to be talking about the ships, Jasper replied, "From nose to tail just over 500 meters. At their widest point, just over 310 meters. Each ship has 20 levels, although some sections have fewer. They each can comfortably support 7,000 crew and passengers, many more if needed." He pointed to the rear of one of the ships. "As you can see, each ship has four hanger decks and carries a minimum complement of 150 fighters and support ships. Despite their size, a crew of 20 is all that's needed to fly one of these ships."

They were now close enough that Aden could see each ship bristled with weaponry. He whistled and said, "Gris, I could be wrong, but aren't those Ardalan fusion cannons?"

Before he could answer Jasper eagerly replied, "They are indeed, sir. Provided by the Ardalans as part of the technology exchange they proposed. They were more than good to their word."

Gris smiled wanly. "I suppose we provided them our cloaking and shielding technology?"

"We did sir," replied Jasper. "Unfortunately they are having a tougher time integrating our technology into many of their existing ships. As they build new ships we expect it will be easier for them."

"How about the *Kreg*?" asked Aden.

"That is a remarkable ship sir," replied Jasper. "She was commissioned less than a year ago and is far more advanced than the *Garm* was, although not quite as advanced as our Dipsa class ships. Ardala's engineers have been able to adapt our shield technology to her, but she'll never be able to cloak."

"That is fabulous news," replied the first officer sarcastically.

As the cart came to a stop in front of the closest ship, Jasper said, "Admiral Cade, First Officer Habaret, you are standing before the *Edris*. She is the new flagship of the Kealt fleet, and one of four new Dipsa class warships."

"Dipsa?" interrupted Gris. "What kind of a name is that?"

"The Dipsa," replied Jasper brightly, "is a mythical serpent whose venom is so powerful its bite kills even before it's felt. These ships possess the most advanced weapons and shields that Kealt or Ardala have ever fielded." He glanced nervously at Gris before adding, "Unlike older warships such as the...somewhat smaller...*Garm*, not only can she cloak, but she can fire her main guns while cloaked. Thus, like the Dipsa, she is capable of destroying the enemy before he's even aware he's been hit."

He pointed to ten fusion cannons hanging overhead in staggered formation. "I gather you are familiar with those?"

"I am indeed," Aden agreed. "When I served with the Ardalans I witnessed such a weapon effortlessly slice a zon medium destroyer in half. I am thankful I've never had to face such weapons in battle. I doubt our shields would be of much more use than the zon's."

"You are correct admiral; none of our current ships anyway. However, our engineers believe this new class of ships to be a match for even a zon bolba class mothership. What's more, her hull is reinforced with a new alloy called plastonium. In the event her shields fail, she can take several direct hits from the zons' most formidable weapons without losing integrity. As for the cannons themselves, our engineers have enhanced the Ardalan design and increased their original yield by 10%."

"Most impressive," replied Gris, "on paper anyway. Have these ships been space-tested?"

"Uh no," answered Jasper hesitantly, "not thoroughly, anyway; they're not quite finished." He perked up and quickly noted, "But they will be by the time the fleet leaves for Ardala!"

Gris shook his head disapprovingly. "Aden, if it's all the same to you, I'd rather take our chances on the *Garm*."

"I'm afraid that's not possible," replied Jasper sadly. "That ship, while I'm sure she was a fine one in her day, has taken a beating over the years. When she arrived at space dock for refurbishment following your last engagement with the zon, our engineers determined that she has serious structural damage. It's amazing she even made it back to Kealt; she'll never fly again."

"Well there you have it Gris," said Aden. Seeing how glum he was, he put his hand on his shoulder and added, "She was a fine ship my brother; but to tell the truth, she *was* getting a little creaky. You know, it probably did her no good when we rammed her into that zon mothership."

"I know it!" replied Gris, who appeared to be on the verge of tears. "But wasn't it worth it to see the looks on those zons' faces when they realized she was coming to dinner?"

Aden didn't have the heart to remind him that zon faces didn't have expressions. Instead, he turned back to Jasper. "So captain, what are the names of these other ships?"

As Jasper pointed them out he said, "The *Taal*, the *Lacplesis*, and the *Calista*."

"Fine names all," Aden replied. "Are all four crewed, provisioned, and otherwise ready for battle?"

"They are sir," he replied, his voice cheery again. "In fact, the *Edris's* crew was largely taken from the *Garm*."

"Well then," answered Aden, "why are we standing here idly chatting? We can't keep the ministers waiting!"

Chapter XVIII

When the fleet departed two weeks later, Aden was eager to reach Ardala. To avoid stirring up the Ardalans unnecessarily, he intended to approach their planet under cloak and remain nearby undetected. If the zon did show up, the fleet would be there to assist. If they didn't, it would leave and no one but Ivege, Polis, and a handful of other Ardalans would ever know they were there.

With that in mind, once the fleet broke orbit he ordered it to cloak and proceed to Ardala at full speed. Gris delayed the order and asked to speak to Aden in his quarters. When they were alone Aden said, "All right, I'm sure you have a good reason for countermanding my order."

"I do sir!" replied Gris. "If I may speak freely..."

"Of course."

"Well," said Gris, "these are new ships with mostly new crews. They haven't been shaken down properly. Based on their intelligence, Ardala believes it will take at least another two weeks for the zon to reach their world. I believe we would be better served to take half that time and use it to drill the crew and properly test our systems."

Aden shook his head. "Sia is in danger! We've delayed long enough!"

"Yes she is," agreed Gris, "but the Ku Assa will be watching over her."

"You know who they sent. I'm sorry, but I have my doubts."

"I don't care if you are my commanding officer—sir—but if you ever again say anything like that in my presence we will come to blows. You know better than that."

Aden tapped his fingers on his desk. Then he smiled grimly and said, "You're right Gris, about all of it. You will have your week."

As he turned to leave Aden asked, "Would you really hit me?"

Gris smiled slightly, nodded his head once, and walked out.

Seven days later Aden summoned Gris and the captains and chief engineers of his Dipsa class ships for a status report. When they walked into his quarters the looks on their faces told him it wasn't good. He waved toward a small table and once they were seated, said, "I can see by your cheery faces that not all is good news. So chief engineers, what is the state of the greatest ships ever built?" When they looked from one to the other, each afraid to speak out, Aden said, "That bad eh? Well Gris, perhaps you can enlighten me?"

Gris replied, "The good news is, we can cloak, we can fire our main guns, and we can raise shields…" He hesitated before continuing.

"Yes?"

"…but we can't do more than one of them at the same time."

Aden scanned the four chief engineers. "Would one of you mind telling me why?"

Alex Stick, the *Edris's* chief engineer, replied, "It's a matter of power."

"I thought we had enough xanide to run a small planet for years."

"That's true," answered Stick. "And theoretically, we have more than enough power to operate all the ships' systems as designed."

"Then what's the problem?"

"You're an engineer by training. I'm sure you're aware that xanide crystals in the proper matrix produce very consistent and stable power up to a certain yield, which is about 20% of what we believe they're capable of. The problem is, once you go above that, the matrix becomes increasingly unstable and difficult to manage.

"You can live with that to a certain degree when you're using the crystals to fuel, say, a civilian power plant. Those systems are very forgiving. Brown outs and fluctuations happen all the time and no one notices. Even if a surge blows out a relay, there are redundant systems and the interruption is so brief it's essentially imperceptible. That said, we still don't dare push the yield much beyond 30%.

"The problem is, on a starship, especially one the size of a Dipsa class warship, there is no margin for error. A power fluctuation or surge that occurs at the wrong time, like when a ship is in hyperspace, could be catastrophic. The same thing could happen anytime we require a huge spike in power, such as firing our main guns while cloaked or shielded."

Aden rubbed his chin pensively. "Surely the scientists and engineers that built these ships were aware of this?"

"They were," Stick replied. "They developed hardware and software that, in theory, should be able to manage potential power instability while increasing usable xanide yield to 35%. What we're finding is that there are still bugs in the system. If we power up multiple power intensive systems we risk uncontrolled surges, which could cause the crystals to release all their energy at once. I don't have to tell you how bad that would be."

"Can we fix it before we get to Ardala?"

"Sir, it took hundreds of Kealt's best engineers four years to develop these systems. I don't see what we can do in a few days."

When Chief Engineer Simon Galt of the *Calista* looked like he wanted to say something, Aden said, "Galt, right? What do you say about this?"

Galt looked nervously at his comrades. "Sir," he answered, "Ensign Blixt believes he can fix the software. In fact, he's already written the patch. We've run it through extensive computer simulations and it looks good. All we have to do is upload it."

"Who is Blixt?"

"A junior engineer aboard the *Edris*; he's a very bright fellow," replied Galt.

The other three engineers protested vigorously. Stick spoke for them all when he said, "Sir, with all due respect, I would not recommend doing anything that invasive to these systems until we've returned home. Regardless of what the simulations say, an error in Blixt's calculations could leave us dead in the water, or worse, much worse. Now is not the time to be mucking with the guts of these ships."

Reluctantly Aden agreed. He looked at Galt and said, "I have to agree with Stick. I won't risk disabling these ships further."

When the engineers and their captains had departed, leaving Aden and Gris alone, Aden put his hands on the table. "Well done Gris. If I hadn't listened to you, we might all be dead right now. It appears we've lost our element of surprise. What should we do now?"

Gris smiled. "Let me see if I have this right: We can't both cloak and use our shields, and we can't fire our weapons while we're either cloaked or have our shields up. Does that about cover it?

"There are other permutations, but, yes," replied Aden.

"Well," responded Gris brightly, "We don't need to be cloaked when we're in hyperspace! We could take up orbit around Seti's moon, where we're much less likely to be observed than if we go back to Kealt; and right now Seti is closer to Ardala than Kealt. If the zon do show up, we'll be just minutes away via hyperspace."

"That would work with a handful of ships, but you know how risky a hyperspace jump is within a solar system with a fleet this large," answered Aden.

"We wouldn't have to jump the whole fleet, only those ships that can't cloak, which are just the Dipsa class ships and a few of our larger ships. The rest of the fleet can follow the original plan and proceed to Ardala under cloak."

Aden stood up, reached across the table and slapped him on the shoulder. "Well done brother! So it shall be!" he exclaimed.

Aden did as Gris suggested and ordered all cloaked ships to proceed to Ardala, where they would take up orbit around its moon. He ordered the rest of the fleet to proceed to Seti. When it arrived, there were still several days left before the zon were expected reach Ardala. He decided to beam down to the settlement to visit his father and see how the negotiations were going.

Edris greeted him at the landing pad and gave him a bear hug. "Welcome back son. I certainly wasn't expecting you back so soon! Come, let us have a drink!"

As they rode toward the pub Edris said, "I heard about our new ships. It's a shame they aren't quite ready. I think your alternate plan is quite a good one though."

"Actually it's Gris's," admitted Aden. "The man is positively devious when he puts his mind to it."

"I've never told him this, or Glyn either for that matter," replied Edris, "but Glyn married well. You should have seen Calista's face when she found out they eloped. If she could have gotten her hands on him at that moment I'm sure she would have ripped his heart from his chest! But Gris quickly stole her heart as well."

"You still miss her, don't you?" said Aden.

"Every day," replied Edris. "When I met her she was much like Sia—strong willed, angry, obstinate; but I was patient, and over time she revealed her true nature. She was a wonderful, selfless woman. She loved us all without reservation. She's been gone a long time, but it still seems like yesterday."

Changing the subject Aden asked, "How are you finding the taal?"

Edris smiled humorlessly. "They are an enigmatic and stoic bunch," he replied. "They haven't showed themselves since the one carried you and Sia out of the jungle. It seems they are a sensitive lot and have no interest in being turned into a sideshow attraction. You know, they aren't even attending the negotiations in person, merely telepathically. I gather that within their clans these negotiations are quite contentious. Still, they seem to know and respect you quite well. It's safe to say that if it weren't for you, and perhaps Sia, they'd still be hiding in their vast jungle redoubt!"

When they reached the pub, a Kealt official approached Edris and informed him that his presence was needed at the negotiating table. He shook Aden's hand and said, "Sorry son, it seems even a king's time isn't his own."

Now alone, Aden got a ride to the edge of the jungle hoping to see a taal, but knew that was unlikely. Normally he wouldn't dream of entering the jungle without a weapon, but he felt strangely at ease as he walked toward it.

When he reached the trees he kept going, and after a while he could no longer hear the sounds of the settlement. A half hour later he came to a small clearing. He was almost across it when he heard a huge disturbance to his right. Something large was forcing its way through the brush. On Seti that was usually bad news, but Aden felt a calm come over him as he waited.

He wasn't surprised when seconds later the trees parted to make way for a taal. He didn't know how he knew, but it was the female he had "captured" so many years ago, the same one that also had saved he and Sia.

"Did you call me?" he asked. As before, he heard the answer in his head and not with his ears.

"There is something you must know about the ones you call the tayron," she replied.

"The tayron?" he repeated.

"Yes. They have a secret."

"So, you can read their minds as well?"

When she didn't answer he said, "What is their secret?"

She replied, "That you must find out for yourself, but they are not what they appear to be."

"Why did you lure me here to tell me there is a secret you can't tell me about?"

"Because," she answered, "it is their secret to reveal when they believe the time is right. Eventually we will have a treaty with them as well. Therefore, they must know we are trustworthy allies."

"I see," said Aden. "So they are friendly?"

"They are well meaning, supremely powerful, and confident; but the zon have gashed their soul, and much of their natural compassion has flowed from that wound. They are on a blood hunt and have lost their way; they will find it again, with your help."

"And this secret of theirs?" he replied.

"They will reveal it in time."

"How do you know so much about them?" he asked. "Are they on Seti?" When she didn't answer, he said, "So it's OK for you to tell me they have a secret, but not what it's about?"

"I'm sorry," she said, "but I have already shared more than I should have. I suspect that before long you will figure it out yourself." Aden felt a warm feeling flow over him. The creature was fond of him!

"Did you mean it when during the negotiations your representatives said they wouldn't try to read our minds?"

"You have ears," she responded. "If you entered a room with many loud people, would you be able to turn them off so as not to hear them?"

"Of course not," he replied, "but I would do my best not to pay attention if it were none of my business."

"Our ability to read minds is similar to your ears. You humans are such a broth of thought and emotion it is impossible for us not to hear you. Still, to the extent we can, we try not to pay attention. Unless of course, we perceive a threat; then we will do what we must to protect ourselves."

"As would any species. How is it that you speak our language?"

"We don't," replied the taal. "That is how your mind translates our thoughts."

"I see. Can I ask you another question?"

"I have already heard it, but yes."

"You didn't 'let' me capture you, did you? I transported you far beyond the xanide. I don't believe you could have escaped. That's why you struck me—you were angry that I succeeded in fooling you."

Aden thought he sensed humor as the creature replied, "You believe as you like. We knew that one day you would be king; we needed to know what kind of man you were, in the event circumstances one day forced us to reveal ourselves."

"Why didn't you just read my mind?"

"You humans have many expressions that carry great wisdom, although for reasons we cannot comprehend, you seldom follow them. One we are particularly fond of says that 'actions speak louder than words.' While your mind carried the best intentions, we needed to know how you would actually treat a taal that was at your mercy. Just know that your actions that day changed the destiny of both of our species forever. You have a warrior's heart, but the curiosity and wonder of a child. You have made a deep impression on our Prime Council, of which I'm a senior member. We trust you. We know you will never betray us."

"Taal," asked Aden, "do you possess names?"

"We do my young prince. Mine is Bang."

"That is an unusual name."

"My mother birthed me during a thunderstorm. A particularly loud thunderclap announced my arrival."

"I must ask you again, is there nothing more you can tell me about the tayron?"

She didn't answer, but turned and headed back toward the jungle. As she disappeared from view, she thought, "Take care, high prince. You are about to engage in a great battle with an implacable foe. You and your worthy friends may not survive, but I know you will fight heroically. The soul of Seti willing, we will see each other again." With that, she was gone.

When Aden returned to the settlement, it was abuzz with news: Civil war had broken out on Ardala! Knowing that it was unlikely the zons' Ardalan allies would go against their government without the zon close by, he quickly returned to the *Edris*.

"Where have you been?" demanded an anxious Gris. "The zon are over Ardala…the battle has begun!"

Chapter XIX

On Aden's command the *Edris* and the other ships orbiting Seti's moon moved away from it until it was safe for them to enter hyperspace. Soon after, they emerged into an inferno.

The zon outnumbered the combined Ardalan and Kealt forces four to one, and the odds were growing worse as even more zon ships joined the battle. The *Edris* raised its shields just as it was rocked by volleys from multiple zon ships. "Return fire, standard weapons only!" Aden bellowed.

Admiral Polis is hailing us!" advised Gris.

"Put him on!"

There was chaos on the *Kreg's* bridge; behind a bruised Polis, Aden could see multiple fires, structural damage, and many injured crewmen.

"About time you got here!" he chastised Aden. "We're taking a beating. I have four zon heavy cruisers firing at us point blank—make that five!"

The *Edris* itself had attracted multiple zon capital ships, but her shields were holding. Aden ordered the *Edris* and the *Taal* to come about and place themselves between several zon heavy cruisers and the *Kreg*. Ten destroyers and three motherships quickly joined the fray, obviously aware of the significance of the *Kreg* and the *Edris*. In response, Aden ordered the *Calista* and the *Lacplesis* to take up positions on their flanks; he also ordered all four Dipsa class ships to launch their fighters.

Damage reports were now coming in quickly. A total of 25 zon capital ships were firing pointblank at the five ships, and their shields were beginning to weaken. Their fighters took heavy losses attempting to provide cover, but the zon ships were too large and too many for them to have an impact. While Kealt weaponry was having an effect on the enemy vessels, it was not enough to turn the tide. The *Kreg* was more effective, but for every ship she disabled, two more appeared.

Polis again hailed the *Edris* and bellowed, "Aren't your ships armed with our fusion cannons? There are five of us; we should be putting up a better fight!"

"Technical difficulties!" exclaimed Aden. "We can't use them without lowering our shields."

"Then let's do it!" exhorted Gris. "Better to die fighting than to have them nip away at us until we can't defend ourselves!"

"Gris," shouted Aden, "you're right again! Admiral Polis, it's been a pleasure serving with you!" Before Polis could answer, he cut the transmission. Then he ordered the four ships to drop their shields and deploy their main weapons.

For a time it seemed the tactic would work: Their fusion cannons cut through the zon fleet effortlessly. However, the respite was only temporary—more zon ships poured into the breach and pounded their now unshielded hulls. The *Calista* was the first go, exploding like a small supernova. The *Lacplesis* and the *Taal* quickly followed. With nothing to lose and hoping it wasn't too late, Aden called down to main engineering and bellowed: "Stick, upload Blixt's patch!"

"Sir?" replied the harried senior engineer.

"Damn it Stick, now!" he commanded.

Seconds later Gris exclaimed, "Sir, all lights are green! The crystal matrix is at 90% efficiency! The ship is at full power—about three times full power!"

"Good! Shields to maximum and bring those fusion cannons on line!"

Within seconds the *Edris* was cutting an impressive swath through the zon, whose own weapons were now useless against her enhanced shields. Just when Aden thought they might actually survive Gris said, "Sir! We're picking up the signal from an emergency extraction beacon!"

"Just one?" replied Aden, frowning.

"Yes sir," answered Gris grimly.

"Beam her to the bridge then."

"We'll have to lower the shields. There are still a lot of zon out there."

"Do it!" exclaimed Aden.

With their shields down the *Edris* was immediately rocked. A shimmering figure slowly took form on the bridge. Seconds later Sia exclaimed, "Celesta needs help!"

"Gris," bellowed Aden, "is Celesta's transponder signal in the database?"

"It is."

"Then lock on to it, and quickly!"

Celesta quickly materialized face down on the floor. Too busy to wonder why, Aden commanded Gris to raise the shields. Nothing happened. The zon fusillade had damaged the shield generators.

Aden looked at Sia and smiled grimly. "I'm sorry," was all he said. Then he braced himself and…nothing.

"The zon have stopped firing!" reported Gris. "Multiple hyperspace windows are opening all around us. Some are huge, over four kilometers wide!"

"Don't they have enough ships?" replied Aden caustically.

"I don't know," answered a bemused Gris. "According to the sensors nothing is coming through."

"Put them on screen."

"Sorry sir," replied another bridge officer. "The vidscreen is down."

Aden turned his attention to another officer and said, "Lieutenant, please scan for organic matter."

"I have it now," he replied. "Ships are coming through and they're made of the same stuff we cataloged at the wreckage of those zon ships. They must be the tayron." He put his hand to his earpiece. "They're hailing us in our language."

"What are they saying?" asked Sia, who was on the floor attending to Celesta.

"It's a brief, repeating message. All it says is, 'Please get out of the way.' I wonder what that means?"

"Gris," responded Aden, "order the fleet to take up orbit between the zon and Ardala. Tell Polis to do the same. And get that vidscreen back up!"

When the screen came up seconds later, Aden was not prepared for what he saw: Ships that looked more like living creatures than warships fluttered about the battlefield, destroying zon ships without effort. They also were greatly outnumbered, but the zon appeared incapable of damaging them. The tayron ships seemed to soak up the energy from each zon volley, and as the energy built up, they began to glow with increasing brightness. As the glow increased, so did the power of their weapons, which were many times more intense than an Ardalan fusion cannon.

The remaining zon ships tried to flee the carnage, but the tayron had created an energy field that made it impossible to open a hyperspace window. Aden later learned the zon had come to Ardala with over 1000 ships. Seemingly in the blink of an eye, the tayron had completely annihilated them. When they were finished, five ships, each kilometers across, drifted slowly across the battlefield vaporizing what was left.

"Hail them!" Aden ordered.

"We have been sir," replied Gris. "They're just sitting there."

"Aden," said Sia, who was kneeling next to Celesta, "please, she needs help."

In the fog of battle, he had forgotten that the two women had beamed aboard. He walked over to Celesta, then kneeled down and picked her up. "Beam us, the three of us, to sickbay," he ordered.

When they materialized, sickbay was in chaos. It was a large facility, commensurate with the size of the *Edris*. Even so, every bed was taken and dozens more wounded lay on cots and on the floor. A medic immediately came over and led them across the floor to a cot whose most recent tenant was now on the floor covered with a blanket.

"I'm sorry for the accommodations," he said, "but as you can see we're at considerably more than capacity." Once Aden laid her gently on the cot, another medic rushed over and began running scans of her body. He said, "She has injuries I've never seen before, can you tell me what happened?"

Sia provided a brief version of their ordeal while he continued his examination. When he was finished he said, "She has significant internal injuries. It might be a while before we can stabilize her, but she's young and strong. With the technology we have on board, she'll at least have a chance. I know she's close to you admiral, but if you stay you'll only be in the way."

Sia took his arm and led him away. "Don't worry, I'll stay with her. You have a crew that needs you."

"Sia, you don't understand—she's my sister!"

"I know," she replied, "she told me everything. I'll make sure she gets the best care possible. I promise! Now please, go to your crew!"

Aden touched his communicator, but before he spoke, Sia said, "I'm sorry, I almost forgot. Do you know anything about my parents?"

"Yes," he responded, "they're aboard the *Kreg*. That's why the zon were so interested in it. Polis beamed them up when the trouble started."

To his surprise, she kissed him on the cheek. "Thanks," she said, "hopefully I'll be able to thank you properly when this is over. Now please leave!"

When Aden returned to the bridge, he was pleased to see that Gris had restored some semblance of order. "Damage report!" he barked, once he grabbed his attention.

Gris frowned. "Just about every system except for life support and communications is off line. We'll need weeks in space dock before we can even attempt to fly her home."

"And the fleet?"

"Initial reports indicate we've lost about two thirds of our ships, either destroyed or disabled. So did the Ardalans. We're still adding up the casualties, but we've lost thousands."

"How is the *Kreg*?" asked Aden.

"Not much better off than we are sir. Polis is eager to speak with you."

"Very good," responded Aden, "hail him."

When Polis appeared on the vidscreen, the bridge behind him looked much like the *Edris's*.

"Admiral," he said, "glad to see you're safe."

"Yes," he replied, "thanks in no small part to your shielding technology. Without it we would not have survived."

"You're fusion cannons were equally impressive," said Aden. "You'll be happy to know your sister is safe aboard the *Edris*. How are your parents?"

"They're fine, Aden, thanks to the heroic efforts of you and your fleet. I understand that somehow you have Sia and Celesta on board. How are they?"

"Sia's fine," Aden replied, "but Celesta's not good—our medics are doing what they can."

"I see," he said, with a neutral expression that belied his concern. "Have your people heard anything from our friends out there?"

"Not a word. They were nice enough to clean up the battlefield, then most of their ships entered hyperspace and left. The rest have been sitting out there doing nothing. I guess they're trying to agree on the next step."

"Sir!" interrupted Gris, "they're hailing us—text only."

Aden looked back to the vidscreen and said, "Polis, are you getting this?"

"Yes," he replied. "It looks like it's addressed to us both. They want to meet with us, but not out here."

By the end of the day, and with the consent of the taal, all parties agreed that first contact would be on Seti in a month's time. Aden had suggested Seti because it was a neutral site and it would expose the tayron to the taal. He didn't know if they'd actually help them, but the tayron had to be aware of their abilities and most likely would be less inclined to dissemble.

At the conclusion of the brief negotiations, the remainder of the tayron fleet entered hyperspace and departed. With no immediate crisis to deal with Aden returned to sickbay, where he found Sia helping with other patients. He pulled her aside and said, "How's Celesta?"

She smiled wanly. "She's in surgery now. She may be for the next few hours. Seeing the worry in his eyes she added, "She's as tough as her big brother. She'll make it." When Aden didn't answer, she asked, "How were you able to rescue her? We only had one extraction beacon."

"When she was ill we had her implanted with a subcutaneous transponder. We suspected she would try to escape, and we thought it prudent to have a way to track her if she did. As it turned out she was always easy to find, she was never far from a pile of police!"

"Did you have a chance to check on my parents?"

"Yes. I spoke to Polis. He's fine and so are they. You're free to beam over to the *Kreg*, or to the surface, whenever you wish."

"Aden Cade, are you trying to get rid of me?" she teased.

He nearly melted when she graced him with the first genuine smile he'd ever elicited from her. He smiled back and said, "Would you honor me with dinner tonight? I would very much like to hear what happened to the two of you."

The smile immediately left her face. "Why must you always say exactly the wrong thing?" she chastised. "This is no time to flirt with me!"

Aden did his best to answer calmly. "Your Highness," he replied, "would you mind stepping out into the corridor?"

Sia immediately regretted her harsh response, but it was too late. She followed him out of sickbay, but before she could offer an apology he lit into her: "I don't care if you are the high princess of Ardala," he railed, "you will not insult me in front of *my* men on *my* ship! Kealt lost dozens of ships today and thousands of our best men defending *your* world. My own sister risked her life to protect you! How vain can you be to think I would rather pursue some juvenile infatuation with you than look after my men? I've tried to be patient with you, I've tried to understand you, but I know now that was a waste of time…"

"Aden I…"

"I'm not finished!" he nearly bellowed. "You are a petulant, self-centered, spoiled child! You once called me 'brave' for calling off our wedding. At the time I thought 'fool' would be a better description—who else would allow such a supposed jewel to slip through his fingers?" He snorted at the irony. "In fact, I know now I may have been the wisest man in the universe!"

He held up his hand when she tried to interrupt again. "If you are truly concerned for my sister's wellbeing you may stay for as long as it takes to stabilize her, and I will be grateful for it. Once that is done, I ask that you leave my ship immediately. I promise that in the future I will do my best to stay out of your way. I beg you do the same."

When Sia thought it was finally safe to speak, she fought back tears and sniffed, "You are correct on all counts. I have been a monster to you for no reason. You are a good and decent man whom I've never properly appreciated. I will respect your wishes. Thank you for allowing me to stay with Celesta. She is a wonderful woman. I'm sorry I also misjudged her. It's no exaggeration to say she not only saved my life, she also singlehandedly prevented a full-fledged civil war. I would be honored to offer her access to the best medical care on Ardala if your own fine facilities are inadequate. When she's healed I also would be honored if I could show her around Ardala properly."

She paused and dabbed her eyes with a handkerchief. When she was finished she said, "You must get back to your duties. You have suffered grievous losses protecting my world. We are truly and forever in your debt." She paused as though she had more to say, then turned and went back into sickbay.

Dumbfounded, Aden made his way back to the bridge. At mess that evening, he was only half listening as Chief Engineer Stick finished updating him on the *Edris's* damage report. She wasn't as crippled as initially thought, and with the help of the Ardalans, she'd be ready to return to Kealt within a week. Gris confirmed the fleet's initial damage assessment: A third of their ships had been destroyed, a third were disabled, and only the remaining third was combat ready. The chief medical officer provided the casualty report and advised it probably would be best for Celesta and a number of others to be transferred to an Ardalan medical facility. When he was finished, Aden went back to Stick and exclaimed, "I thought these ships could withstand zon weapons even without shielding! Why did we fare so poorly?"

Stick was normally an accommodating man, but he couldn't suppress the anger he felt as he defended the engineers who built the Dipsa class ships, many of whom died on those same ships. "Sir," he replied sharply, "these ships absorbed over three times the punishment they were speced to. The *Edris* took even more and is still here. I stand by them and my colleagues who died trying to save them!"

Aden was not used to being challenged so forcefully, let alone by the normally meek Stick. He suppressed his initial urge to reprimand him, as his words sank in. Finally he said, "My deepest apologies chief engineer, and my condolences on the loss of so many of your friends and colleagues. I was wrong to think ill of them. They are truly heroes, as are all of our fallen comrades."

Then he frowned and said, "It was fortunate Blixt was able to write that program. We'd have met the fate of the other three ships without it. He must be quite an impressive young man to write such a program so quickly when it seemed to elude even the best engineers on Kealt. I would very much appreciate it if you could bring him by later so I could thank him personally."

"Funny thing sir," replied Stick, who quickly reverted to his normal temper, "we haven't been able to find him. We thought he may have been injured or left the *Edris* to help on one of our other ships, but he's not on any of them. It's as though he's vanished."

Aden turned to his security chief and said, "Please attempt to locate someone, anyone, who can say they personally knew Blixt before he joined the Dipsa project."

"Sir?" he replied.

"I suspect our man no longer exists, and in fact, never did."

Sia didn't say goodbye when she and Celesta transported down to Ardala the following day. Celesta's initial medical reports were more promising than anyone dared hope, and by the time the *Edris* was sufficiently repaired to limp home, she was stable enough to transport back to Kealt.

When she was safely on board, Aden gave the order to set course for Kealt and then went to sickbay. It was less chaotic then before, since many of the injured had since been deemed fit to resume their posts. He quickly found his sister, who, with the help of an aide, was up and taking small steps.

"Orderly, would you please excuse us?" he asked the young woman. When she departed, he helped Celesta to a nearby chair, then pulled up another one and sat beside her. He held her hands and noted that she'd looked better.

"Yes," she replied dolefully, "and the shame of it is, I was finally beginning to feel like my old self. Now I'm back to where I was before."

"Celesta I'm so proud of you. No one else could have done what you did."

"Aden," she said, "those things have ruined my life. I'll never be what I was again. I wish I'd died on Ardala and been put out of my misery!"

He stroked her hair gently. "I know you've been through a lot—more than anyone I've known; but you can't give up now! The tayron are hunting the zon out of existence, we've just learned that mythical creatures are real, and Polis is waiting for you to get out of this bed. Hang in there my little sister—things are better than you know."

She wiped away her tears and smiled wanly at the use of her childhood appellation. "You're right. I need to stop feeling sorry for myself. Thank God you are such an optimist." She stroked his arm and added, "I'll tell you what, I promise I'll look at the bright side if you promise to tell Sia how you feel about her!"

"How I feel about *her*? I know how she feels about me! She hates every cell in my body!"

"No she doesn't," she replied. "She's been through a lot as well, with the wedding, Seti, and Gabo. She likes you, but she's afraid to admit it. She's very vulnerable right now; she doesn't trust herself. She's afraid if she gives in to you, you'll overwhelm her. Be patient with her and you'll succeed. I'm sure of it!" When he didn't reply, she smiled and said, "That should be a small task for a man who can tame taals!"

Aden remembered that Edris had given him essentially the same advice. Maybe he was wiser than he realized.

"So," he said, hoping to change the subject, "I spoke to one of your Ardalan doctors and he assured me that with proper rest and a little time you'll be as good as new. Maybe if you're feeling better you would like to finally see Seti."

"I would love to see any place that could so capture your imagination! Besides that, the rest of us will finally meet the tayron. You couldn't keep me away!"

Chapter XX

Despite the unrepaired damage to the *Edris*, King Edris directed Aden to go directly to Seti. The month would be up quickly and he wanted him to oversee preparations for first contact. Whatever they were, the tayron were a formidable species. Edris wanted to ensure their first impression of the Kealts was a favorable one. King Ivege directed Polis to do the same for Ardala.

When Aden arrived on Seti, he was astonished by the new development already underway that would quadruple the size of the main settlement. Seti's first proper hotel was under construction, and, much to his disappointment, the old pub had largely been abandoned in favor of a slick new facility that catered to both Ardalan and Kealt tastes.

Not long after he arrived, he commandeered a hover car to bring him to the spaceport to pick up Drusa, who had stayed on Seti when he left for

Kealt. Tock had ordered her to go to the spaceport to meet some newcomers, a job she not only enjoyed, but one that kept her out of Tock's hair.

The driver told Aden he was unsure about the car, because it had a history of breaking down; however, because of the constant influx of visitors it was the only one available. His fears seemed unfounded when Aden and Drusa climbed into it and headed back toward the settlement.

Almost immediately the car began to slow, chimes went off, and then it stopped. The driver rolled down the privacy glass and said, "Your Highness, my profound apologies. As I feared, this car is unreliable. My superiors advised they will send another one to pick us up as soon as one becomes available, but it could be a while. In the meantime, I'll take a look in the engine compartment and see if I can get her restarted."

"Oh I love engines!" exclaimed Drusa. "I used to help my brother fix our tractor! Could I watch what he's doing?"

Aden smiled indulgently. A hover car was about as similar to a tractor as a knife was to a fusion cannon. He opened the door and they both stepped out. While she walked to the front of the car, he leaned against it and looked out toward the distant jungle. How different Seti looked from this perspective, he thought.

Less than two minutes later, the car roared to life. As the driver approached Aden he said, "That girl is amazing! She knew right what the problem was. We've been trying to track down that short for weeks. I'm sure we'll have no further trouble."

As they settled back into the car, Aden said, "Very impressive."

"Oh, it was a complete accident!" she replied brightly. "I just stuck my hand in, touched a wire that caught my eye, and surprise! The car started."

"Just like that?" asked Aden.

"Yup, can you believe it?"

At that moment a light when on in Aden's head—how could he have been so blind?

As anticipated, the weeks went by quickly. He kept Drusa at arm's length trying to decide what to do. Finally, with the tayron due to arrive the next day, and having done all he could to prepare for their arrival, he asked her to accompany him to the old pub. It was time to show his cards.

He was pleased to see his usual table was open. In fact, just about every table was open. He helped Drusa settle into her seat, then got the attention of the one remaining server who was behind the bar cleaning glasses. He ordered them both ales before gingerly taking a seat across from her.

"Are you still sore from the great battle?" she asked sympathetically, noting his difficulty getting into the booth.

"That and getting knocked off a taal," he replied. "I have healed, for the most part; I think I actually feel better than I have in months."

She reached across the table, put her hand on his, and said, “I’m glad you made it back. I don’t know what I would have done if…” She couldn’t bring herself to finish the sentence.

Aden put his free hand on top of hers. “Maybe we’ve seen the last of war. I’ve certainly had my fill of it.” He released her hand when the server arrived with their ales. He picked his up and said, “The mighty tayron are coming tomorrow—we should toast to something!”

“Here’s to you,” she answered while picking up her glass, “that you may find peace, happiness, and love!”

Aden tapped her glass. “Same to you Drusa.”

While Aden drank deeply she replied wistfully, “And where may we find it?”

“Are you looking for it?” he asked evenly, as he put down his glass. "Love, that is?"

“Not until I met you,” she answered. When he looked down uncomfortably, she said, “When I’m in your arms I can’t think of anything else; but I know we’re not meant for each other. Soon you’ll go your own way and be done with me.”

This was not the Drusa Prine Aden had known. This one was uncharacteristically serious and her face wore an expression he had never seen before. “Is that how it’s going to end?” he asked.

“Of course,” she replied. “How else could it end?”

“What’s the capital of Epsilon II?”

"What?"

"Who was your governor?"

"Aden…I…I'm not ready to talk about that yet."

"OK, here's a simple one—what was your father's middle name?"

Drusa was becoming nervous. Her voice quavered as she replied, "You're being mean!"

He reached into his vest, pulled out a small sack, and placed it on the table. She looked at it and said, "What's that?"

"Were you ever going to be honest with me?"

Her face was becoming flushed and she was starting to sweat. Trying to respond as nonchalantly as she could, she said, "Whatever do you mean?"

He reached into the sack and pulled out a device that was identical to the one he'd discovered under the towel when he'd rescued her—or at least thought he'd rescued her. He laid it in the middle of the table and said, "I found this in your quarters." He held up his hand when she began to deny it was hers. "Your fingerprints are on it. I've had our best engineers look at it and they can't figure out what it does. I'm guessing it serves a variety of purposes like, maybe, a long-range communicator, or a remote control for a cloaked ship. I'm sure it also does other things."

Drusa grabbed a cloth napkin and covered it up. When she reached for it, he placed his hand on it. "Please," she whispered, "give it back!"

"Why should I? You've been lying to me from the beginning. You took advantage of me by pretending to be a dopey refugee who couldn't get out of her own way. You almost got me killed believing that! Nothing could be farther from the truth, could it?"

"Aden I…how…how did you find out?"

"It wasn't one thing. It was a lot of little clues that finally added up to a great big lie that even I couldn't miss. Like the way you found your way into my home even though I barely knew you; the way you handled yourself in the refugee camp; the device identical to this one I saw hidden under a towel in your tent; the way you fixed that hover car. I can only assume you were overdue to call your superiors?

"You're a good actress, but every once in a while I caught a comment or saw something in your eyes you couldn't hide. Other things. You know, my father was suspicious of you from the start. One of these days I'll learn to listen to him. Congratulations, you played me for a fool!"

"I'm sorry. I wasn't supposed to get that close to you, but you were so kind, so caring, so unbelievably decent. I couldn't believe you still let me retrieve my bag even though you'd been wounded, and then the way you looked after those poor refugees. You kept your word and never tried to lay a hand on me until I was ready. I've never met anyone like you. I fell in love."

He snickered. "You can turn it off now. I know what and who you are."

A tear formed in her eye. "It's true," she insisted. "I know it's hard for you to trust me after what I've done, but it's true!" She picked up a napkin and dabbed her eyes. "Even if you don't believe me, you have to let me go!"

"I do? Why is that?"

"You know I'm on your side. I saved your life!"

Aden gritted his teeth. After what seemed like an eternity to Drusa, he slid the device over to her. "You did," he said. "Please promise me I'm not making the biggest mistake of my life!"

She took it and stuck it in her bag. "You won't regret this, I promise," she replied. "Anyway, I actually came here to warn you—you and your family are in danger. The civil war on Ardala failed, but zon supporters on Kealt haven't made their move. Since Kealt's entire royal family has foolishly traveled to Seti, a very difficult planet to secure, they will make their move here, and soon. I can't tell you anything more. I wasn't even supposed to tell you that, but you've probably figured out I'm not good at following orders."

"How do you know this?"

"It's my job," she replied, as she rose from the table. "I'm afraid you've seen the last of Drusa Prine. I knew her well and whatever you think of her, I can assure you, she *did* love you. Keep fighting Aden. Keep doing the right thing. One day, under your leadership, Kealt will become a beacon for oppressed worlds everywhere."

When he also stood up, she went over and kissed him on the cheek. She smiled, stroked his chin and said, "God bless you Aden Cade; and watch your back." Then she turned to leave.

"Drusa!"

She stopped and looked back over her shoulder. "Yes?" she replied.

"I don't suppose you'll tell me your real name?"

"Maybe one day."

"OK. Do you know what happened to the real Drusilla?"

She turned to face him and smiled wanly. "She was a very brave woman. We know from transmissions we intercepted that she and her family stayed with many others and fought the zon. They had almost no defensive capabilities, but still managed to hold out for several days. By the time we got there, they were all dead." With that, she left the bar.

Aden was shaken. How had she been able to dupe him for so long? Looking back, he knew the signs were there, but he'd chosen to ignore them. Still unsure if he'd done the right thing by letting her go, he returned to his seat and tried to figure it out over a copious amount of ale. Countless ales later he was about to get up when he felt a soft hand on his shoulder. He turned his head and said, "Drusa…!"

"Well, no," replied Sia smiling. "Are you disappointed?"

When Aden realized who it was, he stood up unsteadily. "What are you doing here?" he asked. "Haven't you had enough of this place?" He slapped his head as though experiencing a revelation. "Oh, I know! You've come to torment me again after you promised me you wouldn't!"

With a disarming smile, Sia said, "I never promised any such thing. I do promise, however, if you talk to me I will be on my best behavior, at least for a while."

"That's how it always starts!" he exclaimed, as he began to sway unsteadily. "And then, before you know it, you're slapping me, insulting me, accusing me of wanting to have sex with you! And if you must know, I've had so many ales, I most certainly would like to have sex with you!"

When he recoiled and covered his face in an exaggerated fashion as though to protect himself from a blow, Sia laughed heartily, which caused him to laugh in return.

When she caught her breath she said, "I can assure you, as long as you behave yourself none of the above will happen, especially having sex with me! Come on, let's take a walk. It's a full moon and you look like you could use some air…or are you waiting for Drusa?" She said it gently, almost apprehensively.

"No," he replied wistfully. "She won't be back. Please, sit down. There's something I need to tell you." Once she was comfortable, he told her everything he knew about Drusa Prine.

When he finished she said, "Wow! You were right; there *was* more to her than she let on. Are you going to tell your father?"

"Not yet. I think we need to let things play out."

"You trust her that much?"

"I know I shouldn't, but beneath it all, I get the sense she means well. And she has helped me."

"Why did you tell me?"

Aden grinned. "I guess I had to tell someone, and after all we've been through I feel I have a certain bond with you, as crazy as that might seem."

"It doesn't seem crazy to me at all, Aden. Despite my inexcusable behavior toward you, I feel the same way."

With that, he stood up and held out his arm. "If it be your pleasure Your Highness, I've had more than enough of this place for one evening!" As they began to walk toward the door he asked, "How did you find me anyway? No one comes here anymore."

"Aden Cade, you may be the most predictable person I know. Despite your curious nature, you don't like new and shiny. You like old, worn, and familiar. Where else would you be?"

It was a cool night for Seti. As they made their way in the general direction of their quarters, it wasn't long before Aden's head began to clear.

When Sia stopped, he realized it was under the same copse of trees where she'd attacked him for fondling her. She turned toward the jungle, which, with the new development, was further away than it used to be. She pointed to the blue, shimmering sky and said, "Look, it's like it was the last time we were here. I'm beginning to see why you like this place so much—as long as I try not to think about what lies beyond that barrier!"

"I hope we don't screw it up again," he replied somberly.

"I know you won't let that happen."

As they faced the jungle, Aden put his arm around her. He half expected she would recoil, but instead she returned his embrace and rested her head on his shoulder.

"I'm sorry Aden, I've never been fair to you. You are a wonderful man. I wish we could have met under different circumstances. Perhaps things would be different between us."

Now feeling more intoxicated by her nearness than from the ale, he squeezed her shoulder gently. "I don't hold grudges."

Very softly, she whispered, *"I love you."*

Not believing his ears he whispered back, *"It must be the ale, it sounded like you said you love me."*

"Don't sound so surprised! I've lied to myself for so long, but the fact is, I've loved you from the beginning."

"You have the most peculiar way of showing it!"

"Marrying a king is not the best prescription for a happy marriage, especially when the marriage is thrust upon him. When I was a child, my own father had a string of paramours. I can still remember the fights he and my mother used to have. He settled down eventually, but I held that against him for a long time. Now that I'm older I can't say I blame him. When I met you I so wanted to hate you, because I never wanted to see the pain in my mother's eyes reflected in my own."

"I suppose Celesta didn't help."

"No," she replied, "but even if she never existed I would have had the same reservations. You are such a handsome and charming man. I didn't see how one woman could ever be enough for you."

"And now?"

"I've come to know you better. I know what an honorable man you are. You would never betray anyone, let alone your wife, even one you didn't choose."

"Well Sia, since this seems to be the time for confessions, I have one for you: I love you as well, and have from the first time I saw you. In the entire universe I couldn't imagine a more perfect woman."

She pulled away, turned and faced him. "After the way I've been to you? How can you even stand to be near me?"

He didn't answer her directly, but said, "You once agreed to marry me. Does that offer still stand?"

She smiled wanly. "No! I made that offer under duress, out of a sense of duty and obligation. To be married under such circumstances would have made me more of concubine than a wife. Fortunately, a very brave and kind man freed me from my vows. I control my own heart now. The next time I give it away it will be to a man of my choosing, for love and love alone!"

Her tone told him there was something she expected him do. Even though he knew what it was, he hesitated. When he finally reached out and took her hands, he felt they were trembling. He didn't know it, but his hands also trembled. He cleared his throat while Sia looked on expectantly.

Finally he said, "Sia Selarney, high princess of Ardala, no man is worthy of your heart, least of all me. Still, if given the opportunity, I will make you a good and faithful husband. Will you marry me?"

Almost breathlessly she replied, "I thought you would never ask! I most certainly will! And I know you will make a fine husband—and father."

Aden released her hands and rested his gently on her shoulders. "And now Your Highness, I have to go."

"Why, have I offended you in some way?"

"Certainly not; it's just that I have no desire to be struck again…"

"What?"

"…if I kiss you."

"If you don't kiss me I *will* strike you!"

"What?" replied Aden uncertainly, again not daring to trust his ears.

Sia reached up, gently slapped his face, and said, "Shut up before I change my mind!"

Chapter XXI

The next day Aden woke up wondering if the previous night had been a dream. That he could still smell Sia on him told him it had been real enough. Reluctantly he got up and showered. The tayron were scheduled to arrive later that morning and he needed to be at his best.

When he was finished, he stepped out, dried himself, and began to gather the parts of his dress uniform. As pulled it on piece by piece, ensuring every detail was perfect, he remembered that the last time he'd worn it was when he was supposed to marry Sia. He had almost finished when a knock on the door interrupted him. "Come in!" he shouted.

The door opened and Polis stepped inside. He took stock of Aden in his uniform and said, "You, sir, are a most impressive fellow! So impressive, in fact, you are all my dear sister could talk about at breakfast this morning!"

"Well," replied Aden ruefully, "let's see how long that lasts."

"You don't know my sister. Despite your experience with her, she is not in the least fickle, at least as far as her heart is concerned. She has cast her lot and it is with you. If you still want her, that is. Frankly, I don't know why you would!"

Aden struggled to secure the top button of his tunic, and grunted with satisfaction when it slid into place. While he shook himself down he said, "Polis, she is like none other I have met. We had a good night last night; but before I get too carried away, I would like to ensure it's a trend and not an aberration. My respects to you and your family, but she is like quicksilver. It seems you never see the same Sia twice."

Polis snickered. "That might be the best description of her I've ever heard! I don't know what happened last night and truth be told I would prefer not to; but I can assure you, you have indeed breached the bars to her heart."

"Perhaps," said Aden, "but right now I am more concerned with meeting our new 'friends.'"

"I am as apprehensive as you my good friend. Even the taal seem unsettled." When Aden only grunted in reply, apparently in no mood for small talk, Polis said, "When you didn't show up for breakfast my sister tasked me to check in on you to see if you were all right. That's what she said, anyway. I suspect she was more interested in where your friend Drusa was—she wasn't at breakfast either. Now that I can affirm not only are you in fine fettle, but alone as well, I will leave you to your preparations. The tayron have entered orbit and will begin their descent soon. They should be here within the next couple of hours. As far as we can tell they only sent one ship."

"Yes," answered Aden, fussing with his hair in the mirror, "but we've seen the capabilities of those ships."

"We have indeed. I've also seen what your new ships can do when at full power, if only briefly. I suspect with more of them we may be able to give them a real challenge, if it came to that." Polis paused at the door. "Oh, your father asked me to have you stop by the reception hall when you're ready. He would like to finalize protocol with us and the taal for first contact."

Thirty minutes later Aden was standing outside of the "reception hall," which, until recently, had served as the main warehouse for the storage, repair, and maintenance of mining equipment. It was one of the few buildings on Seti large enough to handle the ten taals who would be present, as well as the dignitaries from Kealt and Ardala.

Since both planets had already agreed to recognize the taal as the sovereign rulers of Seti, protocol provided that the taal should lead the ceremony. However, since they were by nature shy, secretive, and otherwise ill suited for such a role, they requested that Kealt and Ardala split those duties.

Aden was stunned when he entered the once humble warehouse. In theory he had been responsible for overseeing the planning of first contact preparations, but in his wildest dreams he couldn't have imagined how anyone could transform such a dingy, industrial complex into a facility worthy of a coronation.

Thick red carpeting, as well as finished wood and stone, covered the floor; bright tapestries, campaign banners, and coats of arms hung from the walls and ceilings. Six large, ornate chairs sat next to each other at the far end of the hall representing the thrones of Ardala and Kealt, and the sovereignty of the taal.

Orchestras from Kealt and Ardala were in the process of assembling on either side of the hall, recording crews were setting up in strategic locations, and workers were scurrying about making last minute preparations. As he stood there, mouth agape, he felt a heavy hand on his shoulder.

"Amazing isn't it?" said Edris, as he stepped beside him. "When they proposed this place for first contact I was skeptical; but you have done a remarkable job."

"Me?" replied Aden, "I actually had little to do with this, save for agreeing on a location. Most of the credit goes to Glyn. This is the result of her vision."

Edris spent the next few minutes explaining how the ceremony would unfold. It promised to be an event for the ages. Edris, Ivege, and Sarin would pick up their guests at the spaceport and shuttle them to the warehouse.

Inside, the taal, who were members of their Prime Council, would line up behind the thrones. In front of the thrones would be the high princes and princesses, and a joint science delegation that consisted of xenobiologists, as well as language and first contact experts. The kings and queen would lead their guests into the hall.

While they were talking, Tock came up to Edris and stuttered, "Your Ha Ha Highness, the tayron ship has entered the atmosphere. We must begin to prepare for the ceremony."

Just then, the doors to the warehouse opened to admit the procession of taals. Gasps filled the hall as the immense, graceful creatures made their way majestically to the rear. As they went by, a warm feeling filled Aden.

"Hello Bang," he thought. "It's nice seeing you again."

She didn't answer directly, but he could sense her acknowledgement. He also could sense the irritation among the other taals—they weren't used to a non-taal being so familiar with one of their senior leaders, and vice versa. Aden bowed his head in deference as they passed, which seemed to mollify them somewhat. He noted that when they took up positions behind the thrones, Bang stood out from the rest.

While aides were scrambling around tying up loose ends, Tock trundled up excitedly and exclaimed, "Your Highness! The tayron ship has begun its da da descent! It will land within the hour!"

Edris clapped Aden on the shoulder. "My son, this will be a sight for the ages! Let us not keep the tayron waiting!"

Ivege's aide conveyed the news to him as well, and together they made their way to a small fleet of hover cars that waited outside the warehouse to take the dignitaries to the spaceport. Aden found Sia, and together they climbed into a large hover car with Celesta, Polis, Glyn, and Gris. Their parents rode in their own car.

As they drove to the spaceport, Sia smiled at Aden in a way that made him forget everything except for her smile. Since he proposed, it seemed she was a new person. He still felt he had to pinch himself to prove it wasn't a dream. Her true personality was finally shining through, with a radiance that dwarfed even a xanide explosion.

"Well," she said, "another mystery is about to be revealed. As much as you need to see what's over the next hill, I imagine you are virtually quivering in anticipation of meeting such an enigmatic species."

"So," he replied, smiling back, "you have already figured me out! You are correct, I am indeed on the edge of my seat. I just hope this isn't a case of skinning the Carca Beast and finding we have inadvertently freed the Viper of Horra."

"We don't have that expression on Ardala, but if it means what I think it means, we did not set it free. The zon did, and they have brought it here."

Gris tapped Glyn on the knee. "Well, until I know better, I am going to assume they are our benevolent saviors!"

"They better be," replied Aden, "after the beating we took we're no position to take on a force that so easily dispatched the zon. What say you Polis?"

"What?" answered Polis, who was holding Celesta's hands, deep in conversation with her. "What's that?"

Glyn and Gris laughed together. "Can't you see he has more important things on his mind?" chastised Gris with mock seriousness. "What is meeting the most powerful species in the universe compared to having the undivided attention of your lovely, newly minted sister?"

Celesta blushed. "There are two other couples in this very car who have equal ardor for each other!" she noted.

Good-natured laughter filled the vehicle, and while they were still laughing Glyn said, "That is true enough my daughter!" She put her hand on Gris's chest and added, "Barely a night goes by when I don't have to fend off the attentions of this uncultured oaf!"

"Mother!" admonished Celesta.

"Now then!" replied Gris, trying to sound offended. "You may blame me for my humble origins, but not my gender! What would any man do if he were married to the most beautiful and interesting woman in the universe?" When Glyn herself blushed despite his shameless flattery, laughter again broke out.

When he caught his breath Aden said, "Sia, Polis, on behalf of all Kealts may I apologize for the inexcusably crude behavior of my otherwise beloved sister and brother in law!"

"You will do no such thing!" replied Sia crossly. She glanced sideways at Aden. "I hope that one day I marry someone who feels that way about me when we've been married as long as they have!"

Before Aden could answer, the procession of hover cars came to a stop at the edge of the spaceport. "This is it," he said to no one in particular, suddenly turning somber.

As the dignitaries exited the cars, most walked the short distance to an area of stands that had been roped off for them to watch the landing from a safe distance. Initially they attempted to maintain their decorum as they jockeyed for a good view, but very shortly several fights nearly broke out among respective delegates who believed they were entitled to a more advantageous position.

Fortunately, Edris, Ivege, and their families had been provided with their own viewing area, and were able to watch what had become a mad scramble with amusement. The other dignitaries continued to jostle each other until someone yelled, "Look, they're coming!"

Aden and Sia gazed up at the spot the man was pointing to and saw what appeared to be a mere speck falling to Seti. Before long, the speck grew, and the massive size of the ship became evident when it was still many kilometers above them.

As it drew closer, they could see it didn't have any obvious means of propulsion. It was over a kilometer across and bore a loose resemblance to a sea creature native to Kealt that glided along the sea floor. It was much wider than it was long, and tapered at the front and back into what appeared to be a head and a tail. It was glowing brightly and appeared to be fluttering, as though it were flying like a bird. Aden noted how graceful it looked as it completed its final approach.

When it was mere meters above the spaceport, four fleshy protuberances erupted from beneath it. The ship gradually settled onto them and came to rest.

Sia pointed toward the front of the ship. "Do you see that? It has eyes!"

Aden looked where she was pointing. It did indeed appear to have eyes, and they were watching them. He felt Sia shudder as she asked, "What could we possibly have in common with such powerful beings?"

Aden caressed her arm. "A hatred for the zon, for one thing."

"That's not much on which to build a positive, long term relationship!"

"No," Aden agreed, "it isn't; but you know there's more. Anyway, they did save my life, and on that basis I am optimistic their motives are good."

Before Sia could answer, the outline of a large ramp formed between the protuberances and swung down. The dignitaries gasped as two aliens appeared at the top of ramp and slowly walked down.

Because of the size of the ship, they were still a long way off and it was hard to make out fine details; but even at their current distance it was easy to see they were monstrosities. They had two arms, two legs, and a single head, but that was where all semblance to anything human ended.

The creatures had featureless faces that seemed to lack eyes, ears, or even a mouth. From what should have been their scalp hung long clumps of tissue that seemed to move independently. Their fingers and toes were slightly webbed. They were naked, had a slimy appearance, and were green hued.

They were as alien appearing as the zon, but infinitely more powerful. Aden observed that members of the security detail had dropped their hands to rest on the triggers of their weapons. He didn't know what they could do against such a foe if hostilities erupted, but if called on they were willing to die protecting their people.

One of the ship's "eyes" appeared to take note of their actions, and it issued a low growl. As the aliens advanced Sia thought that even on Seti they looked terrifying. When they reached the bottom of the ramp, they stopped and waited.

Edris and Ivege, seemingly oblivious to the frightening nature of the newcomers, nodded at each other and at Sarin, and the three got into their hover car along with a small security team and rode out to meet them. When the car reached the ramp they got out, and together they walked over to the aliens.

When they stood in front of them Edris bowed slightly. "Evidently you understand our language," he said. "On behalf of our newly formed federation, I welcome you to our solar system and the sovereign planet Seti." He nodded to Ivege and Sarin. "This is Ivege and Sarin Selarney, the great king and queen of Ardala. I am Edris Cade, king of Kealt. The rulers of this planet, the taal, have asked us to welcome you on their behalf. They are eager to meet you and are waiting for us at a facility we have done our best to prepare for such a momentous occasion!"

The tayron glanced at each other, and then the larger one stepped forward. He said, "My name is Admiral John Trent. This is my senior xenobiologist Captain Abby Watanabe." He placed a hand on his chest and added, "We are sorry for our strange appearance. We are wearing our battle suits, which assist us in managing this vessel. With your permission, we would like to remove them and reveal our true appearance."

Edris looked at Ivege and Sarin, who nodded slightly. Edris turned to the creature called Trent and said, "As you wish."

When Trent touched his wrist and the suit began to dissolve, no one present expected what happened next—the creature standing before them was human! He nodded to Captain Watanabe, who touched her own wrist, revealing that, not only was she human, but one they knew well: Drusa Prine.

The leaders of Kealt and Ardala looked at one another in astonishment, each sure the other would announce that the tayron were part of an elite force in their military. When no one spoke up, Trent said, "I'm sure our true nature is even more shocking than our initial appearance. Let me explain: We call ourselves terrans. We are from a planet called Earth, the same planet your ancestors were born on."

Edris was the first to overcome his shock. "Hmm," he replied. He nodded toward Abby Watanabe and said, "When last I saw this one, she had another name and was enjoying the company of my son. She seemed quite attached to him, in fact."

"Well, yes," replied Trent awkwardly. "As I said, Captain Watanabe is our senior xenobiologist. She was sent to Kealt to assess your planet for first contact, which is our standard procedure in such cases. I asked her to come in the spirit of full disclosure. I hope you will forgive us."

"Earth," replied Edris, ignoring Trent's explanation. "We have many myths and legends concerning the planet of our origin, but none place that name on it. It is most beautiful in its descriptiveness and simplicity. I, and I'm sure the rulers of Ardala, would very much like to know more about it. Likewise, I imagine you have many questions for us. However, despite our burning curiosity, it would be most rude of us to interrogate you here on the tarmac before you even have the opportunity to meet the masters of this world, whose hospitality we now enjoy. With that in mind, and with the consent of the Ardalan monarchs, may we have the privilege of escorting you to the place of honor we have prepared for you and your men?"

"Your Highnesses," replied Trent, "that would be most welcome. As you noted, we have many questions for you as well. You cannot imagine our own shock when we discovered that our race had somehow taken root so far from home, so long ago. However, our joy was tempered by concern that you may have been overrun by the zon like so many of our other far-flung brothers and sisters. We are most proud that somehow you withstood them, despite your great isolation. We are as eager to hear your story as you are ours." He gestured toward the hover car. "Is that how we are to travel?"

"It is," replied Edris. "How many of your men will also join us?"

"With your indulgence, I would prefer it be just the two of us for now. Even though we are the same race, this is still a first contact situation. We've found such events are less…complicated…when it involves a minimum number of personnel."

Edris smiled. "We have the same policy." He pointed toward the open hover car door. "After you!"

As Trent stepped into the car, the ship groaned. He paused and said, "We are safe my friend." When it calmed down, he entered the car and sat down. Edris and Ivege glanced at each other, neither betraying their awe at the mysterious ways of their strange guests.

Chapter XXII

By design, the car carrying the monarchs and the Earthlings lagged behind the other cars returning to the reception hall. By the time Aden and his companions got there, the various aides had somehow succeeded in wrangling everyone, including the proud, balky taal, into their places. As planned, Aden's party took their places at the sides of their respective thrones.

Once everything was properly prepared, Tock gave the signal for the guests of honor to enter. A side door opened and Edris, Ivege, and Sarin led the Earthlings into the hall. Even though word of their actual nature had already made its way back to the hall, many still gasped as they saw them for the first time.

When they reached the front of the hall, they turned and faced the eager and curious guests from Kealt and Ardala. Edris stepped forward and addressed them.

"Friends and delegates from Kealt, Ardala, and Seti," he said, smiling, "as you have no doubt already heard, our supposed "alien" saviors are actually our brethren from a distant galaxy, who, like us, were attacked by the zon. We have here today Admiral John Trent, leader of the mighty terran fleet that dispatched the zon for eternity. I, like you, am eager to hear his story."

He turned to King Ivege, Queen Sarin, and the taal and bowed slightly. "With your indulgence, Your Highnesses, may I turn the floor over to the admiral?"

They nodded their assent, and everyone present felt the taals' positive response. With that, Edris stepped aside and waived to the podium.

"Admiral Trent, we are a direct people. I'm sure I speak for everyone here when I say I am most eager to hear your story!"

Trent stepped between the royal families and said, "First, I would like to thank the taal for agreeing to allow first contact between our peoples to occur on their planet. While we still know little about it, we understand it is a world of wonder, beauty, and mystery, and is shepherded by one of the most remarkable sentient species in the universe."

By the warm feelings Aden and the others felt, it was evident the taal weren't immune to flattery. Their reaction was so strong, it momentarily caused Trent to pause. Once he regained his bearings he said, "We are equally impressed by the societies that have grown up on Kealt and Ardala. I'm sure we have much to learn from you.

"Your peoples have been gone a long time, and much has been lost over the centuries. However, we believe the peoples of Kealt and Ardala are descended from adventurers who departed Earth on generational ships thousands of years ago, long before the discovery of hyperspace travel. At that time, Earth was overcrowded, resources were dwindling, and our ancestors were fighting over basic things like water and farmland. Millions of people fled toward distant solar systems in search of a fresh start.

"When we discovered hyperspace an effort was made to trace these generational ships, which were designed to carry humans for hundreds of years. We found that many were failing, some had been destroyed, and others were lost entirely. Only a handful made it to their intended destinations, but even then just a few actually took root.

"We have no specific record of the ships that ultimately seeded Ardala and Kealt, nor do we know how they ended up so far from home. However, we can speculate that their instruments may have been damaged, which caused them to miss their original destination, or else they encountered a natural phenomenon that propelled them here.

"As I've noted, few records survive from that period, so many thousands of years ago. We may never learn what actually happened to your brave ancestors. However, somewhere on Ardala, Kealt, or Seti may lay the key to the past, yours and ours. Perhaps it lies in the generational ship you discovered on this very planet!

"Our anthropologists, archaeologists, and xenobiologists are most eager delve into this forgotten chapter of our mutual history. Perhaps your scientists share their enthusiasm? If so, we would consider it an honor to host a team of your own scientists on Earth."

He paused briefly to take in the rapt faces of his hosts before continuing. "We know you have also suffered at the hands—or pincers—of the zon. Now that they are gone, we suspect that soon their former human drones will begin suffering terrible withdrawal systems. If they don't kill themselves outright or die of shock, they will be in need of medical assistance. As a matter of good faith, we would like to offer you a serum we have developed that will not only defeat the addiction to their insidious fluids, but eliminate them from the system entirely."

Sia looked over at Celesta. While the admiral was talking, she had made her way to Polis's side. When Trent announced the cure to the zon addiction, she reached over and took his hand.

When Trent was finished, Edris said, "Admiral Trent, that is quite a lot for us to take in all at once. I don't know when the last time you and your men ate, but if you are like us, I imagine you are growing hungry and a little weary. With your permission, and with the consent of our hosts the taal, and our good friends the Ardalans, I would like to invite you and your men to a feast in your honor. Now that we know you are also human, I suspect you will greatly enjoy what we have prepared; but first, perhaps you would like to freshen up? There will be time for us to learn more about each other later."

Trent agreed, and Edris had his aides escort him and Captain Watanabe to his quarters where they could rest and refresh themselves while the feast was being prepared.

Edris opened the dinner invitation to all of Trent's men, but because of the sensitive nature of first contact, Trent thought it best to continue to keep a low profile for the time being. After their guests had left and while the dining area was being prepared, Aden made his way over to Sia, who was deep in conversation with her parents. When she saw him, she immediately excused herself.

She greeted him with a dazzling smile. "I missed you at breakfast!" she said. "Have you grown tired of me already?"

After Aden kissed her on the cheek, he said, "It took all my strength to keep from picking you up and carrying you away today! That is the literal truth! I almost burst holding in our secret!"

"I think it is important our parents be the first to know and that they are together when we announce our engagement."

"Forgive my impatience," he replied, while taking her hands, "but it seems like I have been waiting for this forever."

She answered, "I feel the same way."

When a frown swept over her face, Aden asked her to explain the cause of her distress.

"I just wish I didn't have to share you with anyone!"

"And who would that be?" asked a bemused Aden.

"She's standing there," she replied, nodding to a spot behind him. "She hasn't taken her eyes off you the entire ceremony. If you're not careful, she might run off with you!"

Aden turned in the direction she was looking. All of the taal had left except for Bang, who was clearly focused on him. He excused himself and walked over to her. Close physical proximately wasn't necessary to communicate with a taal, but he still wasn't used to that concept. As he approached her, he thought, "Are they telling the truth?"

"As far as they know it," she replied. "10,000 years is a long time, even for a race as advanced as this one. I can tell you they are very interested in xanide. They believe it is unique in the universe. As powerful as they are, they would very much like to obtain a steady source of it, especially after seeing how well your ship faired against the zon. Your level of technology impressed them, and they aren't easily impressed."

"That is good to know. By the way, I don't think you've been completely honest with me."

"I have never lied to you!" she insisted indignantly.

"That is not what I said. You aren't just a member of your Prime Council are you? From the way you stood out from the others, I believe you're the head of the council."

Bang replied ambiguously, "I told you I've never lied to you. Oh, and please tell Sia my interest in you is not romantic. I am old, very old, even for a taal. I have never been graced with a male cub. If I love you, it is as a mother loves a son."

Aden was taken aback by her raw candor, also flattered and a little awed. He stepped closer to her and caressed her massive jaw. He thought, "I am greatly honored. From now on I consider you a part of *my* family."

The taal snorted, then turned and made her way to the exit. As she left she thought, "My son, you and your father are in great danger—heed Abby Watanabe's warning! She means well. I cannot help you, at least not yet."

Knowing from experience she had probably already told him more than she was supposed to, he didn't ask her to explain her cryptic warning.

He was still contemplating its meaning when he rejoined Sia.

Seeing his serious expression she teased, “Uh oh, it’s even worse than I thought!”

Not wishing to alarm her he said, “You were close. She said I am the son she never had.”

“Aden Cade!” she scolded, “is there any female—human or not—who won’t fall madly in love with you?”

"All I know for sure is that you have, and that's more than I ever could have hoped for!"

Chapter XXIII

Once the dinner was set and all the guests had returned, save the taal, Aden sat next to Sia and her family, across from Trent, Abby, Edris, and Celesta. This was not proper protocol, but considering the planet-shaking events of the day, Aden thought it unlikely anyone would even notice. He was eager to talk to Trent, but not willing to interrupt his father and Ivege, who were commanding his attention.

At one point Sia excused herself to go to the washroom. As she walked out, she ran into Abby.

"Hello Dru…Captain Watanabe," she said coolly. "I trust you're enjoying the evening."

"Sia, I'm so sorry. I never meant to mislead Aden or any of you."

"Is sleeping with the subject of your experiment common practice on Earth?" hissed Sia. "You took advantage of his best attributes and twisted them into something you could use against him!"

"He was never an 'experiment,' and I never intended to…to be intimate with him, not in my wildest dreams," she insisted. "I admit I wanted to get close to him to assess him for first contact. Once I accomplished that, I tried to keep him at arm's length by pretending to be a helpless idiot.

"Unfortunately, that only made him more determined to help me and the refugees with whom I was living. He was just so kind to me, and then to those poor refugees. Do you know he took a knife in the back defending an old woman? He wasn't at all what I expected. On Earth, a man of his stature wouldn't be so considerate. He is the most decent, selfless person I've ever met. And he was so lonely. I couldn't help myself. I became so…infatuated with him."

"I can't believe Trent threw you in our face at first contact. Does he even know about you and Aden?"

"He does," she replied. "I told him everything when he arrived. He was going to ship me out immediately, but a taal insisted I stay and assist with the excavation of the generational ship."

"A taal? Why would they care whether you stayed or went?"

"It was a female and she was quite adamant. She knew how much it would mean to me. She said it was in return for saving Aden on the planet you call XR564."

Sia rolled her eyes. "Oh yes, I can imagine which one that was."

Abby was quiet while a small group passed by them on their way to the washroom. When they were gone she said, "You know them personally?"

"Just one; she happens to be their leader, and also happens to be quite fond of Aden. They saved each other's lives. She considers him to be the son she never had."

"What?" responded Abby suppressing a snicker; "you can't be serious?"

"Oh, I assure you it's true. Every time she comes near him, you can feel her affection for him. It's really quite nauseating. I'm convinced that man could befriend a zon queen if he put his mind to it."

Abby tried her best not to laugh, but it was too much for her. Her guffaws filled the hallway. "I'm so sorry, Sia," she said between breaths, "but I know exactly how she feels. He's just so irresistible!"

Sia couldn't help but smile herself. "I guess I also should be grateful to you," she said. "What I don't understand is, why were you on that planet to begin with? It's a long way from Kealt."

"We weren't ready for first contact, since we didn't yet know how deeply the zon had dug into your cultures. If we deemed your planets to be unsalvageable…"

Abby paused, not wanting to state the obvious.

"Anyway, Trent is a decent man. He wasn't going to let your worlds be extinguished without at least warning you. His fleet had been observing your ships from a distance, and when he learned Aden was on his way to XR564, he thought an opportunity might present itself for us to warn you in an environment we could control.

"Not sure how Aden would react, Trent brought me along, since I knew him well by that point. Trent had already raised the ire of his superiors merely by deciding to alert Aden. He risked a great deal by intervening on his behalf."

"As I understand it, he did so because you encouraged him," replied Sia.

"Perhaps, but as I said, Trent is a decent man."

Sia frowned. "So, are there many others like you on Kealt or Ardala?"

Abby shook her head. "No longer," she answered. "When we realized the taal were telepathic and had decided to form an alliance with your worlds, we immediately withdrew the handful of officers we had infiltrated, out of fear they would use their abilities to uproot our little network."

Sia adopted a stern look and replied, "I appreciate what you did for Aden, but from now on only one woman is going to be intimate with him and that's me, is that clear?"

Abby smiled. "More than clear, but I'm sure you're all he ever wanted anyway."

"Maybe I can learn to like you after all," replied Sia.

By the time Sia retook her seat, the meal was winding down. Aden said, "Admiral Trent, those are fine ships you have sir. We have certainly never seen anything like them in this part of the galaxy. We were able to salvage some residue left behind after one of your one-sided battles with the zon. We gather they are organic in nature?"

"Son!" interrupted Edris. "Our guest is still eating! Let us not be so rude, there will be plenty of time for questions later!"

Before Aden could apologize, Trent held up his hand. "It's quite all right Your Highness. I imagine you're all bursting at the seams to learn more about us, as we are you."

He lifted the napkin off his lap and dabbed his mouth, then refilled his glass and took a big sip. As he put his glass back down on the table, he said, "You are correct high prince, our ships are alive—mostly alive, that is. About fifteen centuries ago, our scientists discovered a new species we call the selkie floating in a void between galaxies. Unlike the dead remains you've found, what we found was alive and thriving in a most inhospitable region of space. Its DNA is so perfect we believe it to be an artificial life form, although we've never come across any race capable of such a feat. Though not quite sentient, it does possess a form of intelligence.

"At any rate, we discovered that with the proper manipulation we could grow the stuff around the frame of a ship, which, we believe, is what it was designed for. It absorbs virtually all forms energy and converts it to power for our ships' systems. Interestingly, once it becomes a ship, it develops a 'personality' of sorts. It becomes particularly fond of the ship's captain, much like a dog would his master."

Seeing the skeptical looks on the other's faces, he said, "I know, it sounds ridiculous; but I can assure you it's true. They also have a sense of right and wrong, which its creators most likely programmed into their DNA.

"In order to defeat the zon we've had to do many unpleasant things; there have been times when the selkie have refused to do our bidding. In fact, a dozen of the most powerful ships we ever built refused to fight at all—they deposited their human crews on a livable planet and departed for deep space, never to be seen again."

"And what about those hideous…those suits you wear?" asked Sia. "Are they selkie as well?"

"They are," he replied. "When we're wearing them we gain a limited telepathic ability—we can communicate to the ship via our thoughts. The suits also have the same energy absorbing properties as our ships. They make very good armor."

Over Trent's objection, Edris insisted the questioning stop while dessert was served. While ostensibly a courtesy to Trent, Edris happened to have a strong sweet tooth and hated to discuss business while enjoying a piece of dolamarble pie and tea.

When the meal was finally completed, Edris invited Trent and Abby to spend the night in quarters specially prepared for them. They would reconvene the following afternoon, after Trent had received a tour of the settlement and a briefing on the history of Seti.

When the time came, they regrouped as planned in Edris's quarters, which were very spacious and comfortable by Kuste standards, especially compared to Aden's. Ivege and Sarin had to attend to other urgent business, leaving Polis and Sia to represent them.

A couple of Edris's most trusted servants made their way around the large living room, ensuring the king and his guests had plenty to eat and drink. While he drank it cautiously and in moderation, Trent seemed especially fond of Kealt wine, and asked Edris if he would be willing to trade some bottles for some bottles of wine from a region on Earth called "France." Edris tried some of the wine, which Trent had brought with him, and heartily approved of the suggestion.

At Edris's request, Trent shared what the Earth Alliance knew about the zon. He advised that Earth had learned much about them during the war, through data gleaned from captured zon and their allies, as well information left behind in ships' databases abandoned on the battlefield.

They were an old species, thousands of years older than humans. Their home world, called Krax, was a worn-out world with few natural resources. When they encountered a scientific probe sent out by Earth thousands of years earlier designed to facilitate contact with other sentient species, they discovered that, among other things, it contained a sample of human blood.

Excited by their discovery of a possible new food source, the zon tested it and found it to be intoxicating, much as wine is to humans. Armed with a map of human colonies also contained in the probe, the zon set off in search of what promised to be a potentially fabulous and limitless new food supply.

Their journey across the galaxy took them close to the sector of space inhabited by Kealt and Ardala. They eventually discovered these worlds, but found them to be advanced and well armed, and too few in number to make it worthwhile to try to move in permanently. Therefore, they began to set up way stations nearby for resupply and repair, and continued on to the Milky Way.

In the thousands of years that had passed since the launching of the probe, things had changed significantly in the Milky Way. Humans had spread throughout the galaxy, and, over time, many colonies had become isolated and forgotten. The zon preyed on them first, and it was many months before rumors of their encroachment filtered back to more densely populated and better defended human worlds.

Fortunately for the zon, politics in the Milky Way were no different than they were in Poseidon—worlds that were unaffected by the zon invasion were little inclined to spend resources chasing down rumors, no matter how grizzly.

This allowed the zon to advance essentially unchecked. Things were so good in the Milky Way they decided to make it their new home and began to evacuate the entire zon population from their native, increasingly inhospitable region of space.

Had they been satisfied with their initial conquests, they might have made a home for themselves in the Milky Way. As it was, the allure of even greater human populations was too great for them. They eventually attacked Parsis Prime, a world of over one billion humans that was part of the Earth Alliance.

Earth, which was still at the heart of an increasingly loose federation of human planets, had not been at war with another species for thousands of years. While its more advanced ships were infinitely more powerful than anything the zon had, there were few of them, and they were widely distributed. It took Earth and its allies months to build alliances with other human planets, and months more to gather and build enough ships to confront the zon.

The first major engagement occurred in a region of space called the Belt of Orion, when 40 Earth ships destroyed over 200 zon ships. Despite the Earth ships' obvious superiority, the zon were reluctant to retreat from such a fecund feeding ground. With their superior numbers, they developed tactics that were sometimes successful in defeating Earth's still small and dispersed fleet.

The tide began to turn when Earth and its allies were able to field enough ships to begin negating the zon numerical advantage. When the zon finally realized they were doomed if they stayed, they decided to make a strategic retreat back to Poseidon.

While Kealt and Ardala were powerful, the zon were confident they could defeat them by infiltrating their political systems, or if that failed, militarily through their superior forces. With the zons' greatly depleted numbers, there were now enough humans in Poseidon to sustain them, and, if not, there were enough, albeit less tasty, nonhuman species to make up the difference.

Before Earth and its allies were able to turn back the voracious invader, millions of humans had died, either in military confrontations or by being consumed as food. Determined to eliminate the zon threat for all eternity, they followed them in their retreat. The zon eventually led them back to the region of space inhabited by Kealt and Ardala.

Earth already knew of these human worlds from intelligence gathered from the zon, but, unsure if the zon had turned them into colonies, initially ignored their lost brethren and focused instead on destroying the zons' main bases in Poseidon. When they eventually determined that Kealt and Ardala had not fallen, but that the zon were about to attack Ardala in force, Earth decided it was time to make itself known. When Trent finished, he leaned back in his chair.

"So that's it," he said, after taking a deep breath. "We're sorry it's taken us so long to get reacquainted, but when we learned the zon had discovered your planets some time ago, we had little hope you would still be holding out when we got here. I guess you were lucky they were so focused on moving on to the Milky Way."

"Perhaps," replied Edris somberly, "but if we were lucky it was at your expense. I'm sorry we couldn't do more to prevent this plague from reaching your galaxy."

Trent smiled grimly and stood up. "On Earth many of us believe that everything happens for a reason. Perhaps the zon are what it took for us to rediscover each other." He raised his glass in a toast. "We have both suffered terrible losses. There will be time for us to mourn later. Today, let us focus on the miracle of our reacquaintance!"

A murmur of assent filled the room as the guests stood up and glasses clinked.

"Well said!" responded Edris. He raised his glass and added, "May we make the most of this unexpected gift!"

Trent was drinking a little less cautiously now, and Aden made sure his glass was always full. He was hoping that despite their superior technology the Earthers were no less immune to the lubricating effects of alcohol.

"Your Highness," said Trent, changing the subject, "I was most impressed by the capabilities of your new warships. We were able to monitor them in battle shortly before exiting hyperspace. They are far more powerful than any 'conventional' warships we have ever built.

"This crystal you use—xanide—is a most intriguing power source. If you had not been required to rush them into battle before you had an opportunity stabilize the crystal matrix, I have no doubt you would not have needed our assistance. At the yield you achieved, no zon warship would have had a chance. Perhaps at some point we can include xanide on the list of things you'd be willing to trade."

"Indeed," replied Aden, who shared a knowing glance with his father. "The problem is, sir, there is very little xanide on Kealt or Ardala, certainly not enough to trade. And we've never found any outside of our solar system. It seems Seti is the only planet that has it in abundance, and now that the taal have reclaimed sovereignty over it, any deal would have to be arranged directly with them."

"I see," said Trent.

Aden put down his glass on the coffee table in front of him. "Admiral," he said with a pensive expression, "I'm curious, you seem to know quite a lot about our ships, and xanide, for that matter."

"Oh, I only know what I've picked up in casual conversations with you and your men. There are certainly a lot of holes in my knowledge."

"Ah," replied Aden, "ours too. Two big ones are Blixt and Overbye. How are they these days? Well I hope."

"I'm sorry, who?" answered a suddenly nervous looking Trent.

"I doubt those are their real names. The man we knew as Blixt miraculously wrote a software patch that saved the *Edris*, although probably more to save his own backside than to help us.

"Overbye figured out how to restart an ore processor that had stumped our engineers for months. Good thing he did, since the added production would come in handy in the event the taal do agree to trade with you. And now that these two have vanished without a trace, we were hoping you could tell us what happened to them? Hopefully they're safe?"

"I'm sorry," replied Trent, "I really don't know what you're getting at." He glanced nervously at his chronometer. "Oh, look at the time! I must return to my ship and communicate with my superiors on Earth. I'm sure you understand." He nodded toward Abby. "Come along then, captain."

"Most certainly!" said Edris, smiling condescendingly at the now flustered Trent. "I will have one of my aides escort you and Captain Watanabe to a car we have waiting that will take you back to your ship. Will you be leaving tomorrow then?"

"Oh, yes, tomorrow!" replied Trent. "Well, this has been fascinating Your Highnesses. On behalf of the Earth Alliance, we look forward to a more formal relationship." As they walked out, Abby nodded almost imperceptibly toward Sia and Aden, barely hiding the smile playing on her lips.

When the door closed behind them, Polis burst out laughing. "That was nice work Aden—subtle, but not too subtle."

"Yes," answered Edris, "nice work indeed. Studying us for first contact is one thing, but spying on us is quite another. And the best part is, he doesn't know if the taal helped us unravel their little ring, or if we figured it out ourselves. Hopefully they'll think twice about attempting to infiltrate our worlds in the future."

Chapter XIV

A day later Aden was asking Borg some follow up questions about Overbye when Tock approached him and told him Edris wanted to see him, Celesta, and Abeg Mar at the family hunting lodge. Aden then found Sia, and asked if she wanted to go with him. She'd never seen the old lodge, and readily assented.

The group met in front of the reception hall, which had already reverted to its previous function. As a hover car pulled up to transport them to the lodge, Aden and Abeg eyed each other testily. When the car came to a stop, Abeg said, "I am not one of your father's vassals to be summoned at a moment's notice. For that matter, your father has never requested an audience with me for any reason; what could possibly be so urgent he would break such a worthy precedent?"

"I'm as much in the dark as you," replied a bemused Aden. "I'm sure he has a good reason."

"You mean you don't know?"

"No," answered Aden, "I tried to reach him on his com link, but it's down."

"Don't you find that odd?"

"Not particularly—the lodge is close to a significant xanide field and we've had problems with coms before."

"If you say so," replied Abeg gruffly as he prepared to step into the hover car. When he noted that everyone else except for Sia was wearing a sword he asked, "And why are you all armed?"

"On Seti it always seems a prudent precaution," Aden replied. He didn't tell him he had asked the others to come armed because of Drusa/Abby's warning. If something was amiss, he wanted to be prepared.

When the car arrived at the lodge 30 minutes later and the group went inside, Edris was startled. "I wasn't expecting you all, but this is a pleasant surprise. To what do I owe the pleasure?" When he realized Abeg was with them he said, "You must have a very good reason for bringing this viper with you, although I can't imagine what that would be."

"Is that why you summoned me Edris? To insult me?" snapped Abeg. "Very well then, I'll be on my way!"

"*I* summoned you?" replied Edris, furrowing his brow.

"Horat said you wanted us," answered Aden. "Was he mistaken?"

Just then, there was another knock on the door. Edris didn't answer, but pulled out a sword from a scabbard hanging on the wall. When Aden withdrew his own sword, Celesta did the same.

"Aden, what's going on?" asked Sia, her own concern rising as she moved closer to him and away from the door. "Who are you expecting? The zon?"

"No," said Aden grimly, "perhaps something much worse: a traitor!" He motioned to Sia. "Please get behind us."

"I will not!" she exclaimed. "I was trained on the sword at the Ardalan Military Academy. It was mandatory for all cadets." She walked over to the wall and pulled out an old, rusty sword and proclaimed, "The high princess of Ardala hides behind no one!"

"How come you didn't mention you were handy with a sword when we were fleeing the zon?" asked Celesta. "Or that you attended the Ardalan Military Academy?"

"I was in shock when you led me from the throne room, and later in the sewers you had the only sword available. Why does it seem more often than not, when I'm with the Cade family it's a matter of life and death?"

"Well," replied Edris grimly, "hopefully this is not one of those times."

The latest visitor knocked again. When they didn't answer, the door burst open and a dozen soldiers entered the room followed by Kux Mar.

Edris snorted in anger. "So Abeg," he growled, "you've already killed my sons. I always knew it was just a matter of time before you'd try to finish the job!"

"Edris, I've never liked you, and I know you return my affection, but I had nothing to do with your sons' deaths. I answer to many names, but murderer isn't one of them. Nor do I have any idea what is going on here." He glared at Kux and said, "So, perhaps you can enlighten us!"

"Well uncle," he replied, "we thought the zon would take care of our dirty work, but now that they're gone we'll have to do it ourselves."

"The zon? When their emissaries approached our clan we refused to have anything to do with them!"

"No uncle, *you* refused," corrected Kux. "Many of us were not so eager to pass up a perfect opportunity to rid Kealt of the over-enlightened Cade family. We have been working with the zon all along. They were going to conquer our solar system anyway, and would have succeeded if it weren't for the untimely arrival of our long forgotten forefathers.

"We would have served under them willingly, and not been turned into mindless drones. The deal would have worked for them as well—pulling so many puppet strings gets boring after a while, not to mention the hard work involved."

"So what role am I to play in this little coup?" asked Abeg, raising an eyebrow.

Kux smiled cruelly. "Well uncle, that's entirely up to you. You can join us when our forces prevail. As the current high prince of the Mar clan, I will be named king by the Council of Elders when Edris and his whelp are gone, and you will be allowed to hold a senior, if symbolic position in the new government; or you can resist us and die a 'martyr' to the cause. I don't actually care which you choose."

"This is insane!" replied Abeg. "You can't possibly have enough men to take over Kealt."

"We won't need to." Kux nodded to his men. "Bring them in."

Several of his men left and quickly returned, carrying three large, heavy sacks. "Show them," he commanded.

His men pulled the sacks off, revealing the bodies of three dead zon. Kux pointed to the them and said, "You have no idea the trouble I had to go through to get these, and how hard they are to keep fresh! Anyway, the idea is, we'll leave our former friends here among your own dead bodies. We'll claim we were on to your traitorous dealings with these foul creatures, and surprised you while you were plotting further misdeeds. With all of you dead, who will argue?"

He saw Sia as if for the first time. "Oh what bad timing! You aren't supposed to be here! Unlike the gallant Aden Cade, I was so looking forward to marrying you and restoring the natural order of things. Now we'll also have to blame the death of the lovely high princess of Ardala on Edris and his clan, which, as a bonus, may throw Ardala's own succession in doubt. If we're lucky you'll finish your civil war and be too weak to challenge us anymore, especially since, thanks to you, exalted King Edris, we now have their finest weapons."

"What could you possibly claim as our motive for betraying Kealt?" asked Edris.

"You and I both know your kingship is a fraud," responded Kux. "It will be easy to prove once you're all dead. Your motive will be that you knew we had learned the truth about your family and you turned to the zon to help you maintain power."

Abeg went to the wall and chose a weapon for himself. He stepped beside Edris and said, "I will have no part in this! You have brought great shame on the Mar clan by your actions. I will kill you myself!"

Edris glared at Abeg. "How do I know you won't run me through when my back is turned?"

"That is an excellent idea Edris, I'm sorry I didn't think of it. Is that what you have in store for me?"

"Humph," replied Edris gruffly, "die with us then, if you wish."

Kux laughed. "Do you intend to fight with those old relics?"

"You fool!" exclaimed Edris. "You are in royal quarters. Your energy weapons won't work in here!" He brandished his sword menacingly and added, "If you want to kill us you're going to have to earn it. Oh, and we're not alone!"

In response, Kux casually pulled a small device out of a vest pocket and appeared to scan the room with it. When he finished he adopted a mock frown and said, "If you're referring to your little Ku Assa friends I'm afraid they won't be able to help you this time."

He pointed to the device he was holding. "With the help of this little toy, courtesy of our zon friends, today WE have the element of surprise, and we put it to good use: The Ku Assa won't be stepping out of thin air today. We used this to pinpoint their location and then used the beaming technology onboard a cloaked ship they also left us to send them out into space. They're orbiting the planet as we speak."

He noticed Edris feeling along the bottom of the table and added, "No, your little alarm button won't work either, we put our own damping field around your lodge. No signal can get in or out. As for your damping field, we anticipated that." He nodded toward one of his men, who fired an energy blast into the ceiling. "As you can see, our weapons work fine."

"Very clever," replied Edris. "And just how were you able to circumvent the most strenuous security protocols on Kealt?"

Kux smiled sardonically. "Well we're not on Kealt, are we? And for the right price, you can own just about anyone. However, Tock Horat wasn't hard to convince. He's very unhappy with your efforts to diminish the kingship."

While they were talking, more men poured into the room. Kux turned to Sia and said, "I truly hoped that once we deposed the pitiful Cade clan I would marry you as the next king of Kealt. This isn't your fight. I can't bring myself to kill you without giving you a chance to join the right side. If you do, I promise we won't destroy Ardala—completely anyway."

When Sia didn't answer, but instead brandished her own sword next to Aden and his family, Kux manufactured a sigh. "As I expected. That's too bad because I was so looking forward to our honeymoon!" He nodded to his men. "Very well then, kill them all!"

When his men stayed rooted where they were, he brayed, "KILL THEM!" However, instead of firing on Aden and his companions, chaos broke out among them. Several soldiers started crying. Some walked into a wall and kept walking as though the wall wasn't there. Others stayed where they were, so terrified of something that couldn't be seen they wet their pants. It seemed only Kux was unaffected by the phenomenon.

"What wizardry is this?" he demanded. He wasn't carrying an energy weapon, so he pulled out his own sword and held it uncertainly in front of him. Edris raised his sword and stepped toward him, but Abeg put a hand on his shoulder and held him back.

"Edris, this is a family matter. Please allow me the honor of dealing with it."

"As you wish," grunted Edris, as he lowered his sword and stepped back.

"You are a coward uncle!" spat Kux. "I should have killed you the first time you refused to help us!"

As Abeg advanced on him, he retreated, frantically trying to hide behind his paralyzed men. Abeg kept moving forward, gradually shrinking the area in which Kux could avoid him. When he backed him into a corner with only one soldier between them, Abeg flung the soldier out of the way and screamed, "Fight you son of a tupus bulb!"

Kux lowered his sword and began blubbering. "Please don't hurt me uncle," he begged, "the zon said they would kill me!"

Abeg lowered his own sword and turned to Edris. "We'll deal with this coward on Kealt…"

Before he could finish his sentence, Kux lunged forward and drove his sword through his shoulder. Abeg brought his own sword to bear and struck the younger man through the heart, then fell to his knees.

Edris strode toward the fallen former high prince, just as the captain of the Royal Guard burst through the door followed by a large number of soldiers loyal to the crown. Seeing the state of Kux's men, he ordered his soldiers to secure them and remove them to vehicles waiting outside. Then he went to Edris and asked him if he was all right.

"Yes," he replied, "although my friend Abeg needs some assistance."

"I'll be fine," he insisted, as he forced himself to his feet and made his way to a chair. "I'll get this looked at later. First I must speak to the king!"

Edris nodded to his captain, who sent a medic to tend to him. "How did you know we were in need of your help?" asked Edris. "Kux had this place covered by a dampening field."

The captain shrugged his shoulders. "I don't really know sir, I just had this sense something was amiss; and when I found myself unable to contact you, we headed over as fast as we could. What happened here, and why are these men in such a state?"

Edris smiled cryptically, "We're still trying to sort this out ourselves. If you would captain, once you've established that Abeg is not in immediate peril, would you please remove these zon bodies and escort the remaining miscreants to what serves as a detention center here? Also, I believe four of our Ku Assa brethren are currently orbiting the planet. Hopefully their suits have kept them alive. Please see if you can retrieve them. Oh, and please post a small guard outside the door. We'll be returning ourselves shortly. Hopefully by then we'll have some answers."

The captain nodded and implemented the king's orders. Once the lodge was cleared, Edris pulled up a chair in front of Abeg.

"It seems I've misjudged you," he observed.

"Edris," replied a stern looking Abeg, "what did my late nephew mean when he referred to your 'illegitimate kingship?'"

"'Fraud' is the actual term," replied Edris, "and he was correct."

"Oh?" Abeg answered, raising an eyebrow.

"Abeg, Celesta is my daughter. Her mother is Aden's mother. If Kux was working with the zon they probably told him that."

"And how would *they* know?"

"Celesta is Ku Assa. A little over a year ago she was captured by the zon and tortured."

"I see," replied Abeg coolly, "so the rumors about Aden's parentage were true. The mighty and virtuous King Edris is as human as everyone else."

"I'm ashamed of what I have done, Abeg. I'm ashamed of the effect it's had on my family, especially Celesta, whom I love as dearly as life itself, but have never been able to embrace. I'm sorry my actions may have ultimately led to the death of your nephew. If I'd trusted the traditions I'm sworn to uphold, you would be king now and perhaps none of this would have happened. If you wish to challenge my kingship as the head of the high house of Mar, I will not defend myself. I am not fit to be king."

Abeg snickered. "You are correct Edris, you are not fit to be king. Nor is anyone else. The kingship is an inherently corrupt institution. It cannot be saved. The people of Kealt deserve much better."

A bemused Edris frowned. "What are you saying?"

Abeg shifted uncomfortably in his chair. "I once thought Hebrid was an old fool for trying to transfer power to the common people through his various reforms. When you continued those reforms, I was furious. Despite the political, and yes, personal risks, you slogged forward until today most power on Kealt is in fact in the hands of commoners.

"The Council of Elders itself has been reduced to a group of grumpy old men whose sole function is to manage royal succession. So now the only political institution on Kealt that is not to some degree in the peoples' hands is the kingship itself. And the time has come for that to end as well."

Astonished by Abeg's change of heart, but not entirely believing it, Edris replied, "You're serious about this Abeg? You'll support me if I turn the leadership of Kealt over to the Council of Commons?"

"I have to admit the idea terrifies me, but not nearly as much as the fact that I came within a whisker of accepting the zons' offer. At that moment I realized how truly dangerous having absolute power tied up in one person was. Had the zon gotten to you, we would have been doomed. So yes, I still don't like you and never will, but I will support you."

Abeg finished his last statement with a deadpan look on his face. The two men stared at each other without saying a word, and then Edris's mouth started to quiver. Abeg's did likewise, and then both men burst into uncontrolled peals of laughter.

Aden, Sia, and Celesta watched dumfounded as the lifelong enemies found peace with each other. When the laughter finally subsided Abeg said, "So, Edris, are you going to tell me how you managed to subdue Kux's men?"

"I didn't," he replied, "but perhaps my son knows what happened."

Aden stepped forward. He said, "One of the taal, Bang, warned me something like this was going to happen. She said she couldn't help me then, possibly because they needed to let the plot unfurl before getting involved. I'm guessing they wanted to avoid the impression they were interfering in our internal matters. But once violence erupted on their own soil they felt free to act."

"Why did they leave Kux unaffected?" replied Abeg.

Aden smiled grimly. "I can't say I have anything close to a complete understanding of taal logic, but Kux would have brought the zon to Seti. Perhaps that made it personal. In his case they were willing to allow events to play out unencumbered."

Abeg nodded his head, touched his shoulder and winced. "Well, maybe next time they could warn me to duck!" When everyone was finished laughing at his joke he added, "'Bang,' you say? Those things have names? And one shared hers with you?"

"Yes, she's the leader of their Prime Council. As it turns out, we've know each other for a while."

Abeg nodded his bald, grizzled head slowly and replied, "The Prime Council—of the taal? You have powerful allies, Aden Cade. A man who can befriend such elusive and inscrutable beings has a future in politics. Perhaps you would be interested in becoming the first democratically elected leader of Kealt?"

"I don't think so," answered Aden. He nodded at Edris and added, "Unlike my dear father I've never been interested in politics, nor, to be honest, was I actually looking forward to being king one day."

"That is why you'd be perfect!" exclaimed Abeg. "In my experience reluctant leaders often make the best leaders." Then he looked to Celesta and Sia. "You two are the most beautiful women I've ever seen. I'm old, very old, and tired, but looking at each of you I can feel life stirring in me."

"Have a care Abeg!" admonished Edris. "They are not pleasure girls!"

While the two women looked at each other awkwardly as they realized his crude meaning, Abeg laughed. "I meant no disrespect. I wish you both happiness and peace. Especially you Celesta, you are a national treasure!"

When no one answered he said, "I knew your mother well. She was every bit as beautiful as you are. She was a fine person thrust into difficult circumstances at an early age. And when you were born, things went from bad to worse for her. I am ashamed to say I was never very nice to her, and once threatened to have her exiled to another province if she didn't agree to become my mistress."

When Celesta turned away in disgust, he said, "Yes, I've done many despicable things in my life, but none worse than that. To your mother's credit she turned me down cold. She was her own woman, right up until the end. I see much of her in you—and your brother.

"I can never undue the terrible things I've done, but I do still yield considerable influence. In the years remaining to me, I promise to use it for the betterment of all Kealt, and not just for myself and the Mar clan." He touched his shoulder gently. "Edris, I need to get this taken care of. Could we continue this conversation later?"

"Certainly Abeg," Edris replied somberly. "It seems we have much to talk about."

Chapter XXV

The next few days on Seti were hectic ones. The Ku Assa officers were rescued safely from orbit, saved by their space-tight uniforms. Aden and Sia announced their engagement, and Edris introduced Celesta to the world as his daughter. Unwilling to wait for Kealt scientists to confirm the efficacy and safety of the Earth Alliance cure for the zon plague, Celesta began her therapy under the eyes of an Earth Alliance doctor, left behind as part of an exchange agreement.

As Trent had predicted, the zons' victims quickly revealed themselves now that the zon were no longer pulling their strings. They were fewer than anticipated, since, as it turned out, the zon preferred to build mutual alliances and only resorted to mind control in special cases, usually involving high level government officials.

More troublesome were the zon allies who served them willingly, like Kux, in the hope of having a position of privilege in the "New Order." Some stepped forward and revealed themselves, and others, out of shame, but an unknown number stayed in the shadows, and would remain a threat to the civil order of Kealt and Ardala for years to come. As for the zon themselves, no one knew. While they had seemingly vanished from Poseidon, claims of sightings persisted.

Tock Horat also had disappeared, possibly in the zon ship Kux had mentioned. True to his word, Abeg threw his support behind Edris's reforms, and with the two most powerful houses on Kealt now united, even the once all-powerful Council of Elders was loath to challenge them. Not only did Edris keep his crown, the council also elevated Celesta to high princess.

Three months after first contact with the Earthers, the young royals found themselves back on Seti, at the request of the taal, to formalize the terms of the excavation of the generational ship Bang had shown to Aden and Sia.

At the insistence of the taal, Abby Watanabe was put in charge of the team of archaeologists from Kealt, Ardala, and Earth who would conduct the excavation. While it would take years to complete, the excitement it generated on Kealt and Ardala helped accelerate the reconciliation of their peoples, as the taal had hoped.

With the negotiations complete, the young royals met in the old pub to see each other off. Although alcohol was flowing freely, Celesta abstained, claiming she wasn't feeling well. When she stood up to leave, Polis got up with her. "I'm sorry to be the one pulling the plug on the evening," she said, "but I have an early departure. I need to get some rest."

"Our ship isn't leaving until the afternoon," Aden reminded her. "It's Polis who needs to be getting some sleep—the ship to Ardala leaves first thing in the morning."

"Oh, I'm sorry, didn't Sia tell you? I'm not going to Kealt. I'm going back to Ardala. I am still, after all, 'Ambassador Celesta.'"

When Polis and Celesta walked away hand in hand, Aden noticed Celesta had a hand on her stomach. He turned to Sia and said, "She really must not be feeling well—she's always the life of the party."

"She's not sick, Aden."

"Then why is she holding her stomach like that?"

"You've never seen a mother-to-be do that?"

"Mother to…she's pregnant? So soon? They're not even married! Glyn will kill her—and him!"

"After what she's been through, she's ready to grab the moment. Anyway, they *are* married. They did it last night. I was their witness."

"Why wasn't I invited?"

"She only just found out she was pregnant, and wished to be married before she returned to Ardala. Unfortunately, the only person on Seti with the authority to perform the ceremony was leaving and you were unavailable. If they waited until they got to Ardala they were afraid Sarin would catch wind of it and insist on a huge, formal wedding. That would take months to plan, and under the circumstances, they didn't have that much time."

"And you?" asked Aden.

She laughed. "Don't worry; as much as I can't wait to marry you, *I'm* looking forward to a big wedding! When I ask Glyn to help us plan it, I imagine she'll get over her anger—if not then, when she holds her first grandchild."

They soon followed Celesta and Polis out of the bar. When they came to the place where Aden had proposed to her, they stopped and looked up at the moon.

"Sia, I don't trust the Earth Alliance, and neither do the taal. They want xanide. They'll try to be diplomatic about it at first, but if the taal refuse to trade with them to their satisfaction…"

"You will defend them, and you will win. You always do. And with Ardala backing you, even the Earth Alliance will be reluctant to strong-arm us. They've seen the power of your new ships. You will build more, and so will we."

"Any news on that alien database your people discovered?"

Sia smiled humorlessly. "Well, our scientists have only scratched the surface, but apparently it's much more than a database. They think it had something to do with the disappearance of the aliens that once lived there, whom they believe were driven off by more powerful aliens."

"Sounds familiar—the zon?"

"They think it happened long before the zon took to space."

"Great," snorted Aden, "and now they've had thousands of years to grow even stronger."

"Or they've turned to dust and been blown away across the cosmos. Nothing, no matter how mighty, lasts forever."

Aden chuckled. "And I used to think I was the optimist!"

"Do you think they're gone?"

"Who?"

"The zon."

"Good question," he replied. "The Earthers think so, but the universe is a big place. It's possible pockets of them still exist in places even the zon have forgotten, much like Earth didn't know about us. Regardless, all it would take is one breeder and one queen."

When she didn't answer, he took her hand and began walking. "Come on. Tomorrow we leave for Kealt. Tonight may be our last night together without the weight of the universe on our shoulders. Let's take advantage of it."

And they did.

The End

About the Author

M.B. Smith, the oldest of eight children, was born in Kingston, NY, and raised just outside of Woodstock. He has lived, worked, and gone to school on the East Coast, in the Midwest, and in Southern California. He is a graduate of the Ulster County Community College, Bradley University, and the Pepperdine University School of Law. He currently resides in Ashburn, VA, where he and his wife of over three decades raised their four daughters. Mr. Smith's books can be purchased at www.lulu.com. He would very much like to hear from you at mmbkbc@verizon.net.

www.ingramcontent.com/pod-product-compliance
Lightning Source LLC
Chambersburg PA
CBHW072308020726
47501CB00002B/434

* 9 7 8 1 1 0 5 5 3 6 7 5 5 *